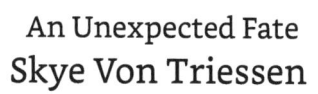

An Unexpected Fate
Skye Von Triessen

Copyright © 2024 Skye Von Triessen
ISBN: 979-8-339479-52-9

All rights reserved.

The characters and events portrayed in this book are fictitious. Names characters, places, and incidents are products of the author's imagination. Any similarity to actual events, persons, living or dead, is entirely coincidental. No part of this book may be reproduced, stored in a retrieval system, or transmitted in any form or by any means — electronic, mechanical, photocopy, recording, or any other without prior written permission from the author.
This book contains content that may be considered sensitive to certain readers, including adult themes and mature situations.

Dedication

For my darling readers.
The past two years have been an incredible journey with you. This book is, in a way, a farewell to all the amazing women in *Meant to Be* and *Unexpected*. This is for you as much as it is for me. May you all find love and happiness similar to what I've written. Thank you!

♥

Table of contents

Chapter 1
Chapter 2
Chapter 3
Chapter 4
Chapter 5
Chapter 6
Chapter 7
Chapter 8
Chapter 9
Chapter 10
Chapter 11
Chapter 12
Chapter 13
Chapter 14
Chapter 15
Chapter 16
Chapter 17
Chapter 18
Chapter 19
Chapter 20
Chapter 21
Chapter 22
Chapter 23
Chapter 24
Chapter 25
Chapter 26

Chapter 27
Chapter 28
Chapter 29
ACKNOWLEDGMENTS
AFTERWORD

Chapter 1

Lane pulled up beside Miranda's Range Rover, still in disbelief that she had agreed to a weekend getaway involving a Broadway show. She blamed her inability to say no on her raging libido, which seemed to override the rational side of her brain when it came to Miranda Hayes. Since their first night together two weeks ago, their opportunities for intimacy had been scarce. Lane quickly discovered that Miranda led a very active life outside the hospital—not only with Found Family, but with other charities, volunteering, and sporting activities. She also made time for her parents and grandparents whenever possible. Their busy schedules had limited them to only one date the first week, and Lane was at the Women in Medicine Conference in New York the following week. Hence, when she called Miranda the previous night to inquire about her weekend plans, she was presented with a choice: wait the entire weekend to satiate the desire that had been building all week, or embark on a two-and-a-half-hour road trip to Portland for Miranda to indulge in one of her favorite pastimes, Broadway. *Nia would have a field day with this if she ever found out I went to watch a Broadway show after refusing her invitations on so many occasions. Christ. Seems my weakness for this woman knows no bounds.*

But Lane knew it was more than just sex. She

genuinely enjoyed being around Miranda and was eager to learn more about who she was beyond her role at Parkwood. There was something irresistibly captivating about Miranda's personality that drew Lane in, making her want to discover the woman behind the bright smile—now that she was no longer scowling at Lane—and keen intelligence. As Lane was lost in thought, the front door opened. Miranda appeared in the doorway, her welcoming smile—the very one Lane had just been contemplating—blossoming on her face as she signaled for Lane to come inside. She was wearing a green and white floral-print slip dress that showcased her gorgeous curves and long, toned legs, instantly reminding Lane of last Wednesday when those very legs were wrapped around her waist. Resigned to her fate but not unwilling, Lane stepped out of her Audi Q7 and walked leisurely toward Miranda. Reaching the doorway, Miranda looped an arm around her neck and pulled her into a salacious, unexpected kiss. Caught off guard, it took a moment for Lane's body to respond, but she soon matched Miranda's fervor—kissing her back passionately. Just as she thought about spinning Miranda around and pinning her against the door, Miranda broke the kiss, her eyes dark with desire and shining with genuine happiness.

"I feel like I haven't seen you in forever," she whispered, her breath warm against Lane's lips.

Lane was taken aback by Miranda's heartfelt admission, even though she was pleased to discover that Miranda had been thinking about her as much as she had thought about Miranda. "Dr. Hayes..." Lane pressed the palms of her hands into the sides of Miranda's thighs, slowly running them up and around to grip her waist and erase any space between their bodies. "Is that your way of telling me you've missed me?" Lane asked, a playful tone coloring her words.

Miranda bit her lower lip, releasing it slowly with a teasing sparkle in her eyes. "Maybe," she replied coyly. "Thanks for agreeing to come with me. I promise you'll have the best time."

Lane, curious and slightly amused, inquired, "Did you just happen to have an extra ticket lying around?"

A fleeting sadness flickered across Miranda's eyes, vanishing almost as quickly as it had appeared. "Kind of." Miranda let out a heavy sigh, before elaborating, "I bought the tickets while I was still with Trevor."

The mention of Trevor stirred an uneasy feeling in Lane's stomach, but she swiftly pushed it aside. "Okay," was all she managed to say, finding herself at a loss for further words.

Miranda observed her briefly, then smiled with a knowing look and let her hands fall from Lane's neck. "I'm ready to go. Just need to put my suitcase in the car." She turned and walked to her bags, neatly lined up by the sofa. Peeking over her shoulder at Lane, she asked, "Do you need anything to eat or drink before we head out?"

"No, I'm fine, thanks," Lane responded, her gaze sweeping over Miranda's living room, taking in the muted, soft tones and stylish decorations. "Your home is exactly as I pictured it," she complimented as her eyes settled on the fireplace across the room.

"And how is that?" Miranda inquired curiously.

"Very feminine and warm, like its owner," Lane replied, her eyes drifting appreciatively over Miranda's curves.

Miranda laughed softly. "Well, I can't say yours is how I pictured it. I expected something more clinical, like a bachelorette pad to match the cold and distant persona you project at work. Not, as you say, warm and feminine. I was utterly surprised the first time I came over."

"I've been known for my unpredictability." Miranda's admission didn't surprise Lane because she wasn't the first who had that impression of what her home would look like. "I enjoy quiet days at home and I prefer the ambiance to reflect comfort and peacefulness so I can relax. I believe a person's home should be their sanctuary and the ambiance should carry the aura of whatever makes them happy," she added, uncharacteristically finding herself wanting to explain her choices—a rarity for her, except when it came to Miranda Hayes.

Again, Miranda studied her intently, as if trying to piece together a multifaceted puzzle. "You're a very complex woman. Definitely not what I expected in more ways than one." Lane could have sworn she saw Miranda wink, or at the very least there was a twinkle in her eyes. "I'm looking forward to knowing the woman behind your many faces."

"I'm not *that* complicated." Lane waved her hand in rebuttal. "My 'many faces', as you put it, are just a part of who I am. It's just that the face is dependent on who I'm interacting with, because not everyone deserves to see the best parts of us."

Miranda shook her head. "See complicated. Although there is some truth to what you said." She picked up her handbag and suitcase. "Let's continue this conversation in the car."

Lane, eyeing the size of Miranda's suitcase, couldn't help but ask, "How much clothes do you need for a weekend?"

Miranda chuckled as she stepped through the door Lane held open for her. "As you said, I'm a very feminine woman." Miranda glanced over her shoulder, a teasing smirk on her lips. "So I need a lot of feminine things and multiple outfits—just in case I'm not in the mood for what I initially planned to wear."

Lane laughed and followed Miranda through the door, her eyes dropping to her swaying ass, thinking about the things she wanted to do to it. "Do you want me to drive?" she offered, stopping at the front of their cars.

Miranda looked at her with surprise, creasing her features. "You wouldn't mind?"

"Nope. Plus, I peg you for a passenger princess." Lane used her key fob to pop the trunk of her SUV. "Let's take my car since my bags are already in there."

"As long as you're sure, because you're right, I am a passenger princess," Miranda admitted with a smile. "While I love road trips, I don't like to drive." She continued to stare at Lane as if she were some mystery she was eager to solve.

"Then it's settled. I'm here to drive at your pleasure," Lane said with a grin, opening the passenger door for Miranda. She took the suitcase from Miranda's hand and stowed it in the trunk. Walking around to the driver's side, she took a few deep, calming breaths to prepare her mind for the long journey ahead.

"Is this gentlelady-like behavior how you get women to fall into your bed?" Miranda asked as soon as Lane slid into the driver's seat and closed the door.

Starting the car, Lane turned her head to Miranda with a cocky smirk. "I don't have to do anything other than be myself to get women into bed, Miranda darling. In fact, women fall over themselves to be with me with just a mere flutter of my eyelashes." Lane huffed in mock vexation, "You're the only one who I've ever had to work tirelessly to get to fall into my bed."

Miranda shook her head in exasperation and rolled her eyes. "So arrogant."

"Naa. Just a simple truth," Lane replied as she backed out of the driveway.

"Are you a music or conversation person during a road trip?" Miranda asked, shifting in her seat to sit with her back against the door.

Lane glanced over at her. "Depends on the company and the mood. I'm flexible."

"Good. I'm the same. I like to start off with music to get in a groove and then conversation later. I also like to sing along, but feel free to tell me to be quiet if my singing bothers you."

Lane laughed. She had never met anyone quite like Miranda, who could match her in sarcasm one moment and then shift to being soft, kind, and an open book with her emotions the next. Miranda was a complex mix—outwardly personable and gentle, which might lead some to underestimate her. But beneath that warmth, there was a solid core of self-assurance and strength. Now that Miranda had let her guard down around Lane, she was beginning to see the bright and sunny disposition that had earned Miranda her reputation among their colleagues—the genuinely warm and caring side that defined her.

"What type of music do you like?" Lane asked, her

voice still filled with mirth.

"90s R&B and early 2000s are my jams. When people were still making real music that touched your soul and inspired you." Miranda snapped her fingers, swaying to an imaginary beat. "Music you could make slow, sweet love to."

Miranda's words sent a thrill through Lane, tightening the muscles in her lower stomach. "You like making love to music?" Lane asked, stealing another glance at Miranda to gauge her reaction. She was almost certain Miranda's cheeks would have been pink if her complexion allowed it.

"Yes, I do," Miranda replied after a brief pause.

Lane was about to delve deeper into what else Miranda enjoyed during sex, but the ringing of Miranda's phone interrupted the conversation. Miranda reached into her bag to answer it, and Lane turned her attention back to the road.

"Hi, Mom."

Lane had been contemplating asking Miranda about her parents' thoughts on her dating a woman, but the right moment hadn't yet come up. From what she gathered, Miranda's parents were quite open-minded and affectionate, having warmly embraced Blake as if she were their daughter.

"Okay, Mom. I'll see you when I get back. Love you too," Miranda concluded her call, placing the phone back in her bag. She then turned to Lane with a smile. "Mom says hi. She's hoping to meet you soon. You somehow missed each other at the baby shower. She's very curious about the woman who has the hots for me," Miranda added teasingly.

Surprised, Lane quickly turned her head to look at

Miranda. "You told your parents about me?"

"Yes, I did. Why do you sound so surprised?"

Lane shrugged, trying to appear nonchalant and not focus on the weird feeling of warmth swimming in her stomach from learning that Miranda's parents wanted to meet her. "Because everything is still so new for you."

"I'm very close with my parents and wouldn't keep such life-changing news from them, especially when I know I'll have their love and support to help me as I embrace this side of myself. Most of my family is very accepting of the LGBTQ+ community, so I have no reason to be afraid to tell them that I'm dating a woman. And the ones who aren't, I don't give a shit what they think. Who I choose to sleep with is nobody's business. Mom even joked that maybe I was destined to be with a woman since I'm so very picky with the men I've dated."

Lane drummed her fingers on the steering wheel, her curiosity piquing. "Are you?" Lane sensed Miranda's eyes on her but they were navigating a busy part of the interstate, so she kept her eyes on the road.

"I wouldn't say that I am," Miranda replied thoughtfully. "I just know what I want and what I'm willing to compromise on. I don't expect anyone to change for me, so I prefer to wait to find someone who possesses the qualities I value most."

Lane wished they were having this conversation face-to-face so she could gauge Miranda's expressions. "I respect that you see it that simply. Not many people do, or have the courage not to settle for less than they think they deserve, just because they want to feel loved. They often end up with people who don't deserve to breathe the same air as them. I personally believe that people are who they are and there's nothing we can do to change them. So why waste your time?" Lane shrugged nonchalantly, continuing to keep her eyes on the road. "A monster is just a monster. It's best to find someone you don't have to waste time trying to change into someone who will make you happy. As you said, find the person with the inherent qualities that will make you happy. It's that simple."

Miranda chuckled, inciting Lane to quickly glance her way, wondering what she said that was so funny. "I'm not surprised that you see people as monsters."

"That's because I've encountered my fair share of them throughout my life." Before Miranda could ask her to elaborate, Lane chose to change the topic. She didn't believe in lying and the last thing she wanted was to talk about past experiences with those "monsters". "What was it like for you growing up biracial?"

"I'm surprised you're comfortable asking me that."

Lane frowned. "Why wouldn't I be?"

Miranda's expression grew thoughtful. "Because in today's society, everything is considered offensive or a sensitive issue, and people are now afraid to ask a question like that out of fear, even if their intentions are good."

Lane nodded in understanding. "I get that. It's unfortunate. But it's a fair question. Despite the racial divide in this country, I think it would be wrong of me to make any assumptions about your life. Nia is black and her experiences growing up here differ from many other black people I know. So, to me, what is offensive is when people generalize someone's life based on the history of their race or what's portrayed in the media."

"I agree." Miranda adjusted her seat to settle more comfortably. "I'm fortunate that my childhood didn't leave any lasting scars. I'm half-black, so yes, I've encountered racism, but my family prepared me well for it. I grew up here in Seattle where my dad's family is from, and my parents chose to live here after meeting in college. They bonded over their shared passion for unique architectural designs, which eventually led them to start their own construction company. Thanks to my grandfather's connections, it was easier for them to launch the company in Seattle, during a time when the market was thriving. Since my mom was the architect, it made sense for her to relocate with him. My mom focused on designing the buildings, while my dad brought them to life." Miranda inhaled deeply before continuing. "I attended predominantly white private schools and then spent most holidays in Atlanta with my mom's family, because she wanted me to connect with my black heritage and bond with my relatives there."

Miranda paused briefly and then continued, "Even though I'm biracial, because of my skin tone, in America I'm just seen as black. Because of this, from a very young age, my parents made sure I understood what being biracial means in this country and my mom's mother instilled in me the values of being a strong black woman. One key lesson I learned early on was that money makes a significant difference in how people treat you, regardless of race. My grandfather's company donated heavily to my high school and employed quite a few of the students' parents. So, I was the 'black' kid whose white grandfather signed their paychecks, so they came correct." Miranda ended with a chuckle. "Outside of my dad's parents, I'm closer to my mom's family. I mean, I get along well enough with other members of that side of my family, but we don't share the same close bond."

Lane found the last part of Miranda's statement weird seeing that she grew up living closer to her white relatives. "Why are you closer to your mom's side?"

"Because while my dad's parents accepted my mom without question, the rest of his family weren't so kind. They thought my mom was just a black gold digger trying to trap my dad, until they found out that my mom's family had more money than them." Lane could hear the disdain in Miranda's voice as she spoke candidly about something that must have been painful for her to learn. "Do you know Corey Carter of Sageco Technologies? He's my mom's dad."

The name instantly registered with Lane, and she turned her head to look at Miranda, managing to keep her expression composed despite her surprise. "Isn't he like one of the richest black men in America? The second richest on the latest Forbes list of African American billionaires. He owns one of the longest-running African American businesses."

"Yes, that's my granddad," Miranda replied with pride in her voice.

This news made Lane admire Miranda even more. In spite of her very affluent background, Miranda carried herself with a humility not often seen in those with similar fortunes. "So, that's how you came about your many trust funds that you're now using to help the less fortunate," Lane jested, recalling their conversation from weeks ago.

Miranda laughed, the sound echoing in the car and warming Lane's body—a rather strange effect that no one else had ever had on her. "Of course, you would remember that. But yes, you're right. I'm the first granddaughter on both sides of my family, and let's just say I'm their pride and joy, who they took pleasure in spoiling when I was growing up. I was the only one for seven years. This resulted in them setting up trust funds for me along with my parents."

"Yes, I could tell that you're a little princess who likes to be spoiled. It's a good thing I like spoiling the women I spend my time with."

"Yes, you're a very generous lover," Miranda said sincerely, her voice lowering in pitch.

The atmosphere in the car shifted, becoming charged with a tangible tension. Lane glanced over at Miranda, catching the suggestive look in her eyes—one that clearly recalled just how generous Lane had been in bed. Lane was tempted to pull over and address the mounting tension between them. However, she knew that a quick release would only fan the flames of her desire without satisfying it fully. What she really wanted was to lose herself for hours in the warm embrace of Miranda's body.

"What about your parents? Have they always been supportive of your sexuality?"

Lane's initial surge of desire cooled at Miranda's question like a bucket of ice water had been poured over her. She paused, considering how to respond. It wasn't that she was ashamed of her childhood, but discussing her egg and sperm donor was not how she wanted to spend any part of her day. But Miranda had opened up about her own life, and fairness dictated that Lane do the same. Choosing to focus on the positive, she spoke of the one person who had always stood by her since the day she gave Lane a home.

"My foster mom has been incredibly supportive throughout my life," Lane confessed, her voice softening with affection. "She even encouraged me to ask the first girl I liked in high school out on a date and gave me money to buy chocolate for our first date. These days, she's always on my case to find someone special to settle down with."

"You grew up in foster care?" Miranda's voice carried a note of surprise. Lane turned to her, half-expecting the pity she had so often encountered as a teen when people heard the words foster care. Instead, she found Miranda's eyes filled with a respectful admiration, as if she were impressed by Lane's resilience.

"That's a story for another time," Lane said gently, not wanting to delve into the darker chapters of her past just then. "I don't want to cast a shadow on our time together with tales of my less-than-charming childhood." While she was open to sharing her history with Miranda, today was just not the day. It had been years since she had spoken about those early years, and she wasn't sure she was ready to revisit them just yet.

Lane braced herself, expecting Miranda to probe further as many others would have, but she was pleasantly surprised when Miranda said, "I understand. But when you're ready, I'd love to hear about your childhood. Given your professional accomplishments, I suspect there's a very impressive success story there." Miranda then placed her hand on Lane's thigh in a comforting gesture, her light strokes sending a fiery tingle throughout Lane's body. She felt it everywhere but mostly in the pit of her stomach— an arousal so rapacious she wondered if it would ever be sated.

Lane cleared her throat to moisten her suddenly dry

mouth before responding. "Thanks for understanding. I'll share it someday." She then turned on the radio, and Madonna's "Like a Virgin" filled the car. She adjusted the volume down slightly and smiled. "Now, I think it's time I introduced you to my eclectic taste in music."

"Like a virgin, huh?" Miranda asked, her tone teasing.

Lane shot back with a playful hint of seduction in her voice. "Is that how you felt the first time I fucked you?"

Miranda threw her head back, laughter spilling out freely. "Oh my god. What am I going to do with you?"

"I'm yours to do whatever you want, Miranda darling," Lane replied, cranking up the music a notch. "Now, how about you let me hear that singing voice you mentioned earlier."

Miranda didn't miss a beat and began singing along as Madonna's classic hit filled the car, a song daringly released the year Lane was born. The rest of the journey unfolded with lighter conversations and more music, and Lane discovering that she could listen to Miranda sing all day because she did have a beautifully captivating singing voice.

Two hours later when they pulled up outside The Heathman Hotel, Lane leaned closer to Miranda and said, "Maybe I should have brought a tie."

"What?" Miranda asked, the space between her eyes creasing in confusion.

Lane's voice dropped to a sultry whisper. "Fifty Shades of Grey."

Miranda leaned in, her lips tantalizingly close to Lane's. "Do you want to tie me up, Lane? Act out some scenes that Ana and Christian indulged in, since we're staying at the hotel they probably made famous?"

Lane closed the gap, her breath mingling with

Miranda's as she gently bit Miranda's lower lip, then soothed the spot with her tongue. "If you'd allow me, it would be my absolute pleasure."

Lane observed the deepening hue in Miranda's eyes and the quickening of her breath, signs of her rising arousal. Just as she was about to respond, the valet opened the car door, abruptly interrupting their moment. Although Miranda didn't get a chance to verbalize her consent, the unmistakable desire in her eyes spoke volumes. A tremor of excitement raced down Lane's spine at the thought of tying Miranda up and doing very wicked things to her.

This trip might turn out to be very fun indeed.

Chapter 2

Miranda chuckled as the elevator doors slid shut, sealing them in a private world after their evening at the Keller Auditorium. "Admit you loved it. You even got teary-eyed at the end. No need to keep up the tough CEO act with me," she teased, watching Lane's reflection in the polished metal.

"I did no such thing," Lane retorted with a half-smile, her denial lacking any real force. "My eyes were glossy from all the champagne I drank while counting down the seconds to leave."

Miranda moved closer, her hands finding Lane's neck. "I thought you prided yourself on being brutally honest all the time," she murmured, her lips nearly brushing against Lane's.

Lane's hands drifted to settle on Miranda's hips. "I *am* honest," she whispered back, her voice low. "You're the one choosing to romanticize my reaction to watching a young woman overcome tragedies that would have broken many people." Her hands slipped further down, cupping Miranda's ass.

"That's because you were moved, and you're just trying to act all tough. But you and I both know that underneath your aloofness, you're a big softie." Miranda's thumb gently brushed the hair at the nape of Lane's neck. She watched as the greenish hue of Lane's eyes darkened with that familiar hunger, a look that always sent a thrilling clench through Miranda's core.

Lane was like a book that surprised her with every page turn. Each new revelation about her was unexpected and compelling, making Miranda eager to keep discovering more, yet dreading the moment the story might end. Miranda's curiosity about Lane's past deepened, driven by the contradictions she observed. Lane carried herself with the ease of someone born into wealth—sure of her place in the world. Miranda had encountered others who had come into wealth awkwardly—some wore it uncomfortably, some doubted their right to it, and others flaunted it cringingly. But Lane was different, and Miranda found herself drawn to the narrative of resilience behind her poised exterior. She loved a good success story and she was intrigued by how someone from Lane's background navigated the challenges life threw at them. It was always inspiring to hear about real-life survival and triumph.

Lane nuzzled her nose against the tip of Miranda's. "No one has ever accused me of being soft before."

"That's because they aren't as adept as I am in getting you to lower your fortresses. I'm *very* special like that," Miranda countered, her fingers weaving into Lane's hair to massage her scalp.

Lane let out a deep moan as Miranda's fingernails dragged along her scalp. "Who's got the big ego now? And are you trying to seduce me into agreeing with you?"

Miranda fluttered her eyelashes flirtatiously. "I don't think I need to seduce you when you clearly can't resist me. You even agreed to come all the way here to watch a Broadway show you don't care for, just to spend time with me." She then ran her tongue lightly across Lane's lower lip, exhilarated by the palpable effect she had on her.

Lane chuckled, her hands tightening on Miranda's hips. "Gloating now, are we?"

"Just stating a fact," Miranda replied. Discovering that Lane wasn't a fan of Broadway made her appreciate the gesture even more. It was clear Lane had joined her simply to spend time together, proving that the activity didn't matter as long as they were together.

Suddenly, Lane steered them back a few steps and pressed Miranda against the elevator wall. Her voice dropped to a seductive whisper. "While there's some truth to your words, you should know I have my own ulterior motives for inflicting such suffering on myself."

"And what might those motives be?" Miranda asked, her voice low and knowing. She had a pretty good idea of Lane's reasons, but she wanted to hear Lane say it. There was just something about Lane telling her the rather filthy things she wanted to do to her that turned her on.

"This," Lane said simply before closing the gap between them and capturing Miranda's lips in a bruising kiss. Her lips were hot and insistent as they parted Miranda's, her tongue exploring fervently, fueling a desire so intense that Miranda wondered if they would even make it to their room before Lane ripped off her dress. Wrapped in the haze of arousal, Miranda realized that she was ready to agree if Lane proposed stopping the elevator to take her right there.

But just as the thought crossed her mind, the elevator chimed to a stop, and their kiss ended. Lane traced Miranda's lower lip with her thumb, her eyes dark with wicked intent. "Now, I get to show you exactly what my ulterior motives are. I hope you can keep up."

The elevator doors slid open, and Lane intertwined their fingers, guiding Miranda out with a sense of urgency. The desire that had simmered during the show now roared back to life, igniting Miranda's eagerness. Miranda could admit she had spent the entire week thinking about sleeping with Lane again, and that was one of the main reasons why she had taken the chance of asking Lane to join her. There was just something about the way Lane touched her that was addictive —the intensity and confidence that made Miranda wetter than anyone ever had. Entering the hotel room, Miranda expected Lane to pin her against the door and continue what she had started. Instead, Lane led her to the bed and sat on the edge, leaving Miranda standing in front of her. Lane's hands then trailed leisurely up Miranda's hips to the zipper at the side of her dress, and tugged it down slowly, her eyes never leaving Miranda's as the dress pooled at her feet.

Lane's voice was soft yet firm as she leaned forward, her breath warm against Miranda's skin. "I told you I like to spoil the women I date, and that includes making their fantasies a reality." She pressed a gentle kiss to Miranda's stomach. "But that requires trust." She looked back up at Miranda, a silent plea in her eyes. "Do you trust me, Miranda?"

Miranda was having a hard time focusing on Lane's words because all her attention was zeroed in on Lane's fingers, which were dancing a few inches from her clit through her underwear. "Yes, I trust you," she managed to say with certainty. She did trust Lane and had never truly felt uncomfortable around her, even from the very first night they met when Lane had looked at her as if she were a gourmet meal.

"Good," Lane continued, her tone serious but caring. "I also need you to tell me to stop if I do something you don't like. Just say 'stop,' and I will, no questions asked." As she spoke, Lane's thumbs hooked into the waistband of Miranda's thong, sliding them down her thighs, her actions deliberate and slow. Bending forward, she traced her tongue along Miranda's hip bone, sliding her hands up to unclasp Miranda's bra to free her aching nipples.

"Yes, I understand," Miranda replied, her voice thick with need as waves of anticipation coiled in every muscle of her body.

"Good," Lane said, rising to her full height. She met Miranda's gaze with an intensity that sent a current down her spine. "Now, lay on your back in the middle of the bed," she ordered.

Miranda obeyed, moving to position herself as Lane directed, her heart racing with the thrilling mix of command and care in Lane's demeanor. As she settled on the bed, her body was alive with expectation, ready for whatever Lane had planned next.

Eyes locked on Miranda, Lane began a slow, seductive striptease, peeling away her dress and revealing more of her skin with each calculated movement. Miranda watched, captivated, as Lane's beauty unfolded, not just in her form, but in the essence she was discovering that radiated from within. Fully naked, Lane walked over to her suitcase and pulled out a silk scarf and a gray tie. Miranda expected some trigger of apprehension; instead, all she felt was a raging inferno of arousal, hotter and more intense than anything she had previously experienced. While she had enjoyed sex with her previous partners, Miranda had never felt the trust necessary to give them such power over her. Yet, with Lane, there was an imbued comfort and willingness to submit to whatever Lane demanded of her. It was as if her body craved to be explored in ways it never had before, and she wanted Lane to be the explorer.

Lane picked up her phone and EarPods from the bedside table, climbed onto the bed, and straddled Miranda's thighs. She ran her fingertips lightly over Miranda's stomach. "Do you still want me to tie you up and fuck you, Miranda?" Lane's voice was a harmonious blend of firmness and gentleness, like a steady breeze that carried both strength and warmth. Each word resonated with authority, yet wrapped in a soothing undertone that invited trust and comfort.

Miranda's breath hitched, her response a breathy, "Yes," that floated through the air. She then added, "Did you just happen to have a tie lying around?"

Lane flashed a sly grin. "Nope. But I'm very resourceful." Miranda watched as Lane unraveled the tie, pulling it taut between her hands, as if testing its durability against straining force. "After our little chat in the car when we arrived here, I figured we might as well leave our own mark on this place, inspired by one of the most infamous pieces of literature in modern times." Leaning over, her breasts tantalizingly near Miranda's mouth, Lane bound Miranda's hands together above her head with smooth, practiced movements.

Miranda, unable to resist the temptation, arched up slightly and captured one of Lane's nipples between her teeth, biting softly. Lane let out a sharp hiss of pleasure. While Miranda savored the taste of Lane, she slipped the EarPods into Miranda's ears. Miranda released Lane's nipple and looked up at her in slight confusion,

Lane explained with a seductive smirk, "You said you like to make love to music. I'm here to serve at your pleasure." She then eased back from Miranda's eager mouth. "And the blindfold," she added while reaching for the silk scarf, "will heighten every touch, every sensation."

"How do you know that? Have you ever allowed anyone to do this to you?" Miranda asked, her curiosity getting the better of her, wondering if Lane had ever trusted anyone so completely.

Lane's eyes sparkled with amusement. "I'm too much of a control freak for that. Though I'm not opposed to the idea, I simply haven't met anyone who I trust enough to give that kind of control. Besides," she added, shrugging casually, "most of the women I've dated tend to be more submissive in bed. They prefer to be dominated, and I enjoy taking charge." She paused, biting her lower lip. "I guess you could say they like to be fucked, and I enjoy doing the fucking."

Miranda couldn't help but feel a fleeting sting of jealousy at the mention of Lane's past experiences. But she quickly brushed aside her irrational feelings, reminding herself of the casual nature of their relationship.

"Yeah, yeah, we all know how bossy you are," she joked, masking her inner turmoil. However, a part of her secretly reveled in the idea that Lane had never allowed anyone else that level of intimacy, sparking a bright hope within her that she could be the first. The notion of being the one to explore uncharted territory with Lane pulsed strongly through her subconscious.

Unable to resist the urge, Miranda asked, "Would you let me tie you up and have my wicked way with you?"

Lane's eyes smoldered with desire as she answered without hesitation, a simple, "Yes."

Miranda was taken aback by the swift and unwavering response, prompting her to inquire further, "Why?"

Once again, Lane replied with certainty, "I want to make all your fantasies a reality." Then, in a softer tone, she added, "And I trust you."

Before Miranda could fully digest Lane's confession and probe further into why Lane trusted her so deeply, Lane closed the distance between them, her lips capturing Miranda's in a ferocious kiss filled with urgency. The force of the kiss had Miranda's body melting into the mattress and all her attention drifting once again to the blood roaring in her clit. Breathless, Lane pulled back, her fingers gently lifting the blindfold to Miranda's eyes. She paused, her gaze searching Miranda's face for permission to continue. Miranda nodded consent.

"Just relax. I promise to take care of you." Lane's voice was a soothing melody, promising an adventure as she draped the scarf over Miranda's eyes, enveloping her in darkness. Lane shifted, her warm breath caressing Miranda's ear. In a husky whisper, she confessed, "Having you at my mercy is such a turn-on. I'm so wet right now that I could come from just one lick of your tongue." She nibbled Miranda's earlobe. "You're so very beautiful, and I'm going to worship every inch of you." The sultry timbre of Lane's voice, laden with lust, shot straight to Miranda's core and she feared she might climax from Lane's words alone.

Just seconds later, Annie Lennox's sultry rendition of Nina Simone's "I Put a Spell on You" began playing through the EarPods. Miranda couldn't help but laugh at the irony of the song choice and the moment, feeling indeed as if Lane had cast a spell over her, leaving her bound and utterly willing to surrender to whatever Lane desired. As the music infused the air, each note stirred her spirit, heightening every one of her senses in anticipation of Lane's next move. The wait stretched, each second ticking by with torturous slowness, ramping up the anticipation until it was almost unbearable. Just as Miranda was about to break the silence and call out for Lane, she felt warm lips claim hers in a hungry kiss. Lane's body stretched out over hers, settling comfortably between her spread thighs. It felt as though Lane were moving in rhythm with the music that only Miranda could hear, her thigh pressing just right against Miranda's clit, eliciting a sharp gasp that mingled with their breaths.

Lane's relentless pursuit didn't falter—she trailed her kisses down to Miranda's neck, sucking greedily at the pulse beating wildly beneath her lips. The scorching lips moved lower, reaching Miranda's breasts. There, each nipple received its share of attention, skillfully teased and tormented with a combination of tongue and teeth. As the playlist shifted seamlessly to Michele Morrone's "Dark Room" the atmosphere thickened with an erotic charge, each note mirroring the deepening of their entanglement, propelling Miranda closer to the edge of ecstasy.

Lane kissed her way down Miranda's body, each touch of her lips fanning the embers kindling in Miranda's core. With a mix of nips and suction, she explored the entire expanse of Miranda's stomach, dipping teasingly into her navel and tracing the delicate lines down to her hip bones. Miranda was so painfully aroused that she felt like crying. When Lane's mouth finally found its target, firmly clasping onto her clit, Miranda's back arched violently off the bed, a cry tearing from her throat and cutting through the music pulsating in her ears. Lane's tongue danced along her, alternating between gentle licks and firm strokes. The contrast of her soft oral caresses against the sharp pinches and rolls of her nipples created a maddening sensory overload. It was a dangerous combination that had Miranda feeling like she was being fine-tuned for a massive explosion. An explosion that she was on the brink of as her body tensed, walls tightening around the rhythm of Lane's tongue as it dove deep, curling and flicking at just the right spot. With each relentless stroke, Miranda teetered on the verge of a cataclysmic release, each wave building higher, ready to crash in an overwhelming crescendo.

"God... yes.. right there!" Miranda screamed as her orgasm crashed over her like a rough current coming to shore, her back bowing off the bed in ecstasy. She felt the muscles in her arm starting to ache and she lowered them, searching for Lane. But as soon as her hands touched Lane's hair, Lane moved. Before Miranda could figure out what was happening, Lane flipped her over onto her stomach, mid-orgasm. Miranda wanted to cry from what she considered a deep injustice.

"I wasn't finished coming!" she protested, her body still throbbing with unfulfilled need. The abrupt removal of the EarPods left her disoriented as she adjusted to the sudden silence and their ragged breathing.

"Don't worry. I promise the ending will be worth it," Lane assured, her warm breath caressing Miranda's lobe as she spoke against her ear before she moved off her body.

Miranda heard movement as if Lane were searching for something in her suitcase, then more shuffling that she couldn't place. A minute later the bed dipped and she felt Lane settle behind her.

"Let's put our yoga practices to good use," Lane said, her voice gravelly and commanding. "Get into the melting heart pose."

Miranda could almost feel the intensity in Lane's gaze and she wished she could see it. With trembling knees, Miranda obeyed, thankful for her yoga practice that kept her steady despite her bound hands.

"I'm going to fuck you hard, Miranda, but please tell me to stop if it's too much." Lane's hands glided over the curve of her ass, spreading her slightly. A sharp smack followed, sending a myriad of sensations through Miranda's body. "Use your words, Miranda."

Miranda was tempted to remain silent, hoping for another spank, but she wanted to come too much to do anything that would delay her orgasm. "Yes," she responded, her voice almost a plea for more.

"Good." A soft kiss was placed on her lower back almost like a reward for her obedience.

Lane gripped Miranda's hips, lifting her slightly, her palm warm against her stinging cheek. A single finger slipped inside her, tantalizingly slow, stoking her need to an unbearable peak. A whimper escaped Miranda as Lane withdrew, leaving her core begging to be filled. In the breathless pause that followed, Miranda felt the presence of something else—presumably a strap-on or dildo—poised at her entrance. It glided along her, distributing her slick arousal, heightening the ache that pulsed insistently between her thighs into an overwhelming crescendo.

"Lane… please, I need you," Miranda pleaded desperately as arousal coiled tightly within her.

Slowly, almost torturously, the shaft pressed into her. The sensation was both exquisite and agonizing as Miranda's body stretched to accommodate the fullness—a rush of crushing pleasure causing her eyes to roll to the back of her head. Lane withdrew slightly only to enter again, each movement more assertive than the last. Again and again, Lane moved within her, each thrust deeper and more forceful, until Miranda accepted her with little resistance due to her increasing wetness. Her body yielded, accepting each motion with a hungry eagerness that blurred the edge of pain into deep, consuming bliss.

"You're so tight. I love how you strain to take me in," Lane rasped, both hands now firmly on Miranda's hips, confirming the presence of the strap-on. "I think you're ready for me now."

Before Miranda could fully absorb Lane's words, Lane pulled back completely and then surged forward with a powerful thrust. There was no time to adjust as Lane tightened her grip, holding Miranda firmly in place while driving into her relentlessly with long, deep strokes. Each thrust sent her into a tailspin, spiraling closer to what she knew would be a powerful orgasm. Lane's technique was masterful as she rotated her hips with each stroke, playing Miranda's body expertly.

"Oh fuck," Miranda gasped as Lane drove in deep,

stars bursting behind her closed eyes. "You feel so good inside me." She pressed back into Lane, meeting each powerful thrust, driving the dildo in completely once again. "Please, don't hold back. I can take it. Fuck me however you want," she pleaded, the overwhelming desire to give Lane whatever she wanted consuming her.

Miranda's words seemed to ignite something fierce within Lane, who fucked her with an intensity that bordered on savagery, leaving Miranda with nothing to do but surrender fully. "Your pussy is so wet for me baby. So fucking wet that I'm sliding in and out of you so easily now." Lane's breathing became ragged, punctuated by many expletives as the slapping sound of skin meeting skin echoed in the room. Suddenly, Miranda felt a finger exploring a sensitive area that no one had ever touched before, sending a shock of unexpected pleasure through her.

Miranda tensed, and Lane instantly removed her finger, her movements slowing. "You've never been touched there before?" she asked tentatively.

"No," Miranda responded, her voice low, once again wishing she could see Lane's expression.

"If you're comfortable with it, I'd like to touch you there. If not, then we don't have to. But I promise, the pleasure will be worth the experience," Lane offered, her voice gentle yet persuasive.

Lane's words piqued Miranda's curiosity, especially after the fleeting pleasure she felt when Lane had briefly touched her there. More than anything, she felt comfortable enough with Lane to explore this new aspect of sex without feeling self-conscious.

"Yes, I want to try it with you," she told Lane, her

voice devoid of fear.

"Thank you." Miranda almost laughed at Lane's politeness, but before she could, she gasped as the wind was knocked out of her when Lane abruptly pulled out and then slammed back into her, resuming the intense pace before their brief intermission.

This time, when Lane's finger touched her there, Miranda welcomed the sensation, feeling her core tighten with desire as Lane expertly swirled around the sensitive nerves.

"Just relax," Lane murmured gently, continuing her skilled ministrations.

Miranda's body obeyed Lane's soothing command, relaxing as a finger breached the barrier, setting her insides on fire as pleasure like nothing she had ever felt before, spread throughout her body. Lane expertly matched the rhythm of her thrusting finger with the stroke of the dildo, driving Miranda into a quivering mess. The passion that always surged through her veins when Lane touched her now erupted like a volcano, leveling all resistance in its wake as her orgasm approached. Lost in a whirlwind of sensation, every touch, every movement propelled her higher until she teetered on the brink of release. Then, suddenly, Miranda was climaxing in two places, overwhelmed by pleasure so intense it felt as though it was ripping her apart from the inside as her body shook uncontrollably. Ecstasy like nothing she had ever felt before blasted through her, setting her entire body ablaze and erasing everything that she thought was amazing sex before the Lane Experience.

"Fuck, yes. Come for me," Lane panted, drawing out every ounce of pleasure from Miranda's body as she continued her onslaught. Lane's grip on Miranda's hips tightened, her movements growing more urgent and primal. The rhythm of their bodies matched the pounding of Miranda's heart, each thrust pushing her closer and closer to the brink again.

Miranda felt as though she had left her body, cast into an endless chasm of pleasure with no end in sight, as another orgasm slammed into her. Her entire body still trembling, moisture running down her thighs as she came and came. Her body sagged into the mattress, and if Lane hadn't been holding her, she knew she would have collapsed entirely. Gradually, Lane slowed her thrusts and then very slowly pulled out. As she did, an abundance of moisture gushed from Miranda, but she had no time to feel embarrassed when it was a result of the most intense orgasms she had ever experienced. Lane released her hips and, as expected, Miranda's knees gave out and she collapsed onto the bed. Lane left the bed, and Miranda found herself dozing off. Moments later, Lane returned and gently shifted Miranda onto her back, laughing as Miranda mumbled incoherent protestations. Then a warm rag was placed between her thighs, cleaning up the mess she had made of herself—or more accurately, the mess Lane had made. Lane disappeared again, and then Miranda felt the tie loosened around her wrist and the blindfold removed. She slowly opened her eyes, grateful to find that Lane had turned off the overhead lights, leaving only one bedside light on.

Lane settled on her side beside Miranda, drawing her into a comforting embrace as they lay facing each other. She pressed a tender kiss to Miranda's forehead and asked softly, "Are you okay?" Her fingers gently moved along Miranda's spine, offering soothing comfort. "There's water on the bedside table if you're thirsty."

Miranda lifted her eyes to meet Lane's, and the tenderness in them took her breath away. She smiled and snuggled closer to Lane, draping a leg over her hip. "Other than the fact that I can barely feel my limbs, I couldn't be better."

"Okay good. You should get some sleep," Lane murmured, her voice soft and caring.

"What about your orgasm? I need to make you come," Miranda mumbled sleepily, fighting the pull of exhaustion.

"I already did from watching the dildo slide in and out of you," Lane whispered seductively, causing Miranda's flesh to pulse, although she didn't have the energy for another orgasm.

"I want to use it on you. Would you let me?" Miranda asked, teetering on the edge of unconsciousness.

"I'll let you do whatever you want to do to me. I'm here to serve at your pleasure, to ensure that you have the most fulfilling experience during our time together. I want you to explore your sexuality without limits," Lane replied in a hushed whisper as if they were trading secrets meant only for them.

Miranda snuggled even closer to Lane, resting her head in the crook of her neck. "Thank you," she mumbled as she finally gave up the fight and allowed sleep to pull her under.

Chapter 3

"And you're having the best sex of your life?" Blake teased, sitting across from Miranda in her office. Blake had an appointment nearby and decided to drop in to see her.

Miranda couldn't suppress the wide smile that spread across her face, though she tried hard not to dwell on said sex Blake was alluding to. "I've had decent sex before."

"But this is better, right?" Blake gave a knowing shrug. "Come on, admit it. We women know what we're doing way better than men," Blake said, her eyes twinkling with amusement.

Miranda felt incredibly grateful to have a friend like Blake with whom she could have these conversations. With Blake, she could be herself without fear of judgment, particularly important now that she had discovered her attraction to both men and women later in life. She was aware of stories where women in her situation were accused of being frauds or merely experimenting due to a mid-life crisis. Miranda couldn't speak for everyone, but she knew she would never treat her sexuality as a mere experiment borne out of curiosity or boredom. She was acutely aware of the challenges faced by the LGBTQ+ community, stemming from homophobes who refused to acknowledge that just as they didn't choose to be straight, homosexuals didn't choose whom they loved.

"I won't make that judgment since I've only been with one woman. Maybe on both sides, you have people who aren't as skilled as others in the lovemaking department."

Blake rolled her eyes dramatically, and Miranda burst into laughter, knowing Blake—who had known from a young age that she was a lesbian—would never see the appeal of sleeping with a man. "Such a 'you' answer," Blake chuckled. "Of course, you'd take the diplomatic route. And while I agree with your statement, it's still better with women."

Based on her experiences with Lane, Miranda could easily agree that sex with women was superior. Indeed, she was having some of the best sex of her life, though Miranda suspected that this might be because of Lane specifically. Lane was phenomenal in bed, introducing Miranda to new experiences and pleasures she hadn't known before. "Ask me this question again in ten years. For now, I'm sticking with my answer."

Blake shook her head, half in amusement. "Yeah, yeah." Her expression then turned more serious as she studied Miranda. "Outside of the best sex of your life, how are things otherwise with Lane? I know everything is casual between you two, but you've never really been a casual type of person."

Miranda exhaled slowly, gathering her thoughts. "I know, but with the way things happened with Lane, it was either explore my feelings for her or go mad with lust. I wanted to sleep with her so badly. I understand she doesn't do relationships, so I have no expectations of us falling in love and running off into the sunset. Plus, with the newness of my attraction to women, maybe starting with something casual is safer than working toward a relationship. That way it reduces the chances of anyone getting hurt because I jumped into something without fully understanding my feelings."

"I understand. But speaking from experience, I know that casual can lead to forever when we least expect it." Miranda suppressed a smile as she caught the subconscious way Blake played with her wedding rings, her eyes brimming with love for Alexandra. *Still so obsessed with her wife.* "I just don't want you to get hurt. I know Lane is honorable and wouldn't intentionally play with your emotions, but sometimes we end up hurting people even without intending to."

"I know, I'm not worried, to be honest. As you said, Lane is honorable. She's so brutally honest that it can be scary." Miranda chuckled. "I can see why some people might think she's an asshole. Not many people like hearing the truth without any sugar coating. But that's exactly why I feel so comfortable with Lane—I always know where I stand with her. There's no bullshit or games—no hot and cold behavior."

Miranda gestured vaguely toward Blake. "And yes, even though it's casual, she's an amazing person to share this experience with. Maybe it's because we don't have relationship expectations that everything feels so simple. I never have to wonder what she's thinking. And she means everything she says. She's also not clingy and doesn't constantly need my attention. If my schedule doesn't allow us to spend time together, she handles it very maturely. Then there's the fact that she's not intimidated by my family's wealth. In the past, once men found out who my grandfather was, they'd get all insecure, realizing that there was nothing they could do to impress me financially. Even though I'm a successful surgeon, it was always learning about Granddad that brought on the insecurities."

Miranda bit her lower lip, pondering another aspect she truly admired about Lane. "There's also the fact that she likes being in control, both in and out of the bedroom. It's refreshing to be with someone who takes charge like that. When she plans our dates, she doesn't constantly ask what I want to do—she just plans it, and it's always something I'll enjoy. I really like that about her. And she's open to trying things I like, even if she's never tried them before. It's like being with a flexible control freak who's also incredibly generous, both in and out of bed."

"That's a whole lot of likes. She sounds like the ideal partner for you," Blake wiggled her eyebrows playfully as a devilish grin spread across her face. "Are you discovering that you're a true submissive in bed who likes to be dominated?"

Miranda threw her head back and laughed. God, she loved her best friend. "What can I say, I'm discovering a lot about myself with Lane. I honestly couldn't have asked for a better person to be my first experience. It's like she wants to leave a positive impression on behalf of all lesbians. But I think the side of her that I'm getting to know outside of work is who she really is at her core. She just doesn't allow many people to get close to her."

"Alexandra says the same thing. Do you know they text each other regularly just to check in? Maybe that's where she's getting information about you to plan those amazing dates." Blake paused, a look of realization crossing her face. "Now that I think about it, I'm right. Since you two started dating, there have been times when Alexandra would randomly ask me if I think you would enjoy doing something. That woman is surely putting in a lot of effort to give you the best experience."

Warmth fluttered behind Miranda's ribs, filled with appreciation. "Yes, she is. So, regardless of what happens in the future, I'll always be grateful for how kind and understanding she has been about my feelings."

"Sometimes we just have to live in the moment and not worry too much about tomorrow. As long as you're happy, that's all that matters. It's been a tough couple of months for you, so I'm glad you're at least finding some much-needed stress relief by having the best sex of your life." Blake rose from her seat. "I have to go. Amara is spending the night with Olivia. I need to prepare for date night so that I can indulge in the best sex of my life later. Alexandra will be returning to work soon, so we're trying to squeeze in as much alone time as possible before she does."

Miranda laughed heartily, loving the fact that they had always been so comfortable talking about sex in their friendship. She knew people who acted like it was a taboo topic not to be mentioned among friends. She got up from her chair, walked around her desk and pulled Blake into a tight hug. "Thanks for being the most amazing friend in the world. I love you."

"I love you too," Blake responded, pulling back to kiss Miranda on her cheek. "You and Lane should come over sometime for dinner."

Miranda nodded. "I'll discuss it with her. Get home safe."

"Okay. I'll text you when I'm home."

Once the door closed behind Blake, Miranda's

thoughts instantly turned to Lane. She picked up her phone from her desk and checked her messages, noticing the unusual silence from Lane—she typically received a morning text from her whenever they hadn't spent the night together. Concerned, Miranda dialed Lane's cell number, but it went straight to voicemail. With a furrowed brow, she leaned against her desk and picked up the office phone to dial Lane's extension.

"Hi, Dr. Hayes," Kelsey answered after the second ring.

"Hi, Kelsey. Does Lane have a meeting now or in the next hour?" Miranda asked, thinking maybe they could have lunch together.

"She didn't come into the office today. She's working from home. She asked me to send an email notifying staff earlier. Didn't you receive it?"

"I haven't had a chance to go through all my emails since I've been in. Thanks, Kelsey. Enjoy the rest of your day and have a good weekend if I don't see you before I leave."

"You, too."

Miranda hung up the phone, wondering why Lane hadn't mentioned her plans to work from home during their text conversation the previous night. She considered trying Lane's cell again, but opted to send a text instead.

Miranda: Hey. Heard you're working from home today. I'm leaving work around 5. Are you open to dinner and a movie at home? I could grab something on my way over. Let me know if you're in the mood for anything specific.

Miranda stared at her screen for a minute, waiting

for the telltale sign of Lane typing. But the three bubbles indicating a response never appeared. Her apprehension increased—Lane was a creature of habit with certain things, and not hearing from her by this time of day felt off. What made it even more peculiar was that Lane hadn't signed off on the reports Miranda had asked her to review and return by noon. It was a tight deadline, but typically, Lane would at least acknowledge the request, even if just to ask for more time.

Chapter 4

Miranda tapped her foot anxiously waiting for the elevator to finish its ascent to Lane's penthouse. She was nervous about showing up unannounced, worried that it might overstep the boundaries of their casual relationship. The last thing she wanted was to give Lane the impression that their expectations were out of sync. She was enjoying their time together and definitely didn't want to scare Lane off. But after not hearing from Lane all day and learning that Kelsey hadn't heard from her since the morning, her concerns were only intensified. Lane was always professional and wouldn't normally ignore attempts to contact her, nor would she neglect to respond to Miranda's messages about work. If Lane was fine and merely needed a quiet day, Miranda would leave her be. For now, though, she decided to trust her gut instinct and check on Lane.

The elevator dinged open. Stepping out and entering the foyer, Miranda immediately spotted Lane lying on the sofa. From her angle, she could only see the top of her head. Expecting Lane to rise and greet her, Miranda was puzzled when she remained still.

"Lane," Miranda called out, moving deeper into the living room. Rounding the sofa, her eyes widened at the scene before her. The floor was strewn with tissues, several water bottles, and half a bottle of cold medicine. Lane's laptop was also amidst the discarded items, indicating she had attempted to work before succumbing to her illness. Miranda rushed to Lane's side, dropping to her knees and placing the back of her hand on Lane's forehead. She was burning up with a high fever. Noticing the redness around Lane's nose and the dark circles under her eyes amplified Miranda's trepidation. Lane had relayed the day before that she felt extremely tired, but she hadn't mentioned any other symptoms that would have indicated that she was coming down with something.

Resting a hand on Lane's shoulder, Miranda gently shook her. "Lane, honey, wake up." Watery eyes slowly opened, and Miranda could see that even this small effort was a struggle for Lane. "What happened? You're burning up."

"It's just a cold," Lane mumbled weakly.

"No, it's more than that. Why didn't you tell me you were feeling sick? I would have come sooner. Are you in any pain? Have you taken anything besides the cold medicine? Did you take a Covid test?" Miranda's questions came rapidly as she soothingly stroked Lane's hair, her disquiet growing.

Lane turned her head into the sofa and coughed, the sound accentuating Miranda's worries. As Lane shifted to face Miranda and attempted to sit up, Miranda quickly stood to help her. "It's just a cold. I didn't want to bother you with it." Before she could continue, she was hit with another coughing fit. "I just need to drink a lot of water and rest. I'm pretty good at taking care of myself. I did it all by myself until I was fifteen."

Miranda eyed Lane skeptically, noting her dilated pupils, slurred speech, and the unusual snippet of personal history—uncharacteristic for Lane to share so casually. "It's not just a cold. You're burning up. Do you have any Covid test kits here?"

"It's not Covid. I took a test earlier." She waved her hand aimlessly like trying to swat an invisible fly. "I'll be fine. I just need to sleep," Lane insisted, her head lulling to one side as she fought to keep her eyes open.

"Okay, let's get you into bed. You have a high fever. Have you had anything other than water and cold medicine? Did you eat anything all day?" Miranda asked, supporting Lane as she tried to stand.

"I'll be fine, Miranda. I'm not hungry. Don't worry. It's Friday night, go have some fun," Lane insisted, leaning heavily on Miranda despite her protests about being helped.

"I should have known you'd be a difficult patient." Miranda wrapped her arm more securely around Lane's waist as they began moving toward the bedroom. "No, I'm not leaving you like this. I'm the doctor here, and you're going to listen to me. I'm going to get you into bed and make you some soup. You need to eat something. It will help you feel better faster."

"Yes, doctor," Lane said with a hint of petulance. "I can tell there's no point in arguing with you, and I have no choice but to let you boss me around while I'm incapacitated."

Miranda chuckled, pulling Lane closer. "Good. I love that you know which battles to pick."

Reaching the master bedroom Miranda noticed that Lane's bed was unmade—a clear sign that Lane hadn't been feeling well all day. The woman righteously made her bed first thing in the morning, even when she planned to stay home. She guided Lane to the foot of the bed, then walked around to straighten the sheets on

Lane's preferred side. Next, she went to the closet and retrieved the softest shirt she could find. Returning to Lane, she removed the sweat-soaked top and dressed her in the clean one.

Lane dropped her head to rest on Miranda's stomach, "You smell so good. If I wasn't so tired, I'd bury my face between your thighs." Miranda could feel Lane heaving against her, her core muscles tightening against the bellow reverberating from Lane's throat. "I especially love the way you smell down there."

A shiver moved through Miranda's body, and she internally chided herself for being so easily affected by Lane, even when she was clearly sick and likely high on cold medicine. "Okay, time for bed," Miranda said firmly, helping Lane up and leading her to the head of the bed. Once Lane was comfortably tucked under the sheets, Miranda sat beside her, resting her hand on her forehead to gauge her temperature. "I'm worried about your fever. It's not anything to be alarmed about now, but if it rises during the night, we're going to the hospital." Miranda smoothed a stray strand of hair from Lane's face, tucking it neatly behind her ear. "I know you're tired, but you need to eat something. Try to stay awake. I'll be right back."

Lane nodded, watching Miranda with half-lidded eyes as she rose from the bed and headed into the kitchen, hoping to find the ingredients needed to whip up some soup. While she could have placed an order, the delay was not an option—Lane needed nourishment before sleep claimed her. Rifling through the cupboards and refrigerator, Miranda found the ingredients necessary to concoct a reasonable facsimile of her grandmother's vegetable chicken broth—though she humbly admitted her culinary skills fell short of her grandmother's.

While she cooked, Miranda's thoughts wandered to why Lane hadn't told her she was sick. It seemed she hadn't told anyone at all. Lane still hadn't shared much about her family, but from what Miranda had gathered, she only had her foster mother and her best friend in Seattle. Lane didn't have many friends and tended to be a bit of a loner. Since they started dating, Miranda had learned that Lane was quite content with her own company—even to the point of going on solo dates to escape her apartment. Lane was an enigma—complicated yet simple in her own way and utterly undaunted by others' opinions of her. She seemed to understand life for what it was, played its games on her own terms, and didn't care much about being liked. Yet beneath that tough exterior, Lane was caring, considerate, and gentle—a side Miranda cherished deeply as she continued to peel back the layers of this fascinating woman.

I really hope that she'll share her childhood history with me. Maybe that will help me to understand her more.

After she finished cooking, Miranda dished the soup into a bowl and set it on the counter to cool while she dashed out to her car to grab her medical bag. She suspected the flu, but Lane's feverish symptoms bothered her. For her peace of mind, she wanted to get an exact read of her body temperature to be on the safe side. Minutes later, Miranda returned to the bedroom to find Lane curled up in a fetal position. She placed the tray with soup, crackers, and orange juice on the bedside table and sat beside Lane, her hand rubbing her back soothingly.

"Lane? Sit up for me, hon." Lane stirred, and Miranda was relieved that she hadn't fallen into an unarousable sleep. Gently, she helped Lane into a sitting position. "I'm just going to check your temperature." Lane—surprisingly compliant—didn't protest. Miranda quickly took her temperature and was thankful to find it was high but not alarmingly so. She then picked up the bowl of soup, scooped a spoonful, and gently blew on it to cool it, much like one would do when feeding a child.

"I can feed myself," Lane asserted as Miranda brought the spoon to her lips. Despite her protest, she accepted the soup, making no move to take the bowl herself.

"No, you can't. You can barely keep your eyes open." Miranda brushed back a strand of hair that had fallen from behind Lane's ear. "Now be a good patient and let me take care of you." Saying those words, Miranda realized how much she wanted to be someone Lane could rely on to care for her when she was sick. Regardless of their relationship's casual nature, she wanted Lane to know she was there for her in situations like this.

Lane quietly accepted another spoonful of soup, her eyes fixed on Miranda with an unreadable expression. From one spoon to the next she silently watched Miranda, her hazel eyes penetrating with that rare vulnerability she didn't often show. After finishing half the bowl, Lane murmured softly, "Other than Anita, no one has ever taken care of me like this. Thank you."

"Anita? Is that your foster mother?" Miranda inquired, careful not to press Lane for more information than she was comfortable sharing in her weakened state.

"Yes." Lane slowly shook her head as Miranda brought the spoon to her lips. "I can't eat anymore. I need to sleep now." She glanced at the bedside table. "May I have some of the orange juice?"

Miranda reached for the glass, gently pushing away Lane's hand when she tried to take it, and helped her drink instead. Once Lane had her fill, she slid down the bed, her gaze lingering on Miranda. She looked incredibly vulnerable and fragile at that moment, sparking a pang in Miranda's chest as she pondered what Lane's childhood must have been like, to have not been cared for until she was fifteen. It was remarkable how strong Lane had become, showing no outward signs of her challenging early years.

"Thanks for stopping by. I really appreciate it. If I survive the night, I'll call you when I wake up to let you know how I'm doing," Lane murmured drowsily.

"I'm not going to leave you here alone. I'll sleep in the guest room and set my alarm to check on you every two hours. If you wake up feeling worse, please call me." Miranda reached out and caressed Lane's cheek as the overwhelming urge to comfort her consumed her. She was saddened by the realization that Lane didn't even think she would stay the night when she was sick. "I'd sleep with you, but I don't want to increase my risk of getting sick any more than I already have. Both of us can't be out of commission."

"Okay. Thank you," Lane managed to say, her eyes fluttering closed as she drifted off to sleep.

The vulnerability in Lane's voice again awakened Miranda's nurturing instincts. Fortunately, she wasn't on call for the weekend, allowing her to devote herself entirely to taking care of Lane. She would just need to cancel her Sunday dinner plans with her parents. Leaning over, she placed a gentle kiss on Lane's forehead, wishing she could crawl into bed beside her and offer more comfort. Once Lane's breathing became steady and even, indicating she had fallen asleep, Miranda quietly picked up the tray and left the room to let her rest. She hoped that by morning, Lane's fever would have subsided.

Chapter 5

By Tuesday, Lane felt well enough to leave bed but chose to work from home, giving her immune system extra recovery time before returning to the office. Since arriving at Lane's on Friday, Miranda had briefly gone home only once—to grab some essentials after work on Monday before returning to care for Lane. Despite Lane's complaints that she didn't want to be a burden and insisting it was just a cold, Miranda had ignored her protests, choosing instead to stay and nurse her back to health. She wanted to show Lane that she could depend on her to be there when needed. Miranda believed no one should have to endure sickness alone, and she was always willing to be there for those she cared about. And she cared about Lane—a lot. Call her a big baby, but whenever she was sick, she always went to her parents' house for them to take care of her.

Now it was Friday evening, and they were lounging in bed, with Lane looking at Miranda as if she were an alien upon discovering that Miranda enjoyed what Lane deemed "trash TV"—The Real Housewives Sagas.

"Why would you waste time watching such mediocre content that depicts women in such an unflattering manner? There's nothing there that seems like it would stimulate the mind of someone with your intelligence," Lane said, her expression one of comical bafflement, as if she truly couldn't grasp how Miranda could find any enjoyment in what she considered one of the worst creations in television history.

Miranda laughed and playfully poked Lane in the ribs, making her squirm away from her ticklish touch. "I don't watch it for mental stimulation. It's actually the exact opposite of why I watch—it doesn't require much brainpower to focus on, so it helps me unwind after a long day. Plus, the ridiculousness of it all is quite entertaining. I see it as a guide on what not to do as women in relationships."

Lane shook her head, still visibly bewildered. "I'm still appalled by the idea of you subjecting yourself to that," she gestured dismissively toward the image frozen on the TV.

"Don't knock it until you've tried it," Miranda teased, tickling Lane's side again.

Lane made a face as if she had just bitten into a sour lemon. "While I'm open to trying new things, some things are simply a no for me. I can't fathom wasting an hour watching women act like brainless puppets, letting men treat them in the most embarrassing ways and being classless and tacky. That's a hard pass for me."

Miranda always enjoyed discovering new facets of Lane's personality. It was refreshing to see her many comical expressions and to hear her critique something she deemed below a certain standard. Lane's sharp wit and humor often left Miranda in stitches. "There's more to it than that," Miranda replied, smiling. "So, what do you watch to unwind after work?"

Lane's response was instant, which was another thing Miranda admired about her—she was so self-aware and uncompromising. "I much prefer to read. But when I do choose to watch TV, it's either true crime stories or game shows that require me to use my brain to solve a puzzle. For movies, it's mysteries, thrillers, or dramas. When I need background noise, it's Judge Judy. I love her level of sarcasm. And if they had a dancing show with only women, I'd probably watch that."

Miranda laughed. "Of course you would." Miranda began to trace slow patterns along the same side she had been tickling Lane on earlier. "What else do you like to do to relax?"

A devilish grin spread across Lane's lips as she playfully pushed Miranda onto her back, rolled on top of her, and settled between her thighs. "My absolute favorite way to relax is to make a woman come," she whispered, dipping her head to tug at Miranda's bottom lip before letting it go. "I think I can help you relax much faster than any housewife ever could, and my methods are far more satisfying." Lane flexed her hips, causing a delicious friction that made Miranda's breath catch. Sitting back, Lane smoothly lifted Miranda's tank top over her head. "Plus, I need to reward you for taking such good care of me while I was sick."

Lane quickly removed her own top and tossed it aside, followed by her underwear. She then ran her hands up Miranda's thighs, hooked her thumbs into Miranda's boyshorts, and slid them off slowly, maintaining intense eye contact throughout. The usual sharp voracity in Lane's gaze was there, but now it was mingled with something softer, something tender that quickened Miranda's pulse. Lane looked at her with reverence, as if Miranda was someone to be cherished and worshipped.

"No reward needed. I loved taking care of you. I hope you know that you can always call me if you're sick and

I'll show up," she told Lane with all the conviction she could muster around all the arousal already coursing through her veins.

Lane offered a shy smile, the kind that always revealed her more vulnerable side "I'll keep that in mind. Thank you. But you do deserve a reward, and you know how much I love spoiling you, my little pillow princess."

Miranda feigned mock offense. "I'm no such thing. It's not my fault you're bossy and get off on bossing me around in bed. I'm just nice enough to give you what you want."

Lane's grin turned mischievous, her eyes twinkling with wicked delight. "Oh, I get off all right—always."

Miranda laughed, sinking deeper into the pillow as Lane leaned in close. "You're incorrigible."

"And you love it." Lane kissed Miranda on her nose. "You're also a pillow princess who loves to be fucked. Don't think I haven't noticed how much wetter you get whenever I'm on top of you. You also love the fact that I dominate you in bed."

Lane's eyes burned with intentions, which Miranda knew would have her thoroughly rewarded. And while Lane's words were true about loving the way she handled her in bed, Miranda wouldn't admit it and give her reason to gloat. "Again, I'm just a very generous woman who likes to make you happy by enabling your controlling ways."

"Whatever you say, Dr. Hayes," Lane teased, her voice laced with knowing amusement. "But I know the truth, and the fact that you're already dripping wet is proof enough." Lane traced a finger along Miranda's swollen folds to emphasize her point, then lifted it to her lips and sucked it into her mouth, moaning softly. "Delicious," she murmured with a satisfied grin.

Miranda's arousal spiked to a painful level, and she felt more moisture run down her ass cheeks. Before she could voice a response, Lane closed the distance between them, their lips meeting in a tender caress. She had expected the kiss to be rough, since Lane had been looking at her as if she wanted to eat her alive—instead, it was soft and gentle, though still passionate. Lane's lips moved over hers carefully, as if Miranda were a delicate treasure she was taking time to discover. Lane's tongue coaxed her lips apart, dancing in a slow, sensual rhythm that was new to them. This was the softest they had ever kissed. Miranda didn't know Lane had it in her to be this gentle, as their lovemaking was usually filled with fiery intensity. At that moment, Lane kissed her not to take, but to give—pouring every ounce of affection into this tender expression of gratitude.

Lane separated their lips and peppered Miranda's face with delicate kisses, then continued down her neck and chest. Not an inch of skin was left untouched as Lane adorned her with an affectionate blend of lips and tongue. Miranda's body felt like it was slowly being lit on fire, each touch stoking the flames higher, and one touch from Lane on her clit would set off the imminent explosion. The softest lips she had ever felt captured her nipple, and Lane's slow reverence persisted as she teased the sensitive buds between her lips, swirling her tongue around them. Her hands, placid and soothing, caressed Miranda's curves, eliciting a feeling so delightful Miranda thought she might purr like a contented kitten. This tender touch from Lane felt like a completely new experience as if it was their first time all over again. Miranda wasn't sure if Lane realized the depth of her tenderness, but she could only call it being made love to in the most artistic fashion.

Lane's exploration continued down Miranda's stomach, her hands and mouth expertly working Miranda's body. Reaching between her thighs, Lane paused and gently blew across her clit, causing Miranda's back to arch dramatically due to how wound up she was from Lane's caresses.

"You're so very beautiful, Miranda. I could spend all day worshipping your body," Lane murmured, her voice filled with awe.

Glancing down, Miranda saw the undeniable lust in Lane's eyes and felt her core tighten in response. "And I could spend all day lying here and have you kiss every inch of me the way you just did."

"And the best is yet to come," Lane whispered, slowly tracing her tongue along Miranda's slit, moaning deeply. She resumed kissing Miranda's quivering flesh with the faintest of touches as if she were making slow, sweet love to her vagina. Lane's tongue slid oh so slowly inside, flicking softly and pushing Miranda close to the edge. Lane continued her tender strokes—each one more intense than the other, despite how delicately she was kissing Miranda. Her lips wrapped around Miranda's clit, sucking dexterously. The tenderness of her touch caused tears to prick behind Miranda's eyes—she was torn between the desire to climax and the wish for the moment to last forever. It was a slow, exquisite torture as Lane savored her with a thoroughness that transformed Miranda's insides into molten warmth.

Just as the pleasure became unbearable and Miranda was on the verge of begging Lane to fuck her harder,

Lane slipped in a single finger. It was all Miranda needed to plunge into the endless abyss of ecstasy as her orgasm crashed over her, its force belying the gentleness of Lane's approach.

"God... don't stop...," she cried out as Lane's finger continued its rhythmic dance, prolonging her climax.

Lane lapped at her quivering folds as if wanting to capture every bit of Miranda's essence. When Miranda's body finally stopped trembling, Lane kissed her way up her body and captured her lips in a deep, passionate kiss. Miranda tasted herself on Lane's lips and immediately felt her need for Lane reigniting.

Lane broke the kiss, staring down at Miranda, her eyes soft. "How was that for relaxation?"

"You're incredible," Miranda whispered, her hands stroking the length of Lane's spine.

"I know," Lane replied, her hazel orbs dark with desire and sparkling with amusement.

Miranda rolled her eyes. "Remind me again why I like you?"

"Oh, I intend to spend all night reminding you, Miranda darling," Lane said, tone low and seductive as she positioned her clit over Miranda's pulsing flesh.

As Lane began rotating her hips, the sensation of their clits—slippery, throbbing, and sliding against each other—was one of the most erotic experiences Miranda had ever felt. Lane captured her lips again in a passionate kiss, moaning deeply, the sound vibrating through Miranda's body and resonating in her core. Their movements synchronized perfectly, and Miranda found herself questioning if any other woman could ever evoke such feelings in her. Or was it simply that she was drawn to Lane, regardless of gender? Was it possible that sometimes you met someone and the desire and lust were so powerful, so deep, that you're irresistibly drawn to them?

After two months of dating, Miranda still hadn't deciphered why, of all the women she had met, it was Lane who stirred such profound feelings in her. No other person had ever made her pulse race with just a look—not even a man. The way her body responded to Lane was unparalleled, a reaction unique to her alone. She didn't know what the future might hold, but as long as she had the chance to feel Lane's touch, she intended to savor every moment. Miranda was a realist—she knew Lane might eventually move on to her next conquest, but for now, she was all in, taking full advantage of their time together.

Chapter 6

"You seem different," Anita said, scrutinizing Lane through the camera. "More relaxed. I've been noticing the changes over the last couple of months. Before then, when you came to visit your brooding was like a dark cloud hovering over you. What's changed?"

Lane pondered Anita's observations, trying to pinpoint the shifts in her demeanor. She hadn't realized the extent of the change herself, but Anita had always been perceptive when it came to her, picking up on nuances even Lane hadn't been aware of. Although, she could admit that the restlessness that had been plaguing her had started to dissipate over the past few months. "I do? In what way?" she asked, still unable to identify the differences Anita was alluding to.

"Yes. It was especially evident when you came to visit after you were sick. You seemed lighter. Less brooding and dark lord aura. You also had a spark in your eyes that I had never seen before. You were actually smiling to yourself when you were staring out the window." Anita's expression brightened as if she had solved some big mystery. "Have you met someone you have been spending time with outside the bedroom? You have everything to make you happy, except love and steady companionship. Is that it?" Anita's words were both probing and caring, reflecting her genuine concern for Lane's well-being.

Lane laughed. "You know I don't need anyone to make me happy. I've always been happy with my life, whether or not I have a woman to spend time with."

Anita narrowed her eyes and shook her head. "I know, Delaney, and that in itself is wonderful. You know how to make yourself happy, so you don't need anyone. But there is beauty in sharing our happiness with someone who makes us just as happy as we can make ourselves. Someone who you can build memories with, not just romps between the sheets."

Lane burst out laughing. She had always loved Anita's candidness and her sense of humor. While she had played the pivotal role of being a mother to Lane, she had always treated her like a best friend—someone whom Lane could tell anything without judgment. "I do take these women out on dates, you know. I treat them very well. Most of them wouldn't have fallen in love with me if I didn't. Those are memories I'm making outside of the sheets."

"You know, you should have been a lawyer. You always have a counterargument, no matter how strong my position is." Anita theatrically rolled her eyes before continuing. Her tone softened with concern. "I know I've been a bit of a nag lately about you finding love, but I just feel like, because of your childhood, you've shut yourself off from allowing yourself to love or experience it without even realizing it. From a very young age, you had no one to depend on but yourself, and that contributed to you becoming so self-reliant that you don't feel the need for anyone else. Now, you're so comfortable with your own company that not sharing your life with anyone feels like second nature."

An acute sadness seeped into Anita's eyes as she

spoke. "My point, Delaney, is just to give someone a chance to get close to you. Give yourself a chance to share your life with someone. I'm not saying you need to run off into the sunset and have babies, but give yourself the opportunity to not be alone so much."

Lane marveled at how fervently Anita always encouraged her to believe in love when she herself raised her children on her own and accepted when they wanted nothing to do with her. And she continued to be just as selfless with Lane, which had earned Lane's undying love and loyalty for Anita. She had more strength and bravery in her heart than anyone Lane knew. "I know you're not lonely because, as you said, you make yourself happy," Anita continued. "But besides me and Nia, you don't have anyone else to be there for you if you're sick or anything, my sweet child. I was hoping that by thirty-five, you would have finished having your fun with women and given someone a real shot. But I was wrong."

I could call Miranda if I'm sick. She would show up. But would she show up if we were no longer sleeping together? She probably would if things don't end on bad terms, because she's inherently compassionate. But why am I thinking about Miranda when I've never considered calling anyone outside of Anita, Nia, or 911 before?

Lane pushed her thoughts aside, aware of Anita's observant eyes fixed on her. She didn't want to reveal any of her errant thoughts. "I'm still pretty young. Who knows what tomorrow will bring? I might find someone who unexpectedly sweeps me off my feet without me even realizing it," she said convincingly. She was still young and had all the time in the world for love if it was meant for her. Contrary to what people thought, forty was just the beginning of the best years of one's life. By then you would have made all the mistakes and knew who you were as a person and not give a damn about anyone's opinion about how you choose to live your life.

"That's if you allow them to, sweetheart." A knock echoed in Anita's background. "Ah, that's probably, Loretta. She's my soap opera buddy."

Despite her initial concerns about Anita opting to live at the assisted living facility, Lane was happy to see Anita genuinely content staying there. She understood why companionship held such significance for Anita at this stage of her life. Anita had always been neighborly —the type to check in on neighbors and offer assistance when needed. It was her kindness that had shown a teenage Lane that not everyone in the world was a monster. And then there was that one person, a few years before Anita, who had extended kindness to Lane by standing up for her against bullies, even though they didn't know each other.

"Remember I'm coming to take you to the spa this weekend. So don't double book yourself with all your new buddies."

Anita chuckled. "Is it the same one we went to last time? My body still felt like liquid days after."

"Yes, it is. But I booked us for a different treatment this time," Lane replied, feeling a sense of fulfillment in being able to treat Anita to the finer things in life. Provide her with the kind of life someone with her generous heart deserved in a world where good people were often the ones who got the shitty end of the stick.

"Okay. I know I'll enjoy whatever you choose. Have a great day. Love you."

"Love you too," Lane reciprocated before ending the call.

Glancing at the time on her screen, Lane's thoughts immediately turned to Miranda, who had texted her earlier to let her know she would be bringing lunch. Then, Anita's words about sharing happiness with someone echoed in her mind. While Lane had always found contentment in the life she had built for herself, she couldn't deny the shift in her happiness since she began spending time with Miranda. It was a different kind of joy, one where someone other than herself played a role. Anita's insight resonated deeply with Lane. She had long believed that true happiness came from within, and she didn't need anyone else to make her happy. She was fully capable of doing everything people in relationships did by herself, and she had done so. But now, she found herself experiencing the pleasure of sharing happiness with someone else. Being with Miranda brought her happiness simply by virtue of Miranda's presence, and she hadn't even recognized it until now.

Perhaps the unorthodox nature of her relationship with Miranda contributed to its impact. Unlike her previous experiences, they spent more time together outside the bedroom than in it. Miranda also possessed an uncanny ability to draw Lane out, getting her to share aspects of herself without even realizing it. In contrast to past partners who showed interest in Lane's life outside the bedroom only after weeks or months of sex, Miranda prioritized a deeper connection from the start. Their time together extended beyond physical intimacy—cuddling during movie nights, attending yoga classes together, and enjoying impromptu lunches at work were experiences Lane had never encountered in her previous dating endeavors. The lines between casual and committed blurred, yet Lane found herself surprisingly unfazed by it all.

Then there was Miranda taking care of her when she was sick. She had never allowed anyone she had dated to see her that vulnerable—to nurse her back to health. Yes, it was partly her fault, because she didn't allow anyone to get that close to her. But what was different with Miranda was that while the others would have just waited until they heard from her or waited until she was better, Miranda had taken the initiative to find out if she was okay. And regardless of Lane's protest, she had stayed and taken care of her. Once again, Anita's wisdom rang true—it was comforting to have someone care for her in such a nurturing way. It had also been nice experiencing the things she enjoyed doing with Miranda. Now that she reflected on it, her restlessness had subsided since they began spending time together; even though that was probably because of all the amazing sex and the endorphins from it.

But it was fine, she wanted Miranda's first experience with women to be positive, so nothing was wrong with them doing things that Lane wouldn't normally do with other women. She didn't believe in "one hat fits all." And she would much rather Miranda's experience be with someone who wouldn't fuck around with her feelings and end up hurting her. Miranda had a big heart and not everyone deserved someone like her. Lane wasn't perfect but she was always honest with the women she dated and respected them.

The commotion outside her office door shattered Lane's thoughts, and her heart sank when the door swung open, revealing the last two people she expected to see barging into her sanctuary.

"Ma'am, you can't just barge into her office!" Kelsey's voice, filled with urgency, echoed from behind the intruders. She hurriedly maneuvered past them, her eyes wide with trepidation as she addressed Lane. "I tried to explain that you were busy and they needed an appointment, but they insisted they were your parents and forced their way in before I could stop them." Kelsey's breath came in short gasps as if she had sprinted from her desk to intervene. "I was on lunch, so I guess security let them up without confirming with me."

Lane scarcely registered Kelsey's words over the raging storm of anger and hatred churning within her. It was a tumult she had long buried, now erupting ferociously beneath her skin in the presence of the two people she despised more than anyone in the world—her biological mother and her despicable stepfather. Lane summoned every ounce of the fortitude she had cultivated over the years, mastering the art of maintaining composure even in the face of overwhelming turmoil. It was a skill she had honed to navigate life's challenges, to remain composed, and never betray her emotions to her adversaries.

She felt a steely resolve enveloping her, her blood turning to molten metal as she erected the defenses she had once needed as a vulnerable child to withstand the cruelty of this woman before her. A woman whom life, by the looks of it, had not treated kindly. Or perhaps, Lane mused bitterly, *karma was a bitch after all*. Barbara's appearance showed signs of aging, with her light brown hair losing its shine, her aquamarine eyes dimmed with fatigue, and her skin marked by the effects of sun exposure. Though she had always maintained a slender frame, her figure now seemed almost frail.

"Lane, should I call security to have them removed?" Kelsey asked—apprehension evident in her tone—likely detecting the tension in Lane's demeanor.

"No. This won't take long. But please, stay nearby," Lane responded, aware of the importance of having witnesses. She had been in situations where it was her word against theirs, and she knew the value of having someone who could corroborate her account. As she spoke, Lane discreetly reached for her phone, activating the recorder and placing it in her lap. Snakes had infiltrated her space, and she needed to be prepared for anything.

"Okay," Kelsey agreed, casting worried glances between Lane and the intruders. With a brief hesitation, she turned to leave, her expression clouded with uneasiness.

"Hello, Sarah. Or should I call you Delaney?" Barbara's voice dripped with contempt. "I love the last name by the way. *Remington*." Her lips curved in a sarcastic demonic smile that only made Lane straighten to her fullest height, shoulders broad and defiant. "Nice touch. I'm proud of you."

For decades Lane hadn't allowed thoughts of these people to occupy her mind, but she wasn't surprised their appearance stirred up a potent mix of anger and resentment—emotions that she hadn't wanted to consume her and make her angry at the world. "How do you know I work here? And why are you here?" she asked, her tone icy but eerily calm.

"Aren't you going to invite us to sit down? Where are your manners, girl?" Dick's words were laced with a condescending authority, as if he had any right to dictate her actions. *A name fitting for the asshole he was.* Motherfucker probably still saw her as the fifteen-year-old girl whose life he had tried to ruin. Looking at him, Lane half-expected a surge of fear remembering what he had tried to do to her, but the overwhelming wave of hatred drowned out any other emotion. She stared at them, her expression unyielding as she awaited their response. While she was on the verge of tossing them out of her office, she needed answers to those two burning questions. It had been twenty-five years since she had last seen them, and Lane was determined to understand why they had resurfaced now.

As the silence stretched, they sank into the chairs before her desk, finally realizing she was waiting for them to speak. "Remember Pearl?" Barbara began, her tone laced with disdain. "Always glued to celebrity gossip. One day, she came running over with a magazine, and there you were on the front page, dating that actress. My, how you've changed." Barbara waved her hand in such dramatic fashion, it's a wonder she wasn't an actress herself. "Filled out nicely compared to the scrawny kid you were when you decided to abandon your family. But I gave birth to you, so I'd recognize my baby girl anywhere."

I was scrawny because you didn't feed me, Lane wanted to scream, but she clenched her jaw and forced herself to remain silent. What family was Barbara talking about anyway? Lane could see that Barbara was still the same narcissistic bitch she had always been, mixing niceties with her cruelty. *Ah, so they stumbled upon me by chance, not because they had been searching for me all these years.*

"And why are you here?" Lane asked again, cutting through any pretense.

"Is that any way to speak to your mother after not seeing me for over twenty years?" Barbara retorted, her voice rough from years of smoking and drinking.

"Why... are... you... here?" Lane gritted out once more, infusing as much ice as she could muster into her tone. It seemed to work, as Barbara flinched momentarily, her confidence waning before quickly returning—the familiar ugliness resurfacing. A monster was always a monster, after all.

"Do you think you're better than me because you have a fancy job, expensive clothes, and fucking celebrities now?" she snarled, a vein bulging in her forehead—a signal of her rage from Lane's childhood. *A snake will always be a snake.*

Dick intervened, resting a hand on Barbara's shoulder to quell her rising anger. "Barb, not now. Since she's intent on treating us like strangers, let's get to the point."

Dick's beady dark blue eyes ran up and down Lane's body, making her skin crawl, just as it did years ago. She had the urge to reach across her desk and gouge his eyes out. He probably thought he could still intimidate her the same way he did back then, and just as he had misjudged her then, it seemed he was making the same mistake now.

"Fine," Barbara conceded like a petulant child. "We need some money. And since you're doing so well, you could help out your family. I raised you for the first fifteen years of your life, so the least you could do is help your mama out."

Lane felt the overwhelming impulse to laugh, but the sheer intensity of her hatred quashed it, leaving her with a bitter taste in her mouth. How narcissistic and delusional could this woman be? To believe she had ever done anything remotely good for Lane, let alone deserve a single penny from her?

Staring both of them down, Lane made sure every ounce of her contempt was visible in her gaze. "No," she stated firmly, leaving no room for negotiation in her tone.

"After everything I did for you? I carried you for nine months, you ungrateful brat! Nine months, and this is the thanks I get. What kind of child abandons their mother?" Barbara's voice rose to a shout, her face flushed red with anger.

It was painfully clear that nothing had changed about Barbara. She remained the same angry, entitled waste of a human who believed the world owed her everything. Now, she had the audacity to demand repayment for giving birth. *A leopard never changes its spots.* Lane kept silent, fixing them with a glacial gaze. If they expected any reaction from her, they were sorely mistaken. Lane had learned long ago that one of the most effective ways to deal with self-important assholes was to ignore them—never giving them the satisfaction of feeding into their egos or bullshit.

"Well, we didn't want to resort to this, but since you're not willing to be reasonable, then we'll go to the media. I'm sure they would be interested to know that Gabriella's girlfriend is just trailer park trash playing dress-up. I heard gossip magazines pay good money,"

Barbara snarled.

This time, Lane couldn't help but laugh. It felt like she was trapped in a poorly written movie, where these two morons had suddenly materialized out of nowhere, pulling one of the oldest tricks in the book—blackmail. But just as they had underestimated her years ago, they were making the same mistake again. If there was a God, Lane couldn't help but feel disillusioned. Because of all the decent women in the world, why did they choose such a pathetic human as her bearer? What had she done in her pre-life to deserve someone so cruel and self-centered?

Lane took a deep breath, attempting to stifle her laughter. "Do you honestly believe that I'm ashamed to let people know that despite my monstrous egg donor and her despicable criminal boyfriend, I've managed to become successful and accumulate more wealth than I could ever spend in this lifetime? You've always been delusional, so I shouldn't be surprised." With a disdainful glance up and down at them, Lane continued, "I survived your tyranny. My story is one of resilience that could inspire countless young girls unfortunate enough to have been raised by monsters like you. I'm not playing dress-up. I chose not to be a product of the environment I was born into and make something meaningful of myself, rather than becoming a worthless bum who did nothing with my life. You're not getting a dime from me. So go ahead and contact all the magazines you want. But chances are you already did and they turned you down since there is no story there." She waved her hand dismissively and glanced toward her office door. "Now, your time is up. Get out of my office."

"You're just a liar!" Barbara's voice pierced the air, punctuated by her sudden rise from her chair and the accusatory finger she pointed at Lane. "You always hated me and wanted to run away, so you made up a story to get those cops to believe you. You owe me for bringing you into this world and for taking care of you. You just said you have more than enough money, so you need to repay your debt."

Money, that was all this woman ever saw Lane as—a means to get money, her meal ticket. Barbara embodied a level of narcissism that surpassed comprehension. She was the epitome of evil wrapped in self-righteousness, capable of inflicting harm and then smiling as if nothing had happened. "You have one minute to get out of my office before I call security to escort you out."

"Listen here, young lady. There's no need for you to speak to your mother like that. We all know you lied, and we have forgiven you. You were young and don't remember things clearly," Dick interjected, his tone deceptively calm in a way that could fool anyone into thinking he was a decent human being. Lane wasn't surprised they had stayed together all these years. *Birds of a feather.*

"Thirty seconds," Lane bit out, recalling all the times this despicable man had addressed her in that condescending tone, as if being a woman made her inferior to him. God, she loathed them. It was that hatred acting as her anchor now, preventing her from sinking into the abyss of fear she had experienced the last time she had been alone with him. It was also this very hatred that had saved her that day.

Lane grabbed her office phone and dialed Kelsey's

extension when neither of them made a move to leave. "Kelsey, please call security to come and remove these people from my office."

"They're already here. I wanted them close by just in case. I'll send them in," Kelsey replied. Lane smiled internally, appreciating Kelsey's quick thinking. She made a mental note to give her a substantial bonus just for taking this initiative.

"Thanks, Kelsey."

"I knew I should have aborted you. Then I would have been able to have another child, instead of an ungrateful brat like you," Barbara shouted, her voice screeching, and almost causing Lane to flinch as memories of when she would come home and start shouting at her for no reason flooded her mind.

"Yes, you should have, because you don't deserve to bring life into this world, and I wouldn't have endured fifteen years of suffering at your hands. Now get the fuck out of my office." Lane switched off the recorder on her phone. "And if you ever come near me again, you won't like what I'll do. I have enough money to pay someone to end you." She didn't trust them to not become problematic for her, so she needed to speak the only language they understood—violence.

Barbara opened her mouth to reply, but the door opened and two security guards entered. Dick rose from his chair, his beady eyes fixed on Lane. She held his gaze unflinching, refusing to be intimidated by him. She wasn't the fifteen-year-old girl he had tried to control and probably would have done even more despicable things to than he had done.

"Let go of me!" Barbara wailed as one of the guards started guiding her to the door.

"Ma'am, you can come peacefully or we'll drag you out. It's your choice," the guard replied.

"I hate you. Giving birth to you was the biggest mistake of my life," Barbara snarled, her words dripping with venom. She waved a dismissive hand around the office. "All of this doesn't mean that you're somebody. Trash is trash, no matter how much you dress it up."

Lane didn't even blink in response, for this was the demon she had grown up around—a woman who wielded words as weapons to inflict pain. But Lane had constructed a fortress of iron walls long ago to block them out. She remained silent, merely observing as they made their exit.

Once they were out of her office, Lane felt her body slowly coming down from the adrenaline rush of slipping into survival mode. Her heart pounded so hard that she wondered if she was having a panic attack. Closing her eyes, she focused on taking deep breaths in an effort to calm her racing heart.

I survived. I didn't end up like her. I'm safe, she repeated over and over losing track of time.

Soft hands, caressing her cheek—the touch like a balm to her broken spirit—interrupted Lane's silent mantra, coaxing her to open her eyes. Miranda stood beside her chair, eyes filled with concern and tenderness.

"Your hands are shaking, sweetheart," Miranda remarked softly, still using the back of her fingers to soothe Lane's cheek, offering a gentle form of comfort.

Lane glanced down at her trembling hands, confirming Miranda's observation. She clenched them into fists to quell the tremor before meeting Miranda's gaze once more.

"Do you want to talk about it?" Miranda inquired, reaching for Lane's trembling hands and holding them in her own, a beacon of light guiding Lane out of the darkness that was threatening to pull her under.

Lane wasn't sure how much Miranda had overheard, but she knew that regardless, Miranda wouldn't judge her. However, at that moment, Lane felt raw and vulnerable, hesitant to let her guard down any further. But Miranda was good and after being surrounded by evil, it was a pleasant reminder that goodness still existed in the world. Still, despite Miranda's steadfast quintessence, Lane couldn't allow herself to become overly reliant on Miranda for comfort—this was a temporary refuge, and she needed to be able to survive on her own, as she always had.

She inhaled deeply, exhaling slowly. "I'm fine. Can we do a raincheck on lunch? I just need to be alone right now," Lane replied, her voice sounding anything but fine.

Miranda gently squeezed her hands. "I won't push you to talk about what just happened. But please know that I'm here for you and will support you in whatever way you need me to."

Lane yearned to pull Miranda into her arms, to find solace in her warmth, but the overwhelming urge to be alone held her back. She managed a forced smile. "Thank you. I'll be okay. I'll call you later if I don't see you again before I leave work."

Miranda nodded understandingly, leaning down to plant a soft kiss on Lane's lips, which was akin to a healing potion that Lane wanted to constantly drink more of. As Lane contemplated deepening the kiss, Miranda pulled away, and Lane refrained from stopping her. It was a comfort she couldn't allow herself to rely on.

Chapter 7

Curled up on her sofa with a glass of red wine, Miranda made a valiant attempt to immerse herself in the book she was reading, hoping its pages would offer respite from her racing thoughts. However, her efforts proved futile. Not even the soothing patter of rain against the window—a familiar comfort on dreary days—could quell her emotional unrest. Setting the book down beside her, she turned her gaze to the dancing flames of her fireplace. Spring was drawing to a close, ushering in Seattle's signature downpour before the onset of summer. The sudden drop in temperature had prompted her to start her fireplace, both for its warmth and ambiance. However, despite her efforts to find peace, Miranda was consumed by worry for Lane. She wasn't one to push others to talk about their feelings, preferring to offer support when it was sought. But as the evening wore on, Lane's absence weighed heavily on her mind. She had hoped their dinner plans would provide an opportunity to offer comfort, but Lane had canceled earlier in the day. Since returning home, Miranda had attempted to reach out, only to be met with voicemail each time she called. The silence left her unsettled, apprehension gnawing at her insides.

And after witnessing Lane's parents being escorted from her office, who could blame Miranda for worrying? She recognized trouble when she saw it, and those two were undoubtedly trouble. But what bothered Miranda most was Lane's demeanor when she arrived in her office. She was trembling with rage, and Miranda had never seen such a distant, vacant look in her eyes. It was as if Lane had erected a stone wall around herself to confront her parents, and Miranda wanted to break through it, to hold Lane close and assure her that everything would be all right. She couldn't fathom the depths of Lane's childhood trauma, but it must have been severe for her to request security to remove her parents. With a sigh, she reached for her phone, contemplating calling Lane again. Though she wanted to give her space, she couldn't shake her distress. She knew herself well enough to recognize that she wouldn't rest properly knowing someone she cared for was hurting. Just as her finger hovered over Lane's name, a notification about activity at her door flashed on her phone, followed by the doorbell ringing.

Who could that be at this hour in such heavy rain? She opened the security app on her phone to see who it was. The image on her screen caused Miranda's heart to race with both trepidation and elation. She tossed the phone onto the sofa and rushed to open the door. Outside, the rain came down in large droplets, splattering relentlessly against the concrete. Lane stood soaked to the bone on her steps, water dripping from long lashes framing sad eyes, as her breath fogged before her, mingling with the chilly rain-laden air.

"Lane, what are you doing out in the rain? Come inside," Miranda said urgently, gripping Lane's hand and ushering her in, quickly closing the door behind them. Rivulets of water dripped from Lane onto the hardwood floor, evidence that she had been walking in the rain for some time. As Miranda studied her pale face, her heart clenched in her chest, seeing the vulnerability and vacant look from earlier in Lane's eyes.

"How did you get here? I didn't see your car," Miranda inquired as she attempted to remove Lane's coat.

"I went for a walk and somehow ended up here," Lane replied softly, shaking her head as if she couldn't believe what she just said.

Miranda's eyes widened. "You walked all the way from your apartment to here. That's almost a two-hour walk." Miranda dropped Lane's coat beside her feet and moved to remove her top.

"Walking always helps me to clear my mind. So, it was nothing for me. I'm used to taking long walks." Lane chuckled softly. "I don't know how I ended up here though. I just started walking, and here I am."

"Well, I'm glad you ended up here. I've been worried about you." Hearing that Lane had set out with no particular direction but somehow ended up at her door, something unfathomable inside Miranda stirred—an ache, a pull she couldn't quite name. It was as if the universe always quietly shifted, drawing Lane to her in a way that felt both accidental and inevitable. The thought of Lane wandering through the rain, aimless but still finding her, left Miranda feeling a bittersweet mix of longing and hope.

Lane lifted her hands for Miranda to remove her shirt, and Miranda's eyes lingered on the sight of Lane's nipples, hardened from the cold. Lane followed her gaze and then looked back up to meet Miranda's eyes. In an instant, Lane's blank expression transformed into that familiar look of unbridled lust, her eyes darkening. And before Miranda could form her next thought, Lane was on her, kissing her like she needed Miranda to save her from drowning in whatever was bothering her. Miranda gasped from the shock, and Lane used the opportunity to slip her tongue into her mouth, sliding all the way to the back of her throat. Lane spun them around and pushed Miranda against the door, her hands pawing at her body to remove her pajama top. Lane's kiss was turbulent and voracious, exploring every corner of Miranda's mouth, claiming her with an urgency that left Miranda's head spinning. Miranda could only cling to Lane's waist, dizzy from the unexpected change of events and the instant spike of arousal.

Lane kissed her with a single-minded focus and intensity, her hands kneading Miranda's bare breasts as if Miranda were the remedy she needed for an incurable sickness. As if she needed Miranda more than she ever needed anything in her life. And while at that moment Miranda was willing to give Lane whatever she needed from her, she wanted them to talk.

Though it pained her due to how turned on she already was, she managed to say, "Lane, stop," ripping her mouth away from Lane's demanding lips.

All actions ceased immediately, with Lane taking a step back from her, apprehension seeping into her features. Lane closed her eyes tightly, breathing heavily. "I'm sorry. I shouldn't have come here. I'll just go."

Miranda shook her head, reaching for Lane's hand. "No, I'm happy you're here. While I'm more than willing to have you fuck me right here and now, I think we need to talk." Miranda, reached up and gently cupped Lane's cheek. "I'm here for you, so let me be. Sometimes talking through our feelings can help."

"I know, but right now I just want to lose myself in you." She closed the distance between them once again, pressing herself against Miranda. "To feel you fall apart on my fingers." Lane swallowed hard, eyes pleading. "Please."

Even if Miranda wanted to deny Lane's request, after hearing the beseeching in her voice and seeing the sadness in her eyes, Miranda would do anything in her power to soothe Lane's troubled spirit. Foregoing a verbal response, Miranda crashed their lips together and kissed her fiercely—just the way she knew Lane loved to be kissed. Lane quickly matched the pace of Miranda's lips as they fought for control. Once again Miranda's back met the door, with Lane urgently pulling down her shorts. Once Miranda's shorts pooled around her ankles, Lane lifted Miranda's left leg and hitched it around her waist. Miranda struggled to keep up with the frantic movements of Lane's hands and when two fingers slipped inside her stretching her walls and immediately began fucking her with skillful precision that ignited a raging furnace inside of her, Miranda could do nothing but submit to Lane's will. She arched into each thrust of Lane's hand, matching her movements, riding her fingers with wild abandon.

Lane broke the kiss, her eyes ablaze with desire as she stared at Miranda—all traces of her previous sadness gone. Her eyes dropped to the hand between Miranda's thighs. Miranda followed her gaze and seeing Lane's fingers coated with her moisture—slipping in and out of her—was the gasoline Miranda needed to explode. Her orgasm slammed into her and Lane joined their lips in another heated kiss, capturing Miranda's screams of pleasure. She clutched onto Lane tightly, riding her fingers hard until her body sagged against the door. Lane lowered Miranda's leg from her waist. Before Miranda's high could subside, Lane was lowering herself to her knees, but Miranda had enough agency to grab her arms and stop her. Once Lane was at her full height, Miranda grabbed her hips, spun them around, shoved Lane against the door, and dropped to her knees. Staring up at Lane, Miranda reached for the button on her jeans, lowering the zipper and pulling the soaked fabric down Lane's hips. Lane kicked off her sneakers and together they removed her pants with shared urgency of the moment.

"It's my turn to take care of you," Miranda said, yanking Lane's underwear down. She marveled at the abundance of moisture that greeted her, knowing that she was the one who had this effect on this enigmatic woman. Miranda knew that Lane got immense pleasure in giving orgasms, but she also wanted to make Lane feel just as good as she had made Miranda feel, even when she was sad.

Lifting Lane's leg, Miranda placed it over her shoulder and buried her face between Lane's thighs. She made a long delicious sweep of her tongue over Lane's clit and then sucked the hard bundle between her lips. An unconscious growl rumbled in the back of her throat as her hands tightened on Lane's hips.

Lane let out a loud moan, her hands gripping Miranda's hair as her hips started to move frantically against Miranda's face. "Fingers. Fuck me hard with your fingers," Lane demanded, thrusting her hips against Miranda's mouth.

Miranda obliged, slipping two fingers inside, curling upward as her tongue swirled ferociously around Lane's clit. Lane let out another loud groan, her fingers tightening their grip on Miranda's hair. "I want more…harder…please," Lane begged.

Lane's begging caused Miranda's core to clench painfully. She had never once begged Miranda during their sexual encounters. She had always told Miranda what to do to her or take whatever she wanted from her—but never once begged. Desperate to give Lane the pleasure she craved, Miranda pulled out to the edge of her entrance and thrust back in. She continued the relentless pounding until Lane clenched around her fingers, her orgasm washing over Miranda's tongue.

"Yes… that's it… fuck me!" Lane bucked against her face, her cries echoing over the pounding of Miranda's heart, urging her on.

Miranda slowed the pace of her tongue when Lane sagged against the door and released the hold on her hair. Lane groaned when Miranda slowly pulled out her fingers. Looking up at Lane, Miranda slipped her fingers coated in Lane's essence into her mouth and sucked them clean. Lane's eyes darkened even more as she reached for Miranda and smashed their mouths together. The tight fist of arousal spreading between Miranda's thighs grew painful, but she forced herself to sever the kiss.

Lane tried to pull her back in, but Miranda stepped back out of her grasp. "We need to talk and I need to dry your hair before you get sick again," Miranda said, panting. "While I don't mind taking care of you when you're sick, I'd much rather prevent it." Miranda reached for Lane's hand and led her into the living room. She pointed to the sofa. "Sit. I'm going to get a towel."

Miranda didn't wait for a response from Lane, who

was watching her with one of those looks that Miranda couldn't decipher. Entering her downstairs bathroom, Miranda quickly cleaned up the slickness between her thighs. She retrieved two towels and rushed back to join Lane. Rounding the corner, disappointment slammed into her when she didn't see Lane on the sofa. But drawing closer, she saw Lane sitting in front of the fireplace on the blanket Miranda had been using.

"What are you doing on the floor?" she asked, dropping to her knees behind Lane and began drying her hair.

"I didn't want to make a mess of your pristine white sofa," Lane said, her voice carrying a teasing lilt.

"It's cream," Miranda replied, her hands moving tenderly over Lane's hair, drying it with careful, nurturing motions.

"Semantics." Lane let out a contented sigh, leaning back further into Miranda's touch, tilting her head to look at her. "Your hands are magic."

"I'm glad you think so, considering what they were doing between your thighs a few minutes ago." Miranda's movements slowed, becoming more deliberate, almost a massage.

"Now who has sex brain? I thought you said 'no more sex.'" Lane turned around, forcing Miranda to stop drying her hair. She pulled Miranda onto her lap, her hands wrapping around Miranda's waist, holding her close. "Thank you," Lane whispered, nuzzling Miranda's cheek with her still-cold nose while her hands traced up and down her thighs.

Miranda eased back to meet Lane's gaze. There was a softness in her eyes, a depth of tenderness that Miranda had never seen before. For long moments, they just stared at each other—a quiet connection, the kind that said more than words ever could.

Finally, Miranda said, "You're welcome." She brushed a damp lock of hair from Lane's face, her touch lingering. "I like taking care of you." Miranda didn't want to scare Lane off, so she rushed to clarify. "Even though our relationship is casual, I don't mind being here for you as a friend with whom you can share anything. I take very good care of my friends and enjoy doing it." She didn't know what the future held for them, but she truly hoped they could remain close friends when Lane decided to move on. She really did enjoy having Lane in her life.

"I know. You're a natural nurturer," Lane said softly, her hazel spheres searching Miranda's face as if seeking a hidden truth. Finding what she was looking for—or maybe not—Lane Lane shifted, reclining on the blanket, bringing Miranda with her. They adjusted their bodies until they were face-to-face, their breaths mingling in the intimate space between them.

Miranda watched the shadows of the flames dancing across Lane's perfectly sculpted cheekbones, magnifying the foreboding atmosphere that had seeped around them.

Lane closed her eyes briefly, taking a deep breath before meeting Miranda's gaze once more, her eyes reflecting a distant contemplation. "I was born in one of the poorest communities in Southeast Seattle." Lane's voice held a somber tone as she recounted her past. "I spent the first fifteen years of my life there with a woman who hated me but refused to give me up. I can't remember her ever doing anything for me other than belittling, screaming, and slapping me for no reason at all—other than that she seemed to derive some pleasure from it. I don't know how I survived as a baby in her care, but somehow, I did."

Lane swallowed hard, her eyes pained and it was the most emotion Miranda had ever seen, except perhaps when they were having sex. "I did everything for myself as a child as soon as I was old enough to. There were days when all I had to eat was dry cereal and tap water. Days when she locked me up alone in the apartment and didn't return until two or three days later." Lane shook her head. "I was probably eight or nine then. The first few times she did it, I was so scared that I turned on the lights in all the rooms and slept under the bed at night. She showed me a video of a little girl locked up in a mental health hospital, strapped to a bed, and told me that if I ever mentioned anything to anyone, she would send me there. I was young and didn't know better so, of course, I believed her." A sad smile formed on Lane's lips. "But over time, I started looking forward to those days of not hearing her yelling at me for something I didn't do right or for breathing too hard."

Miranda snuggled closer to Lane, her heart aching with empathy. They were already wrapped tightly around each other, but Miranda wanted to envelope Lane and shield her from the impending pain as fierce as the storm outside. "I don't know how to explain it, but it was like I was born with this survival instinct," Lane said, her tone wistful. "To prevent myself from starving on those days she would disappear—when she did allow me to go to school—I would collect multiple lunches and hide them in my backpack. Over time, I had weeks of snacks stashed away under my bed."

Lane began drawing aimless motifs with the tips

of her fingers, up and down Miranda's back, as if she was trying to paint an abstract picture of the angst of her past. "When she was gone, it was like having a house party all by myself where I could watch whatever I wanted on TV. Watching shows that I probably shouldn't have been watching at such a young age showed me that there was a better life out there than what I was surrounded by in that neighborhood—drunks, drug addicts, and people who didn't want to work. I remember telling myself I would be one of those women on TV who wore fancy clothes, spoke in full sentences, drove nice cars, and made lots of money."

Miranda smiled and said, "And you did become that woman."

"I did, didn't I?" Lane replied with a soft smile, her fingers now tracing absent-minded patterns on Miranda's forearm. "Even though I didn't go to school as often as other kids, I still did well and managed to pass all my classes and read at an advanced level. The reading was probably because when I was left alone, I didn't just watch TV, I also read whatever books or magazines I could find in the shithole apartment we lived in. Because I did well in school, my teacher noticed my many absences and called my egg donor to the school."

Lane paused, a flicker of anger crossing her features. "She lied and told the teacher that she sent me to school and was surprised to learn I had been skipping classes. I wanted to scream that she was lying, but I remained silent out of fear. However, Mrs. Bucknell must have seen something on my face and told Barbara that she would call child services if I was absent for anything other than being sick. Barbara assured her I'd be in school every day."

Miranda's heart ached for the young Lane, struggling under the weight of her mother's neglect and deceit. She tightened her grip on Lane's hand, silently wishing she could have been there for her back then.

Lane's voice lacked any emotion, causing Miranda to wonder if that was how she survived those years—by shutting down her feelings so that she could focus on surviving. "When we got home, as soon as the door closed, she started pacing and yelling at me. That was when I learned about my father and why she wouldn't let CPS take me away from her. She said I ruined her life because my father wanted a boy, and because of me, she couldn't have any more kids, and he left her. She also said the only reason she kept me around was because she would receive less money from the government if she didn't have a child."

Miranda's entire body flinched, like she was punched in the gut. Lane soothingly rubbed her tense muscles into submission and Miranda, finally, quietly released the breath she didn't realize she was holding. Lane was the one pouring out her heart and soul, and yet Miranda's empathetic nature was triggered by the pain and vulnerability Lane felt both then and now.

"She made it clear she wouldn't allow anyone to benefit from me, because she was the one who suffered through twenty hours of labor. So, if I thought she would ever let anyone take me away from her, I was sadly mistaken. She said a lot of mean things over the years, but for some reason, I've always remembered those words."

Miranda's head spun with so many questions, her heart growing heavier with each revelation. She resisted the urge to interrupt, fearing it might halt

Lane's cathartic flow. "After that day," Lane continued, her voice now laced with bitterness, "she paid our stupid neighbor, Pearl, with cigarettes and beer to check in on me and ensure I went to school whenever she went—wherever the fuck she went—on those days she disappeared. I later found out she was having an affair with a married man who she was meeting up with in a motel."

Miranda's eyes widened in disbelief, her grip on Lane's hand tightening involuntarily. "Anyway," Lane went on, "as I got older, the fear I felt turned into hatred, and it was like that hatred made me stronger and motivated me to escape her. But I had nowhere to go, and she never introduced me to any family."

Miranda nodded sympathetically, her heart aching for the little girl who endured such hardships alone. "She tried in so many ways to break me with her cruel words and physical abuse, but instead she made me more determined not to become like her. Until I was fifteen, we coexisted together. I took care of myself, ignored her as much as possible, and she did what Barbara did best—smoke cigarettes, drink beer with her loser friends, and complain about life being unfair."

As Lane spoke, Miranda could see the resilience shining in her eyes, the strength that had kept her going despite the odds stacked against her. "Her boyfriends appeared and disappeared just as fast. I was free to do whatever I wanted because I had no parental supervision, but by some miracle, I didn't go down the wrong path. I immersed myself in reading and doing well in school while counting the days until I turned eighteen."

Miranda's admiration for Lane grew with each word.

"I loved school even though I was bullied because I never had new clothes and my clothes were always one size too small. Barbara wouldn't bother to get me anything new until I could no longer fit in my clothes. But I wanted to learn, so I weathered the storm." Miranda felt a surge of protectiveness wash over her, a fierce determination to be there for Lane in any way she could.

Lane paused, her fingers now tracing delicate circles on Miranda's hip. "The only advantage of living with Barbara was that I became very self-reliant and resourceful from a young age. By the time I was thirteen, I appreciated her practically ignoring me. I was able to convince a Chinese lady to give me a job in her restaurant washing dishes after school and on the weekends. Even though I wanted new clothes, I saved as much as I could toward my plan to escape the shithole I was born into. Everything was going according to plan until I turned fifteen and Dick moved in with us."

Lane's jaw clenched, the resentment burning in her eyes at the mention of her stepfather. "By then, I watched enough true crime stories to know a creep when I saw one. He was always watching me, wanting to know my every move. All of a sudden, I was no longer free to do as I pleased. He wanted to pick me up from school and all that, pretending to be the doting stepfather. But I refused and stayed away from him as much as possible. I hated his guts. Because while Barbara was shit, I didn't have her constantly breathing down my neck, telling me what to wear, and saying I better not have any boyfriends. He was just always there in my space, making my skin crawl."

Miranda's heart raced with trepidation as she hoped

the unthinkable hadn't happened to Lane. "One day, while walking from school to the restaurant, he pulled up at my feet and demanded that I get in the car. I refused, but he got out and forcibly dragged me inside, warning me to be calm and threatening to make me disappear by selling me to a sex trafficker if I didn't comply. I remember sitting in the car, consumed by fear and uncertainty about what he might do to me. My mind raced with the worst possible scenarios, but I refused to let the fear paralyze me. Instead, I began planning my escape for when the car stopped." Lane's voice trembled slightly.

"After driving for about forty minutes, the car stopped outside a jewelry store in one of the richest neighborhoods in Seattle. I was so lost in my thoughts that I didn't realize where we were until Dick instructed me to go into the store and grab as much jewelry as possible. I refused because I didn't want to go to jail, but he grabbed my arm hard enough to bruise and threatened me again. He insisted that even if I got caught, I wouldn't face consequences because I was a minor. He said he and Barbara needed the money to move us to Texas to escape loan sharks or some shit."

Lane chuckled softly and shook her head, a hint of disbelief lingering in her expression. "I felt like I was living in a bad action movie. But then, I remembered a scene from one of those movies I watched when I wasn't supposed to." She paused, a wistful smile tugging at her lips. "So, I played along and got out of the car. Inside the store, I mustered up all the courage I had and told the owner that he needed to call the cops because the man waiting in the car outside had sent me in to rob them."

Listening to Lane's tale Miranda could understand

why she felt her life had been a bad action movie. "The owner didn't believe me at first, assuming I was just some idiotic teen pulling a prank. But his wife overheard and said she believed me because she could hear the fear in my voice. She made the call. Dick must have sensed something was amiss since he drove off and left me there."

Lane took a deep breath, her eyes reflecting a mixture of relief and lingering trauma. "When the cops showed up, they took my statement and brought me to the station, and because I was a minor, they needed to get CPS involved. That day marked the beginning of the rest of my life, the day I finally escaped from Barbara—my egg donor." She shrugged lightly, trying to downplay the significance of her ordeal. "But that's enough storytelling for tonight. I'm sure you're bored by now."

"What? No! I want to know what happened after. How did you meet your foster mother? What happened to Dick?" Miranda fired off her questions in rapid succession, her eagerness evident as she sought to convince Lane to continue. There was a plethora of Lane's past yet to be uncovered, and now that Miranda got a glimpse, she wanted the full picture to help unravel Lane's many layers.

Lane pushed Miranda onto her back and rolled over on top of her. "I promise to tell you the rest tomorrow." She nipped at Miranda's lower lip. "But right now, I really want to make you come again."

Miranda wondered how Lane could be thinking about sex after sharing events that would have left many people broken. But she knew sex was something that Lane indulged in to settle her mind, so maybe, even though she wasn't showing it, she needed a break from reliving her painful childhood. "Okay. But you promise to tell me tomorrow?"

"I promise," Lane repeated, lowering her head to press her lips against Miranda's.

Miranda opened her mouth and accepted Lane's probing tongue, her body instantly calling for Lane's touch. She pushed away her sorrows about Lane's childhood, deciding to be in the moment with Lane to give her whatever comfort she needed. If Lane said she would tell her more tomorrow, then she trusted her to do so.

Chapter 8

Lane struggled to suppress her laughter, sensing Miranda's eyes boring into the side of her head. They sat on opposite ends of Miranda's sofa, with Miranda's feet resting in her lap as they watched a movie. It was just after midday, and they had opted to spend the day indoors due to the persistent rain. She knew Miranda was patiently waiting for the continuation of her story since they woke up—a promise Lane intended to honor. But she was enjoying the quiet moment they were sharing after the tempestuous events of the previous day. Lane couldn't quite explain why she felt compelled to open up to Miranda about her childhood so easily. However, after arriving unexpectedly at Miranda's house, she had felt an overwhelming urge to share a part of herself that she rarely disclosed to anyone else. Miranda's earnest offer to lend an ear had struck a chord within her, causing something buried deep inside of her to crack open. Once she began speaking, the words flowed freely from her lips. What puzzled Lane most was how she had ended up at Miranda's house in the first place. When she had left home to clear her mind with a walk, she had no particular destination in mind. Yet, her feet had instinctively led her to Miranda, who had unwittingly become the soothing presence amidst Lane's tumultuous thoughts.

Lane reached for the remote and paused the movie.

Shifting her body, she folded a leg beneath her and turned to face Miranda. "You know, if I didn't know better, I'd think you have some superpower and you're just sitting there trying to read my mind, instead of just asking me what you want to know."

"You already know what I want to know. I'm patient enough to wait until you're ready to share." Miranda shrugged. "I'm staring because you fascinate me. You're sitting here watching a movie so composed as if nothing major happened yesterday. Your mother, who you hadn't seen in over twenty years, showed up out of nowhere." Miranda gestured vaguely toward Lane. "And you're just here... seemingly unaffected by it all. Most people would probably be angry or experiencing some emotional trauma, but you're just..." She made another gesture between them with her hand.

Lane found it ironic that Miranda found her fascinating when she herself was fascinated by Miranda—her gentleness, her patience, her empathy. The way she made Lane feel so safe and cared for. But now was not the time to analyze those things. She ran her thumb along Miranda's instep, preparing to continue her story. "I see people for who they are, Miranda—based on their actions. What happened with Barbara wasn't a surprise for me because I knew the monster that walked into my office. Yes, at first I was shocked, and seeing her so unexpectedly after so long triggered all the hatred I felt for her; which I had buried along with all traces of her from my life."

Miranda temporarily closed her eyes and sighed in contentment as Lane continued to massage her feet. Lane chuckled as Miranda let out something almost akin to a purr, before continuing with her story, "But

I'm in control of my life, and I'm not going to waste time being sad about a woman who has never given a shit about me. It's that simple. One of the biggest mistakes people often make is wasting their time caring about people who don't care about them. I invest in those who invest in me."

Miranda's eyes shone bright with compassion. "I understand but after enduring all that you did..." Miranda trailed off with a slight shake of her head. "I don't know... It's just inspiring to see you're not burdened with any lasting trauma."

"Hatred—it can either break you or make you. My hatred for my egg donor and the surroundings I was born into made me strong. Then there was my will to survive and my sheer determination to become successful. I think the fear of poverty and becoming like Barbara kept me going for a long time and I had a single-minded focus that prevented me from breaking, even on days when I felt like giving up. I think I fear being poor more than anything else in this world. Poverty is a disease that I wish no child should ever have to experience." A fond smile formed on Lane's lips. "And then there was a little bit of luck and my guardian angel."

"Your foster mother?" Miranda asked.

"Yes. First, I'll tell you what happened after we went to the station." Lane adjusted her body so that both legs were now on the sofa, bent at the knees, with Miranda's feet between them. "When we got to the station, Barbara showed up to claim me because protocol dictated that she was notified. She told the cops that I was just a rebellious teen seeking attention who often made up stories when I didn't get what I wanted."

The anger Lane had felt at that moment bubbled beneath the surface, but she pushed it down. "I remember sitting there, staring at her, wishing I could grab the cop's gun and shoot her. That was how much I hated her. I prayed that they wouldn't believe her, but the male cop did and suggested they release me into her custody since it was clearly a family matter. But there was a female cop who must have seen the fear in my eyes when they mentioned releasing me to her. She insisted on waiting for the CPS officer."

Reliving those crucial hours—which were the turning point of her life in some ways—made Lane feel numb, but the encouraging warmth in Miranda's eyes softened her. "They left me and Barbara alone in the investigation room, and as soon as the doors closed, she started threatening me. I remember sitting there and staring at her without any fear, deciding that I would rather die than spend another minute living under the same roof with her."

Lane caught the slight momentary tension in Miranda's posture, the same one she had felt the night before when she would share a particularly painful part of her tale. Her heart threatened to burst at the seams from absorbing the endless empathy gushing from Miranda. "When the social worker finally arrived, I told her my entire history with Barbara. The neglect. The abuse. I told her that if she sent me back with her, I'd kill myself, and my death would be on her hands."

Miranda gasped, her eyes widening. "Would you have done that?" she asked, her voice barely above a whisper.

"No," Lane replied firmly. "Despite how shitty my life was, I wanted to live. It was my will to live and be more that kept me going. But I was so desperate and needed the social worker to believe me. I could have tolerated Barbara if she didn't, but I had a growing fear that Dick would have eventually tried to sexually assault me."

Lane sucked in a shuddering breath as she remembered the unease she felt around Dick. "She believed me, and I went into the foster care system while they conducted their investigation since Barbara insisted I was lying. I don't know why she was fighting so hard to keep me when she and Dick were involved in all their illegal shit. Whatever the government was giving her for me couldn't have been that much. But she's a narcissist and believed she owned me because she gave birth to me and would prefer to see me suffer than let me go."

"We've dealt with cases like that at Found Family, where parents would rather see their kids suffer than let them go. I'm glad you got a social worker who chose to believe you. Sometimes CPS workers take the easy way out by disregarding what the child is saying and allowing them to remain in their abuser's home."

"Oh, I know. I had my own bad experience with a horrible social worker. But we'll get there soon. Anyway, I was placed in a group home with other girls. I stayed for two weeks and then I ran away from it. I was so scared that they might decide to send me back after they conducted their investigation that I wasn't willing to leave matters in their hands. Plus, the girls there were horrible and I felt like I had jumped out of the frying pan into the fire. I had all the money I had been saving from my job at the restaurant. It wasn't much because I had to finance myself while living with Barbara. I left for school, went to the bus station, and hopped on the first bus going north. I didn't even check to see where it was going. I just needed to get out of the area. The ride was about an hour and a half, and the final stop was Parkwood Memorial." Lane smiled, knowing this bit of information would intrigue Miranda.

"Parkwood? As in our Parkwood?" Miranda's incredulous expression amused Lane, her features a canvas of comical shock.

"Yes. So, despite what people at work may think of my motives when it comes to the decisions I make, I have sentimental reasons for wanting Parkwood to be successful." Over the years, while Lane had strived to bury her past with Barbara, this particular chapter in her life remained a cherished memory, a pivotal moment that had set her on the path to happiness and success.

"I got off the bus and didn't know where to go, so I went inside the hospital seeing it as a safe place. It was always busy and no one would question why I was there if I didn't bring attention to myself. I lived there for about three weeks. I would check which rooms were empty at night and sleep there. If I got caught, I'd just make up some story."

In her mind's eye, Lane saw clearly the days she spent navigating Parkwood's corridors. "During the days, I went to the library, tried job hunting, or I would walk around the hospital and watch the movement of people. That was when I decided that one day I would be in charge of running a hospital. I've always been good at math, and I would sit in the emergency room and count patients, document how long they waited, and think about ways how I could make the service faster." A soft chuckle escaped Lane's lips, the memory of her humble beginnings saturated with a sense of disbelief.

"Sometimes, it all feels so surreal when I walk the halls there now. Remembering the days when it was my safe haven."

"I can't even imagine what that must have been like for you. You're so brave... and smart," Miranda said, her voice laced with admiration and empathy. Lane didn't feel any pity as Miranda's words washed over her. Miranda's sincerity was a powerful battering ram against her seemingly impenetrable fortress. As if like a marionette, Lane's hand reached down to touch Miranda's foot giving a gentle squeeze and rubbing her thumb along Miranda's sole in silent thanks.

"Anyway, I thought I was being stealth and no one was paying attention to the girl who was at the hospital every day. Until one day, I was sitting in the cafeteria wondering what I was going to do now that I was almost out of money and wouldn't know where to get food." The memory of her clandestine existence within the hospital walls resurfaced, a bittersweet reminder of the challenges she had faced. "I thought about asking someone in the cafeteria if they would let me help out and pay me with food, but I was afraid they would find out that I was hiding in the hospital."

Lane's gaze softened as she recalled the moment that had changed everything, the kindness of a stranger sparking a glimmer of hope in her darkest hour. "Suddenly, a black lady with the kindest light brown eyes I've ever seen sat down in the chair across from me in the cafeteria and said, 'My child what is your story?'" Anita's image filled Lane's mind, her heart swelling with affection for the woman who had shown her unwavering love and acceptance.

"I remained silent, not understanding what she

meant. Then she told me that she had seen me every day at the hospital during school hours for the past two weeks and I was always alone. And that meant only one thing—that I was hiding. I tried to deny it, but she said the first time she saw me, I was sleeping in one of the empty rooms she was assigned to clean—she was a housekeeper at the hospital."

Lane paused, the memory of their first encounter stirring a mix of nostalgia within her. "She told me not to be afraid of her and she would help me if she could. I was very wary of her intentions, but there was this gentleness to her, and the fact that she hadn't ratted me out to the hospital made me lower my defenses."

A faint smile tugged at Lane's lips as she recalled the moment she had confided in Anita. "I don't know why, but I just opened up and told her everything. At the end, she had tears in her eyes. She told me she didn't have much to give, but her kids' room was empty and it was mine if I wanted it. Of course, I declined, because I wasn't going to go home with a stranger."

Lane's voice softened with gratitude as she spoke of Anita's kindness, the memory warming her heart. "She said she understood and it was smart of me, but the room was there. She gave me her address and phone number and told me to call her if I changed my mind. After that, for about a week, she brought me home-cooked meals."

Lane chuckled softly. "She would always taste it first to prove to me that it wasn't poisoned, because the first time she brought me food I had told her to taste it. Then I didn't see her for a few days, and I don't know why, but I became worried. So, I called her. I was expecting the number to be not in service, but she answered.

We talked for a few minutes, and I learned she was recovering from a terrible flu. After we hung up, I had the overwhelming urge to visit her because she was sick and I knew from our talks she lived alone." Lane smiled internally to herself as she thought about how Miranda had come to care for her when she was sick– turns out karma had a good side too. "I used the last of my money to pay the fare to her apartment. She was so shocked when I showed up. And from that day until now, she has been the only real family I've ever had. I agreed to stay with her, and for the first time in my life, I had someone who took care of me."

Miranda shook her head as if in disbelief. Lane wouldn't blame her for finding it hard to wrap her head around Lane's history. Even telling it, she knew how far-fetched it might sound to some people, but it was her truth. The hurdles she had conquered had shaped her into the woman that she was today. She knew many young girls weren't as fortunate as her to have escaped an abusive home and found someone like Anita, who offered a haven of safety and love.

"What happened to Barbara and Dick?" Miranda's question cut through the silence, drawing Lane back to the present moment.

Miranda's curiosity was addictive, and Lane found herself eager to satisfy it by divulging whatever information she desired. "I didn't know what happened to them after I ran away from the group home. When Anita petitioned to be my foster mother, I was afraid that they would find me and cause problems, but they never did. I begged Anita not to, but she said she was a black woman housing a white runaway teen, and if someone got the wrong impression and called the authorities, chances are they wouldn't believe she had good intentions. She promised to fight for me, and she did, even when the racist social worker who was assigned to our case tried to take me away from her, claiming it would be disadvantageous for me to live with a black woman. I love that woman so much because she never had to go through all that she did just so I could stay with her, but she did because she knew how safe I felt with her."

Miranda leaned closer to Lane, her eagerness to learn more about Lane's life palpable. "How did they find you at the hospital?"

"From the tabloids when the incident with Gabriella happened. They thought they could come and blackmail me. They thought I'd be ashamed to let people know about my past. I've never been ashamed or felt like an imposter. I'm proud of myself for achieving everything I did in spite of them." Lane shrugged. "And I love being rich. I've worked very hard for every penny I have. I learned a very long time ago that money was power and regardless of what people say, it can buy you a whole lot of happiness. It sure as hell has made me very happy. It's people that make us unhappy —not money. The people who we choose to surround ourselves with will either bring stress or happiness, whether or not money is involved."

Miranda nodded, her expression thoughtful. "My grandma always says the same thing. She said rich or poor, we should be mindful of the people we allow in our lives because they can rob us of our happiness if we allow them."

Lane's lips curled up at the corners. "Smart woman. That's why I made the decision a long time ago to forget about my egg donor. It would be a disservice to myself to wallow in self-pity, do nothing with my life, and turn out just like her."

Miranda rose to her knees, moving to straddle Lane's thighs and looping her arms around her neck. With eyes filled with tenderness and pride, Miranda regarded Lane as if she had accomplished something monumental, akin to ridding the world of poverty. "I'm so very proud of you. You're incredibly strong. Even though you hide it, you've maintained your humanity and are so very kind behind your iron fortresses. Thank you for sharing your story with me. I know it took a lot for you to open up to me." Miranda planted a gentle kiss on Lane's nose. "I feel like I understand you much better now. And I'm even more impressed by the woman you've become."

Miranda's words and sincerity stirred an unfamiliar sensation in Lane's chest—a fluttering of emotions she couldn't quite define. It was something she had never felt before, but it made her want to draw Miranda close and never let her go. She reasoned that it must be normal to feel this way after sharing a part of herself she had never revealed to any other woman she had been with.

"Yes, you have a way of coaxing things from me that I've never shared with anyone before," Lane murmured, her lips brushing against Miranda's as she spoke. With a playful nip at Miranda's bottom lip, Lane's fingers traced a delicate path along Miranda's spine. "Thanks for listening. Surprisingly, talking about it made me feel better. Because yesterday, I wanted to snap those two fools' necks."

Miranda chuckled softly, her laughter like music to

Lane's ears. "I'm glad you didn't, because you're too pretty for prison, and I would miss you."

That unfamiliar sensation surged through her once more hearing Miranda's admission that she would miss her. Lane decided that the time for talking was over. She pulled Miranda's head down, capturing her lips in a fervent kiss, allowing the newfound connection between them to speak volumes.

Miranda reciprocated the kiss, but then abruptly pulled back. "Before you distract me with your kisses, I have something important to ask. Yesterday, I had intended to invite you to my birthday dinner. Usually, my parents would throw me a big party, but I'm not in the mood for one this year, much to their dissatisfaction. We agreed to a small dinner with them, my grandparents, and a few close friends. I'd appreciate it if you would come."

Lane had no issue celebrating Miranda's birthday, and in fact, she had plans of her own for them. However, the prospect of meeting Miranda's parents in this context unsettled her. It felt like she was being introduced to the girlfriend's parents—a situation she had never been in before—and much to her chagrin, she found herself nervous. They weren't officially in a relationship, so she had no reason to be nervous or maybe she did. But then again, this was Miranda, looking at her with hopeful eyes, and Lane couldn't bear to disappoint her.

"Who am I to disappoint the birthday girl?" She bowed her head histrionically, and then met Miranda's gaze. "I'll be there," Lane replied with practiced composure, and Miranda's smile in response washed away all her apprehensions.

"Thank you," Miranda whispered.

Lane didn't have a chance to respond before Miranda captured their lips in another feverish kiss, their bodies pressing together. Lane surrendered to Miranda's lips, and she couldn't deny the surge of happiness coursing through her veins. Miranda simply made her happy.

Chapter 9

Standing in the foyer of her parents' house, Miranda glanced at her watch again, her apprehension growing. She wondered if Lane had changed her mind about coming to her birthday dinner. Lane wasn't late, but as the dinner approached, Miranda questioned whether inviting her had been a good idea. Their relationship was casual, and Lane would be meeting her family as the woman Miranda was dating. She didn't want Lane to think she was trying to add more significance to their arrangement than it actually had. Over the past few months, they had grown close, but Miranda knew that Lane wasn't interested in committed relationships. She still didn't want to cross any lines that might scare Lane off because she genuinely enjoyed being with her and wanted to continue seeing her, even if it remained casual. Miranda accepted that their arrangement would eventually end because she would one day want to date someone seeking a commitment. For now, though, she was really enjoying what they shared—it was easy and fun. After her disastrous relationship history, what she had with Lane was perfect—no expectations or pressure to jump into a commitment.

"Sweetheart, what are you doing loitering in the foyer? Everyone is out on the patio," Miranda's mom said, approaching her.

The sound of the doorbell spared Miranda from

having to answer, and she sighed internally with relief. She wasn't in the mood to share her anxiety with her mom. She rushed to open the door, a wide smile forming on her lips when she saw Lane standing there, immaculate as ever, in a burgundy jumpsuit—her toned arms bare and instantly causing Miranda to salivate as her eyes roamed over Lane's body. *Breathtaking.* Lane smiled knowingly, raising a perfectly arched brow.

Miranda swallowed to moisten her suddenly dry mouth and to push down the fluttering in her stomach. "Hey, you. Come in," she finally said, stepping aside to let Lane enter.

"Hey, yourself," Lane replied as she stepped through the door, her fingers intentionally brushing against Miranda's thigh.

Miranda took a deep breath, trying her best to appear unaffected by Lane's presence. The last thing she wanted was for her filthy thoughts about Lane to be written all over her face with her mom standing behind her.

Before Miranda could make the introductions, she noticed her mother already studying Lane with a mixture of curiosity and mild surprise, her eyes narrowing slightly as recognition slowly dawned. "I remember you," Caroline said, her expression brightening as she pointed a finger at Lane. A warm smile spread across her face. "Sweetheart, you never told me you had reconnected with Sarah." Her mother's eyes darted between Lane and Miranda, the excitement in them unmistakable. "This is a wonderful surprise. How are you?" Caroline added, pulling Lane into a warm, familiar hug as if welcoming an old friend rather than a stranger.

Miranda's mind spun, scrambling to make sense of what her mother was saying. Her pulse quickened as confusion twisted in her gut—what the hell was her mom talking about? She was on the verge of correcting her, the words forming on her lips, when Lane spoke up.

"Mrs. Hayes, I'm surprised you remember me," Lane said with a soft smile, her tone warm but laced with surprise. "Our paths crossed so long ago, and it was only for a brief moment." The unexpected ease in Lane's response left Miranda even more bewildered, as if a hidden chapter of their lives had suddenly come into play.

Caroline chuckled, staring at Lane as if they were two old friends catching up. "I'm old, but not that old. I mean you've grown into a beautiful woman, but the few times we met, you left an impression. It's not every day you meet fifteen-year-olds who were as articulate and mature as you were back then."

Caroline instinctively reached out and gently grasped Lane's upper arm and rubbed her thumb soothingly back and forth as she continued. "That last day I saw you at the hospital, I sensed something was wrong and wanted to offer my assistance, but you ran out of the room so quickly. I never saw you again until three years later, when I spotted you in the supermarket with a black woman, but she called you Delaney. I didn't bother approaching, wondering if I was mistaken. And I think I glimpsed you a few years later at the airport too, but you weren't close enough for me to say hello." Caroline gave Lane's arm one more gentle squeeze before letting go. "I'm glad to see that things worked out for you."

Miranda had so many questions swirling in her mind, still wondering what the hell her mother was talking about. Why was her mom under the impression that Miranda knew Lane? She looked at Lane, but as usual, her face gave away nothing.

"Yes," Lane smiled cordially at Caroline. "I go by Delaney now. Lane for short," Lane replied smoothly, as if the rug hadn't just been pulled out from beneath Miranda and this conversation was no big deal.

"Lovely name." Caroline's face lit up as if she just had a huge revelation. "Must be fate that you and Miranda reconnected after all these years, and now you two are," she wiggled her eyebrows, "getting it on," she finished with a wink.

Miranda wanted the ground to open and swallow her up. "Oh my god, Mom!"

"Shush now, sweetheart. We're not prudes here. I know what you and Sarah... I mean Lane, have been up to." Caroline looped her arm through Lane's. "Let's go get you a drink. I want to get to know the woman who my daughter has the hots for. You're absolutely stunning, so I can see why she was drooling when she opened the door. But I want to get to know the woman beneath the beauty."

They were already moving to the patio before Miranda could stop her mother from leading Lane away. She needed a private inquisition with Lane, because what on earth was going on? But now wasn't the time, since everyone was pretty much waiting on her to get the dinner started. She followed them, fighting the impulse to drag Lane to her bedroom and demand an explanation.

Arriving on the patio, she forced a smile on her face as Blake approached her and hugged her tightly. "I can't believe you convinced them not to throw you a huge party," she whispered. "I *also* can't believe you got Lane to come. For someone who doesn't do committed relationships, she sure does behave like the devoted girlfriend," Blake added, teasingly.

Despite all the confusion swimming in her head, Miranda couldn't help chuckling. "The convincing wasn't easy. I had to resort to extreme measures by telling them it was either canceling this party or my fortieth." Miranda glanced at Lane, who was now talking and laughing with Alexandra. "As for Lane, let's just say she's full of surprises."

"Okay everyone, dinner is ready," Miranda's father announced, placing a platter of lamb kebabs on the table already laden with too much food for the small gathering.

Everyone moved to their seats, and Miranda held Lane's gaze as she came to sit beside her. She noted that Lane was watching her, but there were no signs of apprehension in her features to indicate that she was bothered by the conversation that occurred in the foyer.

As soon as Lane lowered herself into the chair, she leaned over and whispered, "I know you have questions, but I promise to answer them as soon as we're alone. Now, stop overthinking and enjoy your birthday celebration," Lane paused, her tongue discreetly flicking against Miranda's ear. "You look absolutely stunning, by the way. I hope you'll allow me to slowly peel this dress off your body later."

Even though Miranda's mind was reeling with questions, she couldn't prevent the involuntary shudder that ran through her body.

"Aww, you two are so adorable. Lane, you're looking at my granddaughter like she'll be your dinner,"

Miranda's grandmother—her dad's mom—said, causing Miranda to whip her head around to look at her and trying hard not to groan in embarrassment while everyone laughed. "I'm so glad we live in a time where my grandbaby can date whoever she wants openly and freely, even if it's later in life that you discover that you're attracted to women." Audrey shook her head, her features growing solemn. "There were plenty of women from my generation who were forced to remain in marriages with men. Even when they realized that they wanted to be with women they ended up living unhappy lives, while yearning for what they couldn't have out of fear and judgment." Audrey then gave them both an elated smile, before addressing Miranda. "So, my sweet girl, I'm glad you're giving yourself a chance to explore this side of yourself instead of hiding from it. Happy birthday, my darling. I hope that whatever the future brings, you'll always find happiness."

Miranda felt her face flush, but her heart swelled with gratitude. "Thank you, Grandma," she said, her voice a bit choked with solace and love. She glanced at Lane, whose eyes shone with understanding and affection. She was so very grateful that she grew up in a family that had always been accepting of everyone, no matter their backgrounds, or who they chose to love.

Everyone lifted their glass in a toast, wishing Miranda a happy birthday. More well-wishes followed, and the conversation flowed smoothly throughout the dinner, filled with laughter and plenty of teasing. Miranda's eyes frequently found Lane's as the evening proceeded. Partly, because she kept thinking about what her mom had said, but she was mostly surprised to see Lane so comfortable around her family. She had expected her to be a bit reserved, but it was quite the opposite. Lane openly engaged with her grandparents and parents, even answering their sometimes intrusive questions about their relationship. However, what Miranda had come to realize about Lane was that, despite her natural aversion to people, when she wanted to, she could charm the pants off everyone in a room full of people. The woman was just that magnetic, often holding the attention of people with just her mere presence. It was as if people were drawn to her, even when she kept them at a distance.

A few hours later, after they had cut the cake and everyone was enjoying one of her father's infamous cocktails, Miranda could no longer wait to speak to Lane in private. "I'm going to show Lane around the property," she announced, rising from her chair.

"Is that code for something else, sweetheart," her mom teased, eyes dancing with mischief.

"Mom! I swear you're hellbent on embarrassing me today," Miranda said, glad she didn't have the palette to blush, because she would probably be the color of a beetroot.

Beside her, Lane laughed as she stood up and Miranda turned to glare at her. Lane lifted both hands in surrender. "Hey now, sweetheart, what's a birthday without some teasing from your mother," she said, totally throwing Miranda off guard with the term of endearment in front of everyone. It was something she didn't expect Lane to do in front of her family, as it sounded so much more than casual dating.

"This one is a keeper," her grandmother added, her aquamarine eyes sparkling with amusement.

Miranda shook her head. "The lot of you are just

horrible. I'm going now."

"And you love us," her dad shouted as Miranda retreated, her hands entwined with Lane's as she led her inside the house.

They climbed the stairs in silence to Miranda's bedroom. She sensed that Lane knew exactly why she had excused them from the table and she was giving Miranda time to gather her thoughts. She opened the door and allowed Lane to enter ahead of her. She didn't know what to expect but Lane shoving her against the door and kissing her until her knees felt weak wasn't it. Miranda's traitorous body responded to Lane's touch, her core tightening with need, but before she could stop the kiss, Lane pulled back, eyes dark with desire as she stared at Miranda.

"I've been wanting to do that since you opened the door," Lane breathed out, before turning and walking away from Miranda. Her eyes did a slow appraisal of the room. "So very you. Warm and comforting," Lane said, lowering herself on the bed. She patted the space beside her and said, "I'm ready to answer your questions."

Miranda wasn't surprised that Lane was getting straight to the point. She had never met anyone who was more straightforward than Lane. Since they started dating, not once had she ever had to worry about miscommunication or mind games. This was why she wasn't worried about Lane telling her the truth about how they could have possibly met before—so much so that her mom remembered Lane when Miranda, for the life of her, couldn't recall meeting Lane before that night at Josephine's.

Taking a seat beside Lane, Miranda took a deep breath and looked her in the eye, deciding that an open-ended question was all that was needed. "Can you explain everything that my mom mentioned?"

Lane nodded, her eyes never leaving Miranda's. "My egg donor named me Sarah Learmond, but after I escaped her, when I turned sixteen, I told Anita I wanted to change my name. I didn't want to be associated with anything that would remind me of my life with her. I was still a minor and given my circumstances, it wasn't as easy as I thought. However, we got help from social services and I became Delaney Remington. I chose Anita's last name since living with her was the first time I ever felt maternal love and she had become my family. I've always thought the name Delaney was fancy." Lane smiled and shrugged. "I've always liked nice things, including names." Another shrug. "New life, new name."

Miranda seized the opportunity to ask a question she had always wondered about. "Why do you go by Lane since you like Delaney?"

Lane grinned. "Misogyny and trial and error. Before heading off to college, I started applying for summer jobs close to Berkeley. I didn't hear back from a lot of the companies I applied to." Lane reached out and began to massage Miranda's hand as she continued her answer. "Then one day, I applied for another role at a company I had applied to the week before. I got a callback, but the guy on the phone was surprised to learn I was a woman. When I asked him why, he said that while Lane was unisex, he had only ever met men with that spelling."

Miranda couldn't suppress a grimace, which transformed into a smile when Lane chuckled at her reaction. "After we got off the phone, I checked the application and realized I had applied under Lane. I don't know if I accidentally deleted the rest of my name or if the computer did. You know technology was prone to all sorts of errors back then. So, I decided to test a theory and reapplied to the same jobs under Lane and I received more callbacks. These people assuming I was a man based on my name alone got me more opportunities. So, from that day on, I decided to go by Lane since it could potentially get me at least an interview." Lane lifted another shoulder in indifference. "Plus, Lane means path, and I was on a new path, so it seemed fitting."

Miranda couldn't help smiling. "When have you not been smart?"

"I had to grow up very fast. I had no choice but to be." Lane glanced toward the window, her features contemplative. "There are many things from my childhood I have forgotten, but there are few good memories that have stayed with me. When I was twelve, for some reason, Barbara brought me to a park in one of the richer neighborhoods. She placed me on a swing set and told me not to move. Said she would be right back. She probably went to try and seduce one of the rich dads." Lane rolled her eyes in that adorable way that Miranda loved and she couldn't help laughing softly.

"While I sat there, watching the other kids, a group of girls came up to me and demanded that I get off the swing. I refused of course, because Barbara said not to move. They started mocking me about my old clothes and torn sneakers. Then, out of nowhere, a little girl with the most beautiful hair and eyes I had ever seen came up beside me and told the girls to leave me alone because her mommy said it wasn't nice to make fun of others."

Lane reached out, running her fingers through Miranda's natural curls. "You still have the most beautiful hair." Miranda's heart raced as she tried to recall that moment from their history, it felt like a distant memory, buried under the layers of time—she would have been ten if Lane was twelve.

"I expected the bullies to ignore her, but they just laughed, said a few more mean things, and then walked away. The little girl then turned to me and said she was sorry they were mean to me. She then sat on the swing beside me, told me her name was Randi, and she would be my friend if I didn't have any. She told me about a horse that her grandfather bought her and that one day she was going to be a surgeon."

Lane smiled, her features almost nostalgic. "Then her mom came to get her. She took off her shoes, gave them to me and said, 'I have lots of nice things, you can have these ones'".

Miranda gasped. Although she wasn't particularly astonished that she had taken off her shoes to give to a stranger. She was always a feisty, outspoken advocate for others even as a little girl. Just that, it was Lane. Her Lane, whom she had defended all those years ago.

"I remembered your mom because I expected her to yell or slap you for giving away your shoes like Barbara would have, but she looked at you with so much love and what I can now only describe as pride. I wasn't used to that type of kindness so the little girl and her mother remained in my memory for a very long time." Lane slid her fingers around the back of Miranda's neck, resting her palm against Miranda's cheek, her thumb running back and forth across Miranda's face, as they stared at each other. "It's a memory that I've cherished and held on to."

"Wow. I don't remember any of that." Miranda chuckled and she turned her head to kiss Lane's palm. "But I'm not surprised. I was a little social justice warrior when I was young, and always gave away my things. I used to go by Randi back then because my idiotic cousin used to tease me about Miranda not being a black girl's name." Miranda rolled her eyes at the memory and laughed. "I'm named after my dad's mom. Miranda is her middle name. Apparently, choosing my name was a big deal because both grandmothers wanted to be honored. To keep the peace, my parents drew their middle names from a bowl. So, my middle name is actually my mom's mother's middle name."

"You're still doing those things. Giving so much of yourself to others." Lane's eyes carried that tenderness Miranda was noticing more often these days. "I never saw you again until three years later when I was hiding at Parkwood—you had an appendectomy." Lane reached out and touched the area where the faint scar from the surgery remained. "I was sitting in the emergency room when your parents brought you in. It was your mother that I recognized first. I wanted to know if you were okay, so when the doctors came to get them, I followed. You had to stay overnight and I slipped into your room that night."

Miranda watched the tenderness in Lane's eyes morph into trepidation as she recounted that moment. "I remember just standing there, watching you sleep, praying that you would be okay. Then your mom came into the room and caught me. Surprisingly, she remembered me and was so very kind, making me feel welcome. The next day she saw me again in your room and started asking about my parents. I panicked and told her I had to go. The following day I went back to your room, but you had been discharged."

"So that night at Josephine's, you knew who I was?" Miranda asked, wondering why Lane had asked her name if she already knew her.

"Not really. I recognized you, but I wasn't entirely sure it was you. It had been over twenty years since I last saw you, and you've grown into a rather ravishing, gorgeous woman." Lane's eyes trailed up and down Miranda's body with a heated intensity—she felt the impact in her core. "That's why I had asked for your name when you were leaving to confirm if it was you. It was also why I came to talk to you after you rejected my drink. If you were just a random stranger, I wouldn't have wasted my breath with a woman who so rudely sent back my offered drink." They both chuckled softly. "It was when I saw you and your mother having lunch at Sophie's during the week I started at Parkwood that I was absolutely certain it was you. Your mom hasn't aged that much. She is the true definition of black don't crack."

"Why didn't you tell me?" Miranda asked, trying to make sense of the serendipitous chain of events. What were the odds that they had met over twenty years ago and ended up where they were now? Miranda narrowed her eyes. "So let me get this straight. Instead of coming over to introduce yourself as someone I met years ago..." Miranda lifted a skeptical brow... "You instead tried to seduce me into your bed. I think that night would have ended on a better note if you had taken that route."

Lane laughed, her shoulders shaking. "You were absolutely too gorgeous for me to resist, and I was more interested in bedding you than reminiscing about our brief childhood encounter. But..." Lane briefly tapped her index finger against Miranda's lips. "Maybe if you hadn't been so rude in refusing my drink, then we would have had a civilized conversation and I would have brought it up. But I much prefer where me trying to seduce you got us."

"Of course, you do. But you also had plenty of opportunities after that to tell me."

"Are you forgetting that until a few months ago, you couldn't stand my ass? If I recall, you thought I was arrogant and insufferable. You probably would have thought I was spinning some tale to get into your pants." Lane shrugged. "I didn't see the point of it. We met briefly when we were kids and grew into different people. It was clear that you didn't remember anything from our brief encounter. And I don't believe in all that destiny and star-crossed-lovers nonsense. Life just happens and sometimes we run into people from our past. That doesn't mean that we're destined to be together and all that."

"You don't believe in relationships, so of course, you wouldn't believe in fate bringing two people with our history together."

Miranda didn't expect everyone to crave the grand romance she wanted, so she didn't judge Lane for living her life on her terms, unconstrained by societal norms. As long as Lane was happy, that was all that mattered. Still, Lane would make such an excellent life partner if she ever chose to settle down with one woman.

"And I still think you're arrogant and insufferable.

Just that now, I also see how much of a softie you are beneath it all," Miranda continued teasingly.

Lane leaned closer to Miranda, her hand resting provocatively between her thighs. "Softie?" Lane's fingers flexed ever so slightly against Miranda's legs, causing her to momentarily shudder. "I'm no such thing, Dr. Hayes. I think the way you begged while bent over my bathroom sink a few nights ago proved as much." She nipped at Miranda's lower lip, igniting a rush of heat between her thighs as she remembered what exactly Lane was referring to. "Will you come home with me tonight? I have a gift for you there."

Miranda pulled back from Lane's lips, feeling intoxicated by her signature scent, something she would never forget, and just her overall presence. "You gave me my gift yesterday, or should I say gifts."

Lane had surprised her with a weekend getaway for two to New York, to watch a Broadway show Miranda had mentioned wanting to see. In her own way, Lane had even offered to accompany her, by telling Miranda she was willing to suffer through another Broadway show for her. It was such a considerate gift that spoke volumes about Lane's thoughtfulness and attentiveness to Miranda's desires. But it was Lane's willingness to share in Miranda's interests that meant the most. She had also gifted Miranda seeds for a rare plant, something else Miranda had mentioned being interested in acquiring. Then there was the exquisite pair of diamond earrings that Miranda had felt was too much from someone she was casually dating, but Lane had insisted on her accepting them.

Lane leaned back in, her hand running up and down Miranda's thigh. "I saved the best gift for last."

"Well, my curiosity is piqued. How can I say no?" Miranda could no longer resist Lane's lips. She wrapped her arms around Lane's neck and kissed her deeply. Unlike Lane, she did believe in destiny, and regardless of how things might end between them, maybe it was fate that they found each other again. Everything happens for a reason, after all. Maybe they were meant to be of some significance to each other, even if it was just friendship.

Chapter 10

Miranda stared at the items in the black box on Lane's dining table, her pulse hammering as excitement and anticipation coursed through her body. She turned to face Lane, who stood behind her, but her words caught in her throat. Lane had stripped out of her jumpsuit and now stood in nothing but her heels and a black two-piece lingerie set—one of the sexiest Miranda had ever seen, with her long, toned legs and sculpted arms on display. Miranda tried to speak, but she was at a loss for words—mesmerized by Lane's exquisite body. The woman was sex on heels, and Miranda could already feel the inferno roaring to life between her thighs. *Jesus, mother above. Will I ever be able to give this up when the time comes?*

Miranda pointed to the box. "You said you saved the best gift for last. That's what you consider the best birthday gift?" Miranda asked, her voice heavy with desire as she tried to control her urge to reach for Lane and kiss her.

Lane lifted her hand to her neck, slowly tracing her fingers across and down to her stomach. Miranda's eyes tracked the movement of Lane's fingers, wishing she were the one touching her. "No. Those are just accessories for the gift." Lane waved her hand up and down her body. "I'm your last gift—the best one." Miranda raised a questioning brow, even though she found Lane's arrogance irresistibly sexy-as-hell in this setting. Well, in every setting nowadays. "When we were in Portland, you said you'd like to tie me up and fuck me with a strap-on. Tonight, I'm going to make your fantasy a reality." Lane placed both hands on her hips, shifting her weight to one side, and flashing an unabashed wink toward Miranda. "I've been waiting for you to take the initiative and take what you want from me, but since you haven't been proactive about it, I thought I'd take the initiative for you." Lane smiled—stunning, and so fucking seductive. "Though I understand, since you much prefer when I tie you up and fuck you, my little pillow princess."

Miranda mock-glared at Lane, though she knew she was failing miserably since she couldn't prevent the excitement, which was clearly visible in her expression. "Again. I'm no such thing." She glanced over her shoulder at the strap-on and handcuffs. "I guess I'll just have to prove to you that I can be just as dominant as you."

"Oh, Miranda darling," the drop in octave pushed the firestorm within Miranda to the verge of eruption, "I'm *absolutely* looking forward to it." Lane closed the distance between them, wrapped her hands around Miranda, and started pulling down the zipper on her dress. "But first, I really want to slowly peel this dress off your body." Miranda could feel the heat from Lane's slow, increasing breaths—the heaviness of her exhalations reverberating on the shell of her ear. "I don't know how I managed to keep my hands to myself during dinner." Their gazes shifted till they were staring into mirrored amber-flecked olive irises eclipsed by blown pupils. "This dress fits you like it was designed specifically for your gorgeous curves." Lane's hands caressed said curves as they traveled up her body to her shoulders, slowly pushing the straps down her arms. Next went her bra and underwear. Their eyes remained locked, Miranda's stomach tightening with desire as Lane palmed her breasts and toyed with her aching nipples.

Lane took a step back, her lust-filled gaze scorching Miranda's skin as she appraised her. She reached behind her back and removed her own bra, then her underwear. Miranda's eyes immediately dropped to Lane's firm breasts, salivating as the need to have them in her mouth consumed her. "You're breathtaking, and I'm so tempted to bend you over the table, and fuck you." Miranda was hypnotized by the deep rise and fall of Lane's heavy sigh. "But tonight is more about your pleasure than mine." She stepped beside Miranda, retrieved the handcuffs from the box, handed them to Miranda, and extended her hands to be cuffed.

"Aren't we going to the bedroom?" Miranda asked, her voice husky.

A devilish grin spread across Lane's lips. "Where's the fun in that when we have a perfectly sturdy surface right here on the table?" Lane patted the glass and positioned herself on the edge. "Let's be adventurous."

Miranda gulped, her mind instantly picturing the scene Lane was setting up. Her hands shook slightly as she clasped the soft leather cuffs around Lane's wrists, securing them with a resolute click. "Yes, we all know you love to live on the wild side."

"Only in the bedroom, Miranda darling. I tend to be a little more calculated in other areas of my life," Lane replied, her voice a low, seductive purr. She lifted her foot and placed it on the table, opening herself up invitingly. Miranda's eyes widened as she took in the sight of Lane's glistening sex, the sheer eroticism of it causing the throbbing between her own thighs to intensify. Lane gestured toward her body. "This is all yours to do with as you wish. I got you the panty harness since it's your first time. They tend to be a little sturdier," she said, flashing a teasing grin that Miranda had come to love and anticipate. "Great for beginners."

Miranda felt a surge of determination. Lane's teasing only fueled her desire to prove that, while she might be new to experiences with women, she wasn't a novice when it came to sex. "Oh, you're going to pay for all this teasing," she said, her voice thick with intent.

Lane's eyes sparkled with challenge, as if she was daring Miranda to live up to her words. "Do your worst, darling."

Miranda picked up the harness, the lace material soft against her fingers. She was secretly grateful that Lane had already attached the dildo, as her hands were shaking slightly while she pulled the harness over her hips. She felt a bit nervous as it was her first time using it, and she wanted to please Lane—who wielded a strap-on as if it were an extension of herself. But as Miranda's eyes met Lane's, all her nerves evaporated. Lane's gaze was brimming with that familiar hunger that always made Miranda's knees tremulous, drawing her in like a strong tide pulling her into a rough sea. Allowing her passion for this amazing woman to guide her, Miranda grabbed the back of Lane's neck and smashed their lips together. The kiss was rough and urgent, tongues and teeth clashing in a fervor that left them both breathless. Lane wrapped her legs around Miranda's hips, pulling herself closer to the edge of the table, her hips flexing against Miranda's pelvis, seeking friction. Miranda's hand trailed down Lane's body, each touch igniting sparks of desire as she positioned herself.

Breaking the kiss, Miranda eased back to stare at Lane. "I'm in control tonight. No topping from the bottom. We go at my pace." Her fingers found a nipple, pinching hard, cutting off whatever retort was on the tip of Lane's tongue. Lane moaned deeply, her eyes darkening to a molten shade of golden green.

"Okay boss," Lane rasped, eyes twinkling with amusement.

Miranda had every intention to wipe that smirk off Lane's face and have her begging by the end of the night. With this in mind, eyes still fixed on Lane's face, she reached between them and slowly circled Lane's clit. Lane moaned when Miranda slipped inside and groaned in frustration as her thumb grazed the side of the sensitive nub. Lane tried to move her hips but Miranda placed her other hand there, keeping her in place. "Don't move or I'll stop." A satisfied smirk now crossing her own face as she continued her ultimatum. "And since you can't use your hands, I can leave you cuffed all night, hot and bothered without an orgasm." Miranda brought her mouth to Lane's ear, bit into the lobe, and whispered darkly, "You're at my mercy, so it's in your best interest to do as I say." She bit down again, her teeth pressing firmly as she used her tongue to tenderly caress the spot, a soft, deliberate motion meant to soothe the sting. Then, with a gentle, reluctant retreat, she pulled back, leaving behind a lingering warmth.

Lane arched a brow, her chest heaving as Miranda continued to tease her clit. "My, my, my, what have I created?"

"You'll find out soon enough," Miranda replied, her voice dripping with promise as she decided that the time for talking was over.

She joined their lips in another searing kiss, slipping two fingers inside Lane to prepare her for the sizable dildo. She knew Lane was very tight and wanted to ensure she was ready. The abundance of moisture coating her fingers assuaged her worries. Miranda broke the kiss and pushed Lane onto her back on the table. Lane lifted her hands above her head, giving Miranda a tantalizing view of her hard pink nipples. Miranda's gaze traveled down to Lane's pussy as she slowly pushed the dildo inside her. Exhilaration and lust surged through her, making her knees buckle. This was quite possibly the most erotic thing she had ever experienced. Lane's channel tightened around the intrusion, and Miranda pulled out slowly before re-entering. She filled Lane over and over with long, deliberate thrusts until her body accepted the appendage with ease. The room was thick with the sound of their bodies moving together, wet and rhythmic, the air charged with the raw intimacy between them. Lane's soft moans slipped out in quiet gasps, blending with the slick sounds of their connection, creating an almost hypnotic rhythm that filled the space. Each breath, each movement, seemed to draw them deeper into a shared moment, electric and undeniable. Miranda threw her head back, savoring the moment as she rocked into Lane—each thrust drawing a gasp or a moan from Lane as she writhed under Miranda's control.

My god, this feels so fucking good. I can definitely get used to fucking her like this a whole lot.

"Miranda... please..." The whine in Lane's voice was symphonic to Miranda's ears. "Fuck me harder," Lane begged, her voice trembling with desperation, each word thick with longing and need. Opening her eyes, Miranda found Lane watching her, arousal painfully evident in her eyes. Miranda rolled her hips slowly, not immediately giving into Lane's demands. And even though she wanted to drag this out, to tease Lane until she was a quivering mess—her own need for Lane's surrender overpowered her. Grasping Lane's hips firmly, she pulled out and then plunged back into her, causing Lane's back to arch off the table. Miranda's movements became more assured, her hips rolling in a steady rhythm that had Lane panting loudly. The sight of Lane's flushed face and the feel of her tight, welcoming heat drove Miranda wild with desire. Lane's cries of pleasure grew louder as she threw her head back, lost in the throes of passion. She was so incredibly beautiful in the grip of ecstasy, and even if she wanted to, Miranda couldn't tear her gaze away.

The table shook with the force of each thrust, the sound of skin slapping against skin echoing around them. Miranda lost herself in the pleasure of bringing Lane to orgasm like this, reveling in the primal nature of their connection. As she drove Lane closer to the edge, Miranda felt a sense of power coursing through her veins. The carnal intensity of the act made her blood sing, and she felt as though she were soaring above the ground. Now, she finally understood the appeal of wielding a strap-on—the raw passion of the moment, intoxicating her. Was sex with women always this intense? Or was it just Lane who ignited this kind of lascivious passion within her? Miranda didn't have the answers, and at that moment, she didn't care. All that mattered was the fire between them, burning bright and fierce, consuming them both in its passionate embrace.

"My clit, Miranda. Play with it," Lane demanded, her voice a frantic plea.

Miranda wanted to deny Lane's request, to prolong her agony and make her beg even more. But the desperation on Lane's face told her how much Lane needed it. With a flicker of satisfaction at having Lane at her mercy, Miranda obeyed, her fingers finding Lane's clit and circling it with increasing speed. Lane choked out a loud cry, her body curving like a tight bow as Miranda's touch sent waves of pleasure coursing through her. Her cries grew louder, mingling with gasps and moans as she begged Miranda to fuck her. At that moment, Miranda felt like the most powerful woman in the world with one of the most formidable women she had ever met, surrendering to her, begging for release.

"Don't stop… feels so fucking good," Lane moaned out, her back lifting off the table with the grace of her yoga practices. "Miranda, oh fuck… I'm so close. Please don't stop."

Lane's pleas were like the sexiest music Miranda had ever heard, fueling the fire that burned beneath her skin. Her own need for release was building, the pressure of the harness driving her closer to the edge with each thrust. As Lane's pleasure intensified, so did Miranda's—the flames in her stomach burned hotter with every moan and gasp that escaped Lane's lips. Miranda could feel the tightening of Lane's muscles beneath her palm, a sure sign that her orgasm was imminent.

"I'm going to come...don't fucking stop!" Lane screamed, her voice echoing through the room as her body began trembling uncontrollably.

It was the loudest Miranda had ever heard Lane, and she had no intention of stopping if it meant hearing her scream like this over and over again. But more than that, she felt her own orgasm barreling toward her like a tornado. The overwhelming urge to cry consumed her, driven by the intensity of the moment and the sweet bliss spreading throughout her body. Miranda didn't let up, grinding herself harder into Lane until she too exploded, her knees almost buckling as her orgasm slammed into her. It was as if she were plummeting from the sky, her stomach flipping with the weightless sensation, teetering between exhilaration and terror. Her rough breathing seemed to tear through her, making her feel alive and utterly vulnerable all at once, suspended in a moment where anything could happen. To prevent herself from collapsing on the floor, Miranda slumped forward, resting her head on Lane's stomach.

For a while, they remained still, the only sound filling the silence was their labored breathing as they came down from the euphoria that accompanied amazing sex. Moments later, Miranda felt Lane's fingers playing with her hair. She lifted her head to look at her, finding Lane's eyes soft and glowing with tenderness. Miranda was always awed by this softer side of Lane that emerged after sex. It was as if all her walls came down in those moments, allowing Lane to be fully vulnerable with Miranda. Now that Miranda had learned of Lane's history, she understood why she was built the way she was. Lane had no choice but to be strong to survive, and in doing so, she had erected walls to protect herself.

Though to be fair, Lane had never hidden her true self from Miranda.

"I guess you could say you proved your point that you're not just a pillow princess, even if it's your preference," Lane said, her voice raspy from all the screaming.

Miranda softly bit Lane's stomach. "I've always been very flexible in all aspects of my life."

"That you are. Now, how about you help me up and remove the cuffs, so that I can reward you for your hard work."

Miranda could hardly feel her legs but she managed to lift herself up and rid Lane of the cuffs. Lane slipped off the table and returned the chair she had moved in front of the table. She sat on it, reached for Miranda, and positioned her between her legs. Slowly, she removed the harness coated with their essence—her hands cool on Miranda's heated skin—and dropped it to the floor.

Miranda was shocked to see the intense desire in Lane's eyes, as if they hadn't just had sex moments ago. Despite still coming down from a powerful orgasm, Lane's hunger seemed insatiable as she said, "Sit on the table."

Wordlessly, Miranda followed Lane's instructions. What was the point of pretending that she wasn't eager to experience whatever Lane had planned? Once she was settled on the table, Lane pulled the chair closer, placing Miranda's feet on either side of her—exposing her naked flesh to Lane's hungry gaze.

"You can watch or you can lay back," Lane said before lowering her mouth to Miranda's throbbing pussy, moaning deep in her throat from the first taste.

Miranda watched, initially drawn to the captivating

sight before her. But soon enough, overwhelmed by the intensifying pleasure, she surrendered and reclined back on the table as Lane slowly lavished attention on her pulsing center. At that moment, Miranda reflected on her past experiences, comparing them to the unparalleled satisfaction Lane effortlessly delivered. With Lane, everything seemed heightened, intensified —a revelation that had dawned on Miranda after months of passionate lovemaking.

Despite the undeniable chemistry and the insatiable lust she felt for Lane, Miranda was acutely aware of the transience of their arrangement. She harbored no illusions about the nature of their connection. It was meant to be purely physical, devoid of any emotional entanglements or expectations beyond the confines of their carnal desires. Moreover, there was a stark contrast between superb sex without relationship expectations and the complexities of a committed partnership laden with expectations and obligations. For now, what they shared was simple and she wouldn't complicate it by thinking about the future.

Chapter 11

The insistent buzzing of her phone on the bedside table roused Lane from a deep slumber. She groaned, trying to reach out and silence the offending object—it was too early on a Sunday morning to be disturbed. But a warm body lay draped over her, keeping her in place. Lane buried her nose in Miranda's hair, inhaling the sweet scent of vanilla and shea butter. *She always smells so good*, Lane thought, pulling Miranda closer and savoring the comforting weight of her body. Before Miranda, she never knew that cuddling while sleeping could be so... enjoyable. So much so that, whenever they didn't sleep together, she missed the feeling of having someone wrapped around her—a sensation she had never experienced before. Lane had always preferred sleeping alone, but with Miranda, there was a natural closeness that drew them together during the night. She could blame Miranda for conquering her and the bed, but Lane had realized that she, too, now sought out Miranda's warmth while they slept. The phone started ringing again, its persistent noise breaking the peaceful moment. Sighing, Lane gently eased Miranda off her body and reached for it.

Lane's eyes widened in alarm when she saw multiple missed calls from the assisted living residence before she quickly answered Nia's incoming call. "Nia?"

Before Lane could say anything else, words that

caused her heart to momentarily stop beating came rushing out. "It's Anita. She collapsed on her way to an early morning walk. They have rushed her to Parkwood. When you didn't answer, they called me since I'm her second emergency contact. We're on our way to the hospital now."

Forgetting that Miranda was still entwined around her, Lane abruptly sat up, her movements urgent and unthinking. Words tumbled from her lips in a frantic rush, her heart tightening in her chest as if it were being squeezed. Each breath felt shallow, her pulse quickening with an almost panicked intensity, the weight of her emotions pressing down harder than she could contain. "What do you mean she collapsed? I saw her yesterday in the morning and she was fine."

"That's the only detail that I have, hon. We'll know more once we get to the hospital," Nia said, her voice heavy with worry.

Lane's pulse raced erratically as dread pushed down on her shoulders. "Okay. I'm on my way," she replied, disconnecting the call. She swung her feet off the bed, her movements controlled despite the urgency of the situation.

"What's wrong?" Miranda, awakened by Lane's movements, asked as she sat up.

"It's Anita..." Lane paused, swallowing hard as she tried to push away the fear that always threatened to consume her whenever she thought about losing Anita. She was her only family, after all. "She collapsed this morning. I have to go to the hospital," she continued, rushing to her closet to grab some clothes.

Miranda immediately slid out of bed, her concern etched across her face. Without hesitation, she moved to Lane's side, her bare feet padding softly against the floor. "Do you have any more information?" she asked, her voice laced with worry as she gently placed a hand on Lane's lower back, the warmth of her touch offering silent support while her eyes searched Lane's face for answers.

Miranda's touch was a quiet balm, her fingers tracing gentle circles on Lane's lower back, grounding her in the midst of rising panic. The care in Miranda's voice wrapped around her like a lifeline, calming the storm that threatened to take over. "No," Lane murmured, her voice strained yet steadied by Miranda's presence. "Just that she collapsed while walking earlier."

"All right. I'll need to borrow some clothes to accompany you to the hospital. I don't know how long we'll be there and I don't want to be in my dress from last night," Miranda said, reaching for a pair of Lane's sweatpants.

"You don't have to come with me," Lane replied, hastily pulling a sweatshirt over her head. Miranda was right—she didn't know how long she would be at the hospital, therefore comfortable clothing was the smart choice.

"Yes, but I'm coming," Miranda said, her voice resolute and tender. "I'm not going to let you face this alone." She reached out with both hands, her fingers clasping Lane's with a firm, reassuring grip. Her eyes were filled with earnest concern, a silent plea as they met Lane's. "Please, let me be there for you. Don't shut me out."

Even if Lane wanted to, she couldn't deny Miranda's request when she stared back at her with so much care and concern. But more than anything, she realized that she wanted Miranda there with her. Even though she had Nia, she didn't want to face whatever was ahead alone. But Miranda's presence offered a different kind of comfort, something deeper and more intimate than what she got from Nia. She couldn't explain the reason for the difference, but it just felt like more—a profound need to have Miranda with her. These were things that she needed to analyze, but now wasn't the time.

"Okay. Thank you," she replied softly, her voice sounding foreign to her own ears.

Miranda nodded and continued getting dressed. They worked around each other with ease as if they were two people who had lived together for years. Despite the situation, Lane couldn't help but notice how endearing Miranda looked in her clothes. After a quick stop in the bathroom, they were on the way to the hospital, with Miranda driving after a short debate about Lane not being in the frame of mind to drive. Once again, Lane relented to Miranda's request—something she seemed to be doing more and more each day.

During the ride, Miranda insisted on a complete rundown of Anita's medical history. Lane shared that Anita had a history of high blood pressure and she had collapsed a year ago because of it. The doctor had said that Anita had been lucky that someone found her when they did. Another hour, and the outcome could have been different. Lane had been so scared of a repeat incident with no one finding Anita on time, since she lived alone, that she immediately decided to break her contract in L.A. and relocate to Seattle to take care of her. Anita had seen it as Lane overreacting but agreed to the assisted living facility after Lane told her it was either that or she would break her contract. Other than that, her health had been in good condition for her age.

Once they arrived at the hospital, they learned that Anita was in the cardiac unit undergoing tests. Miranda offered to find out more information while Lane went to locate Nia in the waiting room. She spotted Nia and Kenya sitting at the back of the room, huddled together in quiet conversation, and made her way over to them. Sensing Lane's presence, Nia rose from her seat and pulled Lane into a tight hug. Lane wrapped her arms around her friend and accepted the comfort she provided. Other than Anita, Nia was the only constant support she had ever relied on. *That's not true. Miranda has become a steady support system and you have never refused her support.*

"Have you received any updates?" Nia asked, releasing Lane, but keeping her hands on her forearms.

Lane shook her head, her voice steadier than she felt. "They're running tests in the cardiac unit, so it must be heart-related. Miranda went to find out more. If it's her heart, then she has the best heart surgeon on her team. I have faith in Miranda's capabilities." Lane's words were more for her peace of mind than Nia's. She needed to remain positive and not think the worst. Yet, despite her valiant effort, fear clung to her like sweat on a hot humid day.

Nia wiggled her eyebrows, playfully. "Miranda seems to be the best at a lot of things for you these days. If I didn't know better, I'd say you're smitten." Nia exaggeratedly countered her rhetorical statement before Lane could answer, "But we all know you don't do smitten."

Lane rolled her eyes dramatically, her gratitude for Nia's attempt to distract her visible in her expression.

"I'm just speaking facts. She's one of the best in her field. She has the statistics to prove it."

"Hey, Lane," Kenya greeted, pulling Lane into a quick. "I'm going to get us some coffee from The Junction. Do you want something to eat?"

Lane swallowed down the rising tide of dread and unease, trying to prevent her voice from wavering. "Thank you. No food. Just my regular Americano. Double shot of espresso."

Kenya shifted her attention to Nia. "Babe, do you want anything in addition to your regular combo?"

Nia shook her head, eyes shining bright with love for Kenya. "Thanks, love. I'm good with just that."

Kenya nodded and leaned in to give Nia a quick, affectionate kiss. "I'll be back soon," she said, her eyes mirroring the care and affection in Nia's. Then, she turned and headed out, leaving Lane and Nia to wait together.

Lane moved to sit on one of the chairs, suddenly feeling too exhausted to remain standing. It could be hours before they hear anything, and though she was desperate for updates, she knew she had to give her staff time to do their job. They were some of the best doctors and nurses she had ever worked with and she knew they would do everything to save Anita's life.

Miranda is there. I have faith in her.

Just thinking of Miranda brought a sense of comfort that washed over Lane, making her heart feel strange. Maybe it was just gratitude for having her support, a feeling so overwhelming it bordered on something deeper. But now wasn't the time to dwell on that, she reminded herself yet again. Right now, her focus had to be on Anita.

She decided a distraction was needed to keep her mind from drifting into places she didn't want to explore. "Tell me about what's going on with our latest investments. The market has shown some volatility in the last few weeks. But last I checked, you made us a few million."

"That's because I'm the best at what I do. My predictions have been ninety percent accurate for the past ten years, and I don't miss on the big moves," Nia replied, understanding that Lane was seeking a diversion from her worries.

Lane listened intently as Nia delved into the details of Lane's stock portfolio that she managed. She tried to focus on the numbers and trends, anything to keep the impending dread at bay. The thought of losing Anita was unbearable, and Lane clung to the hope that everything would turn out all right. Having Nia and Kenya with her helped, but the true anchor she found herself needing was Miranda—a steadying force in her tumultuous thoughts. *She will be fine. She has to be. I'm just not ready to lose her.*

******

Lane stared at Anita's fragile form in the hospital bed, her eyes studying every wrinkle and laugh line. Anita had suffered a heart attack brought on by a surge in her blood pressure, which had damaged her artery. Fortunately, it hadn't been a massive one, and she had reached the hospital in time to prevent further damage to her heart. Miranda, who had performed the surgery herself, had reassured Lane that Anita would make a full recovery if she followed all of Miranda's post-op recommendations. The first time Anita had collapsed,

Lane had been frightened, but it hadn't been as serious as a damn heart attack.

Nonetheless, it had prompted Lane to reflect on her life. For the past twenty-five years, this woman who had saved her had been a constant beacon for Lane, reminding her that there was goodness in the world. Thanks to Anita, Lane had always had someone to confide in, someone who listened without judgment. As a result, she had never felt the need for anyone else to share that part of her life. Now, as Lane looked at Anita lying there, she couldn't shake the overwhelming sense of loneliness that would grip her when their time together ended. The prospect of facing life without Anita's presence was a daunting one, casting a shadow over Lane's heart. Without Anita, Lane would be left with no other family, and only Nia would remain as her support.

Still, she harbored no regrets about her life choices. She found solace in the simplicity of having fewer people in her life, knowing that disappointment often accompanied human relations. Anita's kindness had been a guiding force for her, shaping her worldview from a tender age, and reminding her that not all humans were monsters. She had encountered the darker facets of humanity throughout her life and career ascent, witnessing firsthand the cruelty and ruthlessness that pervaded certain circles. As Lane grappled with these reflections, her thoughts involuntarily drifted to Miranda once more. Miranda's unwavering kindness and support echoed Anita's—a comforting parallel that Lane couldn't ignore. Before she could dwell further on Miranda's presence in her mind, a soft knock interrupted her thoughts. Lane turned to see the woman in question entering the room, bearing takeout bags.

Miranda approached Lane, raising the bags. "I brought you food. And I don't want any arguments about you not being hungry. You've been here all day, barely eating. You need sustenance to keep your strength up since you insist on not leaving Anita's side."

Lane regarded Miranda, a sarcastic response lingering on the tip of her tongue. But as she stared at Miranda's caring expression, she couldn't help but feel grateful for her steadfast support. Regardless of their non-committal status, Miranda had consistently shown Lane a level of care and consideration that her usual casual encounters didn't entail. Moved by this fact, Lane reached for Miranda's hand, drawing her closer, and enveloped her in a tight embrace. Nestling her head against Miranda's stomach, Lane sought consolation in her presence, a source of comfort she had come to rely on. She didn't know why or could explain it, but there was something about Miranda's presence that had a calming effect on her.

Miranda's fingers gently caressed her scalp, eliciting a contented moan from Lane as she snuggled closer. Lane allowed herself to bask in Miranda's nurturing for a few precious moments before reluctantly withdrawing. Looking up at Miranda, she whispered softly, "Thank you." Swallowing against the lump in her throat, she realized she was not just anxious about Anita—she felt vulnerable in a way she had never experienced before. Emotions she couldn't quite identify or name surged within her, threatening to overwhelm as she gazed into Miranda's hazel eyes, burning with tenderness solely directed at her.

"You're welcome," Miranda replied, her voice soft and soothing. "Thanks for letting me be here for you. I know you're strong and used to handling everything on your own, but that doesn't mean you always have to do it alone. I'm always here whenever you need me."

Miranda's eyes shimmered with sincerity, reflecting a rare goodness that not many people embodied. Lane recognized that even if they were to part ways at that moment and she found herself in need of Miranda's assistance, she would be there for her, setting aside any differences between them. However, Lane also acknowledged her own tendency to weather every storm alone, a habit ingrained from years of independence and self-reliance. She knew reaching out for help wasn't her instinct, even when it was readily available.

Lane released Miranda and glanced at Anita, feeling her heart tighten in her chest. "The day I left for Berkeley when we were saying our goodbyes at the airport, she gave me an envelope with a check," Lane began, the memory vivid in her mind. "I was shocked when I saw the amount, knowing her financial situation and that her job didn't pay much. She had saved every penny from the government stipend she received for fostering me. For three years, she clothed and fed me out of her own pocket, expecting nothing in return."

Lane shook her head, the weight of that moment heavy on her. "Because of her history with her kids, she expected me to abandon her, just like they did. Her final words to me that day were, 'If I don't see you again, always remember that I love you as if I gave birth to you. Go and be great, and remember you'll always have a home with me.'"

Lane turned back to Miranda. "But I could never abandon her, Miranda. She saved my life. I can't imagine what my path would have been if she wasn't the kind soul that she was when our paths crossed. She's more than a mother to me. She's my best friend. My only family," she ended with a whisper, her voice cracking. Lane bit her inner cheek, fighting back the tears that threatened to spill. She couldn't remember the last time she cried—it had been years, and she refused to do so in front of Miranda. She was stronger than this.

Miranda's expression overflowed with empathy. "Why doesn't she have a relationship with her kids?" Miranda asked, reaching out to tuck a stray lock of hair behind Lane's ear.

Lane scoffed with a mixture of frustration and disdain. "You know how society likes to look down on women who choose not to have kids and often say we should have kids because who will be there for us when we're old?"

Lane let out a humorless laugh. "That's a load of bullshit, because despite Anita being the best mother her moronic son and daughter could ask for, once they graduated college and got their fancy jobs, they became too good for their housekeeper mother who had worked tirelessly to take care of them when their useless father abandoned his family. Yes, she may not have gone to college, but Anita is one of the most well-read and knowledgeable individuals I've ever met. Speaking to her you would never assume she only has a high school diploma."

Lane shook her head. "If she was a horrible mother to them, I could understand their behavior, but she's genuinely a good person. So, they have no excuse other than that they're pieces of shit." Lane then laughed with bitter sarcasm. "Life is so fucking unfair, you know? I was unfortunate enough to be given a piece of shit for a mother, and those pieces of shit got someone as good as Anita, and don't appreciate her."

Miranda chuckled softly, the sound drawing Lane away from the dark thoughts that plagued her whenever Anita's ungrateful children, who didn't deserve her, crossed Lane's mind. "You know, I've never heard you curse outside of the bedroom. In fact, you only use the f-word while doing the actual act or referencing it."

Lane loved Miranda's keen observation, appreciating how she noticed the subtleties of her character that often went unnoticed by others. "That's because it's so unbecoming for people to walk around cursing for no reason at all. But I think my aversion to cursing unnecessarily is because my egg donor constantly did when I was with her. I've tried my best to not be anything like her."

Kneeling before Lane, Miranda tenderly cradled her cheek, their faces inches apart. "And you've succeeded marvelously. You're nothing like her," she murmured softly before pressing her lips to Lane's, her kiss a balm to Lane's broken spirit.

Lane surrendered to the kiss, allowing herself to be shrouded in Miranda's tenderness. With each movement of Miranda's tongue, her heart seemed to perform acrobatics in her chest. Kissing Miranda had always been pleasurable, but this time it felt different. More profound. More intense. It was an entirely new sensation—unlike anything she had ever experienced before. At that moment, a whirlwind of euphoria and nervousness swept through her heart, swirling like tennis players volleying a ball with no end in sight. Perhaps it was the shock of Anita's situation stirring up the emotional tumult within her. Yet, in Miranda's embrace, she found peace, a sanctuary amidst the storm.

Miranda slowly withdrew from Lane's lips. "You need to eat before the food gets cold," she murmured softly.

She rose gracefully, retrieving the bag she had set beside Lane's chair. With practiced ease, she began to unpack the containers of food, arranging them neatly on the small table in the room. The tantalizing aroma filled Lane's nostrils, reminding her of her hunger as her stomach rumbled in agreement. Miranda selected a container of shrimp Pad Thai—a dish Lane had once mentioned was one of her comfort foods—and handed it to her. Lane's heart fluttered at the considerate gesture. Miranda then pulled another chair closer to Lane and settled down with her own container, willing to keep Lane company without her needing to ask.

"I also got you some spring rolls," Miranda mentioned before taking a forkful of food.

"Thank you," Lane replied softly, touched by Miranda's thoughtfulness.

"Tell me more about your time with Anita," Miranda requested.

Lane felt a twinge of reluctance at the request, knowing that delving into her past might heighten her already fragile emotional state. However, she recognized that confiding in Miranda had always been a source of comfort. So, between bites of food, she shared anecdotes from her formative teenage years. With each revelation, a new thread—as formidable and resilient as Kevlar—was woven into the invisible connection with Miranda, a bond unlike any she had experienced before.

Chapter 12

"Delaney, I'm not coming home with you. I'm sure you want to get back to your life after fussing over me for the past week. I'll follow Dr. Hayes's instructions." Anita waved her hand as if she were brushing off Lane's insistence like it was a nettlesome fly. "Besides, I need the comfort of my own bed and getting back into a normal routine is what's best for me. You know mental health is just as important as my physical health. And I don't want you constantly worrying about me when you're at work," Anita argued, sitting on the edge of the hospital bed while Lane finished packing her bag.

"I'll hire a PSW to keep you company while I'm at work. That way, you won't be alone," Lane countered. Anita was still a bit frail, but Miranda had given the all-clear for her to be discharged with a follow-up scheduled in a month.

"You'll do no such thing." Anita sighed, reaching for Lane's hands, enveloping them in her own. "I know you're scared, but I'll be fine being back in the comfort of the environment where I'm happy. I love spending time with you, but I don't want to be stuck in your glass tower with some stranger breathing down my neck."

Lane swallowed hard, trying hard not to think about the mind-numbing fear that had gripped her since Anita's hospitalization. The whole ordeal had been tumultuous for Lane in more ways than one, but also eye-opening in many others. "Okay fine. I know there is no arguing with you since you're as stubborn as they come."

"Pot calling the kettle black," Anita replied with a chuckle, raising her brows at Lane in playful mockery.

Lane cast a playful glare at Anita, inwardly grateful that despite everything, Anita's joyful spirit remained undimmed. "Yea, yea, yea. I know I can be just as stubborn as you are. That's why I know when to throw in the towel and let you have your way."

"Good. Plus, I know you want to get back to spending time with Dr. Hayes," Anita teased, her eyes sparkling with mischief as she gave Lane a knowing look.

At the mention of Miranda's name, an indescribable warmth spread through Lane's veins, an unfamiliar yet comforting sensation that left her yearning for Miranda's presence. This was one of those eye-opening experiences—realizing how much she had relied on Miranda's unwavering support over the past week, and welcomed it. A soft knock on the door spared Lane from responding to Anita's taunt. She turned toward the sound, only to see the very woman she had been thinking about materialize in the doorway. A bright smile was already forming on her lips as her eyes flicked between Anita and Lane, lingering longer on Lane with affection. That simple look made Lane's heart perform a strange, joyful dance in her chest.

"How's the patient doing? All set to head home?" Miranda asked Anita, drawing closer to the foot of the bed.

"Dr. Hayes, you came to say goodbye to your favorite patient?" Anita responded, her face lighting up with a broad grin.

Miranda laughed. "You're such a charmer. But yes, I could agree that you're one of my favorites. And you'll remain my favorite if you follow my instructions. As much as I'll miss your delightful company, I'd rather not see you back here under these circumstances."

"Well, you can always accompany Delaney to visit me," Anita suggested, her eyes still sparkling with mischief as they darted to Lane. "Isn't that right, Delaney?"

Lane narrowed her eyes at Anita, then shifted them to Miranda. "Don't fall for all that liquid honey dripping from her lips. She's just a smooth operator," Lane replied, trying not to dwell on the fact that Miranda was the only woman she had ever introduced to Anita. Yes, it had happened under unconventional circumstances, but when Anita had awakened, Lane hadn't introduced Miranda as just her doctor, but as the woman she was romantically involved with. Since then, Anita hadn't missed an opportunity to bond with Miranda, who had visited her daily.

Miranda chuckled. "Indeed, she is."

A gentle knock on the door preceded the entrance of a nurse aide with a wheelchair for Anita. "Are we all ready to go?"

"Yes, I am," Anita replied, accepting Lane's hand as she helped her off the bed. The nurse aide moved closer to assist Anita into the chair. Once seated, Anita reached for Miranda's hands, clasping them gently before he could wheel her out of the room. "Dr. Hayes it was so wonderful to finally put a face to the name I've heard so much about. Thanks for taking such good care of me while I was here." Anita glanced in Lane's direction. "But more than anything, thanks for taking care of my

Delaney and being there for her while I was sick. I'll be forever grateful."

Anita's words struck a tether deep within Lane, and she felt her heartstrings strain against the known and unknown emotions assaulting her. Her eyes drifted to Miranda's face, noting the kindness and warmth that mirrored the very qualities Anita had always embodied —a constant reminder that goodness still thrived in the cruel world they existed in.

"The pleasure was all mine. I'll always be there for Delaney, as long as she allows me to be," Miranda responded, her eyes briefly meeting Lane's before she leaned down to envelope Anita in a warm embrace. Something inside of Lane went molten hearing Miranda proclaim that she would always be there for her.

Lane could only nod, her voice lost in the swell of emotions stirred by the tender exchange between Miranda and Anita. She couldn't quite put into words what she was feeling—maybe it was Anita's health scare that was making her sentimental.

Once Anita was wheeled out of the room, Miranda closed the distance between them, looping her arms around Lane's neck, and pressed a soft, reassuring kiss to her lips. When she pulled back, her eyes searched Lane's with gentle concern. "You look exhausted. Are you planning to stay long at the facility after you drop Anita off?"

"Maybe for a few hours, unless she kicks me out before then," Lane replied, feeling submerged in a flood of vulnerability under Miranda's tender gaze.

"I'll be with my mom, but call me once you're home, okay?"

"Will do," Lane promised, their lips meeting again in

a brief but comforting kiss before they stepped out of the room.

Lane felt a strong temptation to ask Miranda if they could spend the night together—not for sex, but just so that she wouldn't be alone. But she suppressed the urge, knowing how much time with her parents meant to Miranda. She didn't want to burden her, especially when Miranda had already been so generous with her time and support. So, Lane remained silent, reminding herself that she shouldn't rely too heavily on Miranda, given the nature of their relationship.

Four hours later, as Lane stepped off the elevator into her penthouse, the exhaustion of the past week hit her like a tsunami. The weight of it made her feel as though she barely had the energy to climb the stairs to her bedroom. At the same time, her stomach grumbled, reminding her that she hadn't eaten anything since an early lunch, which had also served as breakfast. She'd intended to have dinner with Anita, but when Anita's friends at the facility organized a welcome-home celebration, Lane had opted to give them some space. After bidding Anita goodnight, she headed home, thinking only of a shower, a quick dinner, and bed. Reaching her bedroom door, Lane nearly yelped in surprise. There, amidst the soft light of the room, was Miranda, comfortably dressed in yoga shorts and a camisole, folding laundry strewn across Lane's bed. The sight of her, so at ease and at home, sent joy billowing through Lane, easing the longing that had been building since they parted ways at the hospital.

Sensing her presence, Miranda turned, her lips curving into that beautiful smile Lane adored. "Hey, you're finally home."

Lane stepped further into the room, stopping beside Miranda. She glanced at the bed, assessing the sight of her neatly folded clothes, and then back at Miranda. "You did my laundry," she stated, unable to hide the surprise in her voice or the avalanching relief and alleviation tightening in her throat.

"I did," Miranda replied, her tone warm and soothing. "I also cleaned the apartment. I know you're very particular about how your clothes are washed, but as you so eloquently pointed out the other day, I'm more particular than you and I'm probably the only one you'd trust to do your laundry."

Lane swallowed around the lump forming in her throat, overwhelmed by the quiet thoughtfulness of Miranda's actions. Miranda was someone who didn't just care for her in words but showed it in every action, in every reassuring smile. It was a rare and beautiful thing, and it made Lane's heart swell with an emotion she couldn't quite name but knew she never wanted to lose. No one, except Anita, had ever done anything like this for her—taken such initiative to ensure her comfort.

"I thought you were going to spend the weekend with your parents," Lane managed to say once she found her voice.

Miranda wrapped her arms around Lane's waist, her gaze soft. "Yes, but I changed my plans. I didn't want you to be alone on your first night home after Anita's release. I know sometimes once the adrenaline associated with a traumatic ordeal wears off, it can be difficult for the loved ones of the patient." She closed her eyes and leaned her forehead against Lane's, the touch eliciting a silent transference of benevolence and sympathy between them. "After I left the hospital, I called my mom to cancel our plans and came straight here. I know you haven't had a chance to clean or do laundry with everything going on." She shrugged. "So, I thought I'd do them. That way you can just relax this weekend without worrying about anything."

Lane lifted a hand, cupping Miranda's cheek, marveling at the depth of her thoughtfulness. Her heart expanded with gratitude. "Thank you for being here for me," she whispered, unable to disguise the vulnerability in her voice. "It means more to me than you could ever know." She felt unguarded in a way she rarely allowed herself to be, but with Miranda, she felt safe. After all, how could she not be vulnerable with a woman who had such a remarkable heart, someone who gave so much of herself to those she cared about without ever expecting anything in return?

Miranda kissed Lane gently on the tip of her nose. "You're welcome." They nuzzled their noses together, small smiles on each of their lips. "I love taking care of you." She let out a contented sigh and continued, "Now, why don't you take a bath while I finish putting the clothes away? Have you eaten dinner yet?" Lane shook her head, still overwhelmed by the tenderness in Miranda's gestures. "I'll order something for us then, because I'm starving. Do you have a craving for anything specific?" When Lane shook her head again, Miranda smiled softly. "How about pizza and wings?"

"Okay," Lane finally managed to say, her voice barely above a whisper as she tried to process the flood of emotions surging through her.

Miranda dropped her hand to Lane's, intertwining their fingers, and led her toward the bathroom. Lane followed silently, watching as Miranda turned on the faucet and added two bath bombs. The fragrant scent began to fill the room, but Lane's focus remained on Miranda. She stood still as Miranda began undressing her, powerless to do anything but watch as the woman who had been her rock throughout Anita's hospitalization continued to care for her with such unwavering devotion. Lane was at a loss for words. She didn't know what to make of what she was feeling as she stared at the woman, who had been there every single day, sharing the weight of her burdens, offering strength when Lane felt her own falter. Even now, Miranda was by her side, providing the support Lane hadn't realized she needed.

She tried to rationalize it, telling herself that this was simply who Miranda was—kind, thoughtful, nurturing. Therefore, it was nothing for her to overthink. But regardless, she couldn't form the same opinion about how receptive she was to Miranda's support, how much she wanted it, and how happy it made her. The last time Anita had been hospitalized, Lane had faced it largely on her own, save for Nia. She had been strong enough to weather the storm alone, but having Miranda by her side this time made all the difference. It wasn't just easier, it was better, more comforting.

Lane forced herself to quiet the thoughts swirling in her mind, she was too exhausted for such omnibus introspection. Instead, she pulled Miranda close and kissed her ardently. Physical intimacy was something she understood well. And it was a far more immediate way to unwind, even when she was bone-tired. She reached for Miranda's camisole and began to pull it off, but Miranda stopped her, catching Lane's wandering hands in her own before stepping back from the kiss.

"Later," Miranda said with a soft smile. "After you've eaten and had a chance to relax." She pointed to the tub. "Bath, dinner, cuddles, and then maybe, if you still have the energy, we can think about sex."

Lane pouted playfully. "You know, you can be very bossy."

"I know," Miranda replied, her eyes sparkling with affection. "Especially when it comes to taking care of the people I care about. And you wouldn't want me any other way."

Lane had never heard truer words. There was nothing she would change about Miranda. She followed Miranda's command and settled into the tub, the warm water drawing a deep, contented sigh from her as it loosened the tension in her muscles.

Satisfied that her orders were being obeyed, Miranda blew Lane a kiss and turned to leave. But just as she reached the door, Lane called out, "Miranda, darling." Miranda paused, turning to face her. "When it comes to fucking you into oblivion, I'll *always* find the energy."

Miranda's eyes darkened momentarily before she shook her head with a soft chuckle. "I have no doubt."

Lane watched Miranda leave, incapable of suppressing the smile that spread across her lips. Contentment began to settle over her, a soothing balm after a week of anxiety and stress. And she knew, deep down, that while she was relieved Anita was out of harm's way, it was the woman in her bedroom who was the major source of her happiness.

Chapter 13

"Hey, Miranda. Everly won't be able to make it—she's dealing with an emergency concerning her son. She's deeply sorry and offered to come in on another Saturday to give her speech," Daria informed Miranda just as she stepped out of her office at Found Family.

"Damn. That's unfortunate," Miranda replied, her mind racing to find a solution. "I guess we'll have to scrap the guest speaker segment. We're too close to the end of the event to find a replacement, and I know some of the girls were really looking forward to hearing her speak." She paused, frustration evident in her tone. "We should inform Ava about the change in plans. I could give the speech myself, but I'm not sure I have anything new to say since the last time."

"They love hearing you speak, Miranda. You always manage to inspire them, and those girls adore you," Daria encouraged.

Before Miranda could respond, Daria's phone rang, and she excused herself to take the call. Sighing, Miranda continued walking toward the main hall, where everyone was gathered. As she reached the lobby that connected the executive offices to the general area, the main door opened, and Lane stepped inside. Despite the stress gnawing at her, a wide grin spread across Miranda's face the moment she saw Lane.

Lane returned her smile, shaking her head in playful

exasperation as she approached Miranda. "You seem awfully happy to see me," she teased, pulling Miranda into a brief embrace before kissing her softly on the lips.

"I won't deny the obvious," Miranda replied, her smile widening. "What brings you here? I thought you were spending the afternoon with Nia."

"Kenya's coming down with something, so Nia's staying home to take care of her. Rather than heading home, I decided to come by and bask in your glorious beauty." Lane's hands lingered on Miranda's hips, a subtle gesture of affection that never failed to surprise Miranda. Despite Lane's usually reserved nature and her strong preference for privacy, she had always been openly affectionate with Miranda, even in public.

Miranda let out a soft chuckle. "Still such a charmer." Then she sighed heavily. "Everything was going smoothly until now. We've lost our guest speaker for the 'Inspirational Women Leaders' section. Everly had a family emergency and had to cancel at the last minute. It's not the end of the world, but I hate the thought of disappointing the girls who were excited to hear from someone who's overcome challenges and built a successful life."

"I can step in for her if you'd like." Lane offered, her tone confident yet understated. "We might be in different fields, but given my background and what I've achieved, I think I could come up with something meaningful to share." A small smile tugged at the corners of her lips. "I'm pretty good at improvising speeches, so I'm sure I can wing it."

Miranda blinked, momentarily taken aback by Lane's offer. Knowing how much Lane valued her privacy and how reluctant she was to revisit her past, she couldn't help but ask, "Are you sure? I know how much your privacy means to you." Miranda slid her hand up to cup Lane's jaw, her thumb gently caressing Lane's cheek. "And I don't want you to relive those painful memories."

Lane's expression softened, a tender look that always seemed to surface when she thought Miranda was being particularly endearing. "I'd do anything for you," she replied softly. "And I don't want you worrying about letting down those girls who are looking for hope." She shrugged, as if to downplay the significance of her words. "Besides, if my story can inspire even one of them to rise above their circumstances, then it's worth it."

Miranda felt a wave of gratitude envelope her, mixed with a touch of awe. Even after months of getting to know Lane, she still found herself surprised by her in the best possible ways. "Thank you," she whispered, closing the distance between them to press a gentle kiss to Lane's lips.

It had been two weeks since Anita's health scare, and in that time, they had grown even closer, spending nearly every night together. It wasn't something they had planned, but somehow, they always ended up in each other's arms after a long day. This was her first casual relationship, but in many ways, it didn't feel casual based on how they treated each other. However, she understood the terms of their arrangement and Lane's expectations, so she refused to assign too much meaning to it. They simply enjoyed each other's company and didn't mind spending time together.

A discreet cough behind them prompted Miranda to pull away from the kiss, her attention shifting to Daria, who stood a few feet away with a look of surprise and curiosity. Smiling, Miranda slipped her arm through Lane's and said, "Daria, this is Lane Remington, Parkwood's CEO. She has kindly agreed to step in for Everly, saving us from a last-minute change of plans."

"That's wonderful news," Daria responded, though her gaze flicked between Miranda and Lane with unspoken questions. After a brief hesitation, she added, "I don't mean to intrude, but I always thought you were straight. In all the years I've known you, you've only ever mentioned boyfriends."

Miranda laughed softly. "I thought so too—until a few months ago. I'm still figuring things out." Having been with Miranda since the inception of Found Family, Daria was more than a colleague; she was a friend, so her curiosity was met with understanding rather than offense.

"Well, as long as you're happy, that's all that matters," Daria said warmly before turning her attention to Lane. "It's a pleasure to meet you, Lane, and thank you for stepping in to help." Her gaze turned ever so serious before she added, "Just know that if you hurt Miranda, you'll have a lot of angry people to answer to."

Lane chuckled, the sound light but sincere. "I have no intention of doing so."

"Good," Daria replied, her tone firm but friendly. "We should get inside, it's almost time." She gestured toward the entrance and began walking ahead.

As Lane prepared to follow, Miranda leaned in, her lips brushing against Lane's ear as she whispered, "I plan to properly reward you later for saving the day."

Lane stepped back slightly, her eyes meeting Miranda's, a playful grin tugging at her lips. "Then I guess I'd better make sure I knock this speech out of the park."

"I have no doubt you will," Miranda replied confidently as she entwined their fingers and led them into the assembly.

The room hummed with quiet anticipation, a soft buzz of conversations weaving through the space as the girls settled into their seats, waiting patiently. Miranda made her way to the front, where Daria and Ava were engaged in conversation with one of the therapists.

As they approached, Ava's face lit up with a welcoming smile. "Lane, it's wonderful to see you again. Not only did Miranda manage to get you to open your checkbook, but here you are, stepping in to save the day," she said cheerfully when they reached the group.

"It's great to see you too, Ava. What can I say? Miranda has a way of bringing out the best in people," Lane responded with a confident smile, seamlessly slipping into the extroverted charm she often reserved for occasions like this, where her usual reserved demeanor needed to be set aside.

Ava nodded, her admiration evident. "Yes, she certainly does. She's the driving force behind this incredible facility, which has made such a difference in these girls' lives."

"Miranda, I guess you'll have to introduce Lane," Daria added. "I don't think I could do it justice since my speech was tailored to Everly's background."

Miranda smiled at the suggestion, then turned to Lane. "Well, when you put it like that, how can I refuse?" She met Lane's gaze with a reassuring smile. "Are you ready?"

Lane gave a confident nod, her expression calm as the self-assured CEO mask slipped into place. "As ready as

I'll ever be."

Miranda approached the front of the room, her mind racing with thoughts of how best to introduce Lane. There was so much she admired about her—qualities that were not only impressive but genuinely inspirational. As she picked up the microphone, she decided to keep her words succinct, allowing Lane's presence and story to speak for themselves.

"Good afternoon, everyone. I know you're all eager to hear from Councilwoman Johnstone, but unfortunately, she had a family emergency and couldn't join us today." A ripple of disappointment swept through the audience, punctuated by a few groans. "I understand, but I believe we have someone equally remarkable—if not more so—with us today. Now, I may be a bit biased because she's my boss, but I assure you, I have every reason to be biased. So, without further ramblings from me, please welcome Parkwood's CEO, Lane Remington."

The room erupted in applause, and as Miranda stepped aside, she couldn't help but let her gaze linger on Lane as she approached—her fitted black pants hugging every curve in a way that made it impossible for Miranda to look away and, the crisp white button-down shirt with sleeves casually rolled up, adding a casual sharpness to her confident stride. Her thoughts wandered, taking a decidedly inappropriate turn as her eyes roamed over Lane's form, imagining tracing every inch of her with her tongue once they were home. Lane, perceptive as always, caught the look and flashed a knowing smirk, as if reading Miranda's thoughts effortlessly.

As Lane reached her, she leaned in as though to

greet Miranda casually, but before pulling back, she whispered, "Remember, your beautiful face gives away everything you're thinking. You might not want to be thinking about fucking me with a room full of teenagers watching."

A shiver ran through Miranda, and she quickly masked her expression with a professional smile as she handed Lane the microphone. Taking a deep breath, she retreated to join Daria and Ava at the side of the room, trying to ignore the knowing glance Daria shot her. But who could blame her? Lane was utterly captivating, her allure impossible to resist.

"Are you sure you're not a model? You're way too hot to be working in a hospital. No offense, Dr. Hayes, you know I think the same about you!" Someone from the audience shouted, breaking the momentary pause with a playful tease.

Miranda turned towards the voice, her smile widening as she recognized Harper, one of the girls she was very fond of. Despite the challenges of a troubled home, Harper was determined to get accepted into MIT and pursue her dream of becoming an aerospace engineer.

Lane chuckled, her demeanor inviting and approachable. "Thanks for the compliment, and thank you for having me. I promise I won't bore you or take up too much of your time, but I do want to use this opportunity to share a little of my journey with you," she began, her voice carrying a blend of authority and empathy. She paced the stage thoughtfully, her eyes scanning the room, engaging each person as if she were speaking to them individually.

"How many of you want to be rich when you grow

up?" Lane asked, pausing to let the question sink in. Every hand shot up. "And how many of you believe you can become rich?" This time, less than half the hands went up. Miranda's heart sank a little, knowing how many of these girls struggled to see beyond the limitations of their environment.

"For those of you who didn't raise your hand, I want you to know something," Lane continued, her voice steady but filled with conviction. "No matter where you come from, no matter what challenges you face, if you believe in yourself, you can achieve anything."

The confidence Lane commanded in a board room seemed to captivate every young impressionable girl as she glided across the stage. "I wasn't born into wealth. In fact, I grew up with very little—there were many days that I didn't even have a proper meal. I didn't even have a parent figure who loved and cared for me until I was fifteen. The environment I was born into didn't offer much hope of a better life than what I saw around me. And maybe the majority of society has looked down on you because of your circumstances. But I never let that stop me from dreaming. I dreamt of a better life, and I worked tirelessly to make that dream a reality. It wasn't easy."

Lane paused and pivoted to face the crowd squarely. "The world can be a harsh place, and the odds might seem stacked against you, but I'm standing here today to tell you that if you believe in yourself, if you keep dreaming and never give up, anything is possible."

Miranda felt her heart tighten, overwhelmed by the raw honesty in Lane's words. She could see how deeply speaking about her past affected Lane, and an almost overwhelming urge to comfort her surged through her.

Lane's story wasn't just about success—it was about resilience, hope, and the power of belief, and Miranda couldn't help but feel an even deeper admiration for the woman who had overcome so much and still maintained her humanity behind her tough exterior.

"As you journey through life, you'll inevitably encounter people who, by virtue of their privilege, will try to make you feel small, as if you don't belong. But life is an ever-revolving cycle, and I speak from experience when I say that one day, you might find yourself sitting across from those very people in a position of power—perhaps even as their boss." A mischievous grin played on Lane's lips as she paused, letting the idea sink in. "And believe me, there's a certain satisfaction in watching them squirm, knowing that their future rests in your hands."

Lane paused center stage, her gaze resolute and her demeanor exuding the confidence of a successful CEO who had outmaneuvered her male counterparts to reach the pinnacle of her field. "Society will try to tell you that because you're a woman, there are certain parameters you must meet in order to be considered worth something. A woman's worth is often what she can give to society, and even more often how much society can continue to take, and take, and take from her. Ladies, they...don't... owe...you...anything. And they definitely won't give you anything. It's up to you to determine your self-worth and never lower your standards to appease them. They have to earn your respect. They have to earn your trust. They have to earn your love. They will always try to say that you need to have the most complacent, submissive, and passive personality to remain nurturing, compassionate, and successful. But I am here to tell you that with the love and support of the right people, you can rise above the ranks just the way each of you are. Every trait and personality that defines you is capable of becoming a successful woman."

Lane glanced at Miranda, her smile softening as she continued. "But along your path, you'll also encounter kind strangers, people who will extend a helping hand when you need it most. It's up to you to seize those opportunities, to make the most of every chance you're given. Because no matter how many doors open for you, true success only comes to those who want it deeply enough to pursue it relentlessly. Success is not reserved only for the privileged, it's for anyone willing to work for it, even if that means working ten times harder."

Lane pointed her index finger toward the audience. "Yes, you will have times when you feel disconnected and alone. But fate unexpectedly always finds a way to put the right people in your path to mentor, guide, support, and love you. Family is not always blood. Hang on to those people, and when you become the woman you dreamed of, become that person for another young soul like yourselves."

She paused again, her gaze sweeping the room, ensuring her words resonated with each person. "Mohadesa Najumi said, 'The woman who does not require validation from anyone is the most feared individual on the planet.' Ladies, you are the driving force of your own future. You are the queens of your own empire. You just have to own it. You set the example of what it is to be a strong, beautiful, independent, intelligent, and hardworking woman who is going to change lives. No one is allowed to take that from you. So, keep dreaming, keep believing in yourself. There are no limits to what you can achieve. The only person who can stop you is you. You hold the pen that writes your destiny, and with belief and hard work, you can create a future that surpasses even your wildest dreams."

Lane offered a final, sincere smile as she concluded, "Thank you for allowing me to share a bit of my journey. I wish each and every one of you all the success this world has to offer. Go out there and grab it with both hands. It's yours for the taking." The group of young women gave a standing ovation as Lane gracefully made her exit, stage left.

"Did I perform well enough to still earn my reward later?" Lane asked playfully, stopping just in front of Miranda.

"Yes, you did," Miranda replied, her voice soft with affection. "You'll be *thoroughly* rewarded." The urge to pull Lane into her arms, to hold her close, was almost overwhelming, but she resisted, conscious of the eyes on them. Instead, she asked quietly, "Are you okay?" She needed to know how Lane was feeling after speaking so openly about her past.

Lane squeezed Miranda's hand, a reassuring pressure that steadied them both. "Yes, I am," she said gently. "Stop worrying."

Miranda nodded, though her heart still ached with a tenderness she could hardly express. "All right," she agreed, her voice laced with understanding. "Some of the girls will probably want to ask you a few questions. We'll spend another thirty minutes here, and then we can go."

"That sounds good," Lane responded, just as Harper

approached them, her youthful enthusiasm evident in the sparkle of her eyes.

"Hey, Dr. Hayes. Do you mind if I ask Lane a few questions?" Harper asked, her gaze fixed on Lane with an unmistakable admiration that made Miranda smile. If Harper's skin tone wasn't a beautiful bronze, her cheeks would undoubtedly have flushed with the blush of a teenage crush.

Miranda chuckled softly, recognizing the moment for what it was. "She's all yours," she said, stepping aside to let Harper engage with Lane.

Miranda left Lane with Harper and headed back to her office to wrap up some paperwork before they could leave. She made quick work of the tasks at hand, her mind frequently drifting to what she wanted to do to Lane when they got home. About thirty minutes later, feeling satisfied with her progress, she gathered her things and headed toward the lobby. As she approached the corner, she could hear muffled voices drifting through the hallway. Curious, she slowed her pace, straining to catch the details of the conversation just before rounding the corner. The voices grew clearer, and Miranda caught snippets of a discussion that made her pause.

"I'm currently seeing someone," Lane said, her voice calm and composed, with a subtle edge of finality.

"Is it serious or open? Because I wouldn't mind sharing if it means I get to be with you," a woman responded flirtatiously.

That familiar pang of possessive jealousy surged within Miranda, a sharp, uncomfortable jolt that always surfaced when other women showed interest in Lane. It was a visceral reaction, as if a hidden part of her was suddenly on high alert, bristling at the intrusion and feeling an intense, almost protective flare of envy.

Before Lane could reply, Miranda rounded the corner with purposeful steps, immediately making her presence known. "Well, I don't like to share," she interjected, her voice carrying an icy edge as she slipped a possessive arm around Lane's waist. Her gaze, sharp and unwavering, locked onto the redhead—an all-too-familiar face from their yoga class, whose attention toward Lane had always struck Miranda as overly friendly.

The woman's eyes widened in surprise. "Oh, you attend our class as well. I didn't realize you two were together."

Miranda fought the urge to retort 'obviously' but maintained her composure. "Yes, we are together. May I assist you with something?" she asked politely, but with a clear edge of warning.

The woman shook her head dismissively. "No, I was just walking by and saw Lane standing here. I thought I'd invite her to dinner, but since she's already taken, I guess that's a 'no.'" A sultry smile played on the redhead's lips. "However, if you're ever inclined to share, I'd be more than happy to join both of you for a little adventure."

Miranda minutely slid her arm an inch further around Lane's waist. Reflexively, Lane erased any nanospace between them, leaning enough into Miranda's side that they literally looked joined at the hip.

"See you in class next week. Have a great weekend," the woman said with a wave and a wink, then exited the building.

Lane chuckled as she turned to face Miranda. "You don't like to share, huh?"

Miranda wanted to brush off the moment with humor, but a pang of unease had settled in her stomach. It was the first time since they had been together she had seen Lane interact with another woman who was openly interested in her, and it made Miranda acutely aware of the boundaries of their casual relationship. Despite her feelings, she knew she had no claim over Lane, and there was nothing she could do if Lane chose to sleep with someone else.

"Miranda, are you okay?" Lane's concern was visible as she stared at Miranda.

"I'm sorry if I overstepped," Miranda said, uncertainty coating her words like a thick oppressive fog. "I know our relationship is casual, so I shouldn't have been so territorial."

Lane placed a gentle finger under Miranda's chin, lifting her gaze. "But I love it when you get all jealous and territorial. It makes me want to push you against the wall and bury my fingers inside of you," Lane said seductively, eyes blazing with desire. "Even though our relationship is casual, I have no interest in being with anyone else. Please don't apologize for wanting to claim what's yours." Lane leaned forward, placing her lips lightly on Miranda's and bestowed a slow, reassuring kiss on her lips. "And... I *don't* want to share you either —not even in a threesome."

Miranda felt her unease dissolve as she smiled. "Good."

Lane entwined their fingers and led Miranda through the door. "Let's get you home so you can unwind. You've had a long week, and I'm planning to spend the entire weekend pampering you."

Miranda arched an eyebrow playfully. "And what does this pampering entail?"

Lane's grin widened with a touch of mischief. "Where's the fun in giving it all away? Just know that I intend to take *very* good care of you."

Miranda shook her head, a smile lingering on her lips. She knew Lane well enough to understand that surprises were part of her charm, and she had come to cherish these moments of playful mystery. As they walked together, Miranda reflected on Blake's insight that Lane was precisely what she had been seeking in a partner, so that was why she had been attracted to her. Their time together had felt effortless, and she reveled in the bliss of being with Lane. Miranda realized she had never felt so free and content in a relationship. Maybe it was the casual nature of their arrangement that had somehow made her feel more at ease, without the weight of expectations. And her attraction to Lane remained as strong as ever, growing with each revelation Lane shared.

From their very first date, she understood why so many women had fallen in love with Lane, even when Lane had been upfront about not wanting a serious relationship. At the same time, how could Lane expect those women not to fall for her, given how caring and attentive she was? Miranda could also imagine herself in a committed relationship with Lane, but she quickly pushed those thoughts aside, determined not to make the same mistake those women did by expecting more than what Lane offered. It would be foolish to envision a future with Lane when she had always been clear about her intentions. Miranda knew their time together had an expiration date, so she would simply live in the moment, enjoy their time together, and continue having the best sex of her life.

Chapter 14

Lane studied the picture of Miranda posing on the deck of a yacht, her white two-piece bathing suit accentuating her resemblance to that of a Greek goddess descended from the heavens to grace mortals with her timeless beauty. Miranda's brown skin glistened under the sun, but it was the radiant smile on her face that caused Lane's heart to do strange, fluttering things. Miranda was in Italy, celebrating her grandparents' sixtieth wedding anniversary with her mother's family. And let's just say that Lane missed her more than she had ever expected. It was a longing she couldn't quite comprehend—only two days had passed, yet it felt like months. She had never missed anyone so intensely, to the point where her heart ached. What the actual fuck was happening to her? What did these feelings mean?

She knew she cared about Miranda, but this was more than just caring. In the ten years she had spent sharing her bed with Gabriella, she had never once yearned for her during their separations. Yes, their affair was casual, devoid of expectations for such emotions, but so was her relationship with Miranda. Yet, here she was, missing Miranda so deeply that her bed felt empty without her. She even missed the way Miranda practically slept on top of her—a closeness that had become a source of comfort. Lane's thoughts swirled with confusion and that unfamiliar complexity of longing, security, and hope that she had been noticing for a while now as she stared at the picture, realizing that Miranda had come to mean so much more to her than she had ever intended or expected.

As Lane studied Miranda's beautiful face smiling at her, it dawned on her that it was everything about their relationship that was different from all her previous encounters. She had accommodated Miranda in ways she had never done with any other woman. She had allowed Miranda to see parts of her that she typically kept hidden, not by design, but by choice. She didn't believe everyone was worthy of the best parts of her. However, with Miranda, sharing so much of herself felt natural, woven seamlessly into their dynamic to the point where she didn't even recognize she was doing it. Lane reflected on how Miranda had been there for her emotionally during Anita's health scare. Even after Anita was released from the hospital, Miranda had remained by Lane's side, accompanying her on visits to see Anita. Lane never had to ask for Miranda's support —she just instinctively took charge and provided the emotional comfort Lane needed, often before Lane realized she needed it.

Then there was the constant longing—her constant need to be around Miranda, not just in the bedroom but outside of it as well. She had never craved spending time with a woman beyond the confines of sexual intimacy, yet with Miranda, even existing in comfortable silence felt fulfilling. They could simply be together, and that was enough. And while she found satisfaction in the activities outside of the bedroom, the primal desire to fuck Miranda remained undiminished. Lane had thought her intense attraction might wane over time, but after nearly six months, her desire for Miranda was as insatiable as ever. It was a hunger that hadn't lessened one bit.

What did it all mean? Lane couldn't help but wonder. She was in uncharted territory, experiencing emotions and desires she had never felt before. The constant need for Miranda's presence, the comfort she found in their shared moments, and the relentless passion, all pointed to something deeper than a casual affair.

Lane continued scrolling through Miranda's photos, her mind racing as she tried to make sense of her feelings. She stopped on a photo of them together in Vancouver, British Columbia, where she had surprised Miranda with a weekend getaway. In the photo, Lane looked genuinely happy, a kind of happiness she had never seen in herself before. She appeared lighter... more relaxed. The next photo was a selfie of them cuddling in bed on a lazy Sunday morning. *Jesus Christ, when did I become this person who takes selfies in bed? That's right, it's because Miranda loves to take a million photos and I insist on indulging her whenever she demands we take pictures together, simply because it makes her happy. Yes, I seem to do a lot of things to make her happy, even things that I wouldn't normally do. God almighty. What's next? Becoming a fan of those ridiculous reality shows she loves to watch?*

Her phone vibrating with an incoming message shattered Lane's rampaging train of thought. Noticing the sender, Lane's heart literally galloped in her chest, and she couldn't prevent the smile that formed on her lips. Opening the message, a warm feeling that only Miranda could elicit ran through her veins, making her yearn for her even more. Her heart felt like it was doing a happy dance.

Miranda: *I miss you.*

Three little words that left Lane breathless, stealing the air from her lungs. Three little words that hit her like a tidal wave as emotions she couldn't fully grasp crashed over her, leaving her paralyzed in their wake. Lane felt both terrified and exhilarated as she stared at the words. Her fingers actually shook as she typed a response.

Lane: *What do you miss, Miranda darling?*

The reply was instant.

Miranda: *Everything.*

And then,

Miranda: *I would call you now just to see your beautiful face and hear your voice, but we're out in the city. I really wish you had agreed to come with me.*

A bittersweet mix of longing and regret surged through Lane, tightening her chest as the weight of Miranda's absence continued to wrap itself around her like a dark cloud. She could almost hear Miranda's voice, feel her presence, and it made her ache even more. Miranda's words were simple but packed with an intensity that Lane found both disarming and comforting. Her heart was beating so hard as her eyes scanned each word, seeking to find hidden clues that could help her understand why a few words were making her feel so off-kilter, while at the same time making her feel like she was coming down from an intense orgasm. She attempted to write a response that was less intimate than the tone of the conversation, but in the end, she decided on honesty. She had never played games with a woman and she didn't intend to start now, especially with Miranda.

Lane: I miss you too. I wish I was there with you as well.

Miranda: I'll call you as soon as we're back on the boat. xoxo

Lane: Okay. Later.

Minutes after hitting send, Lane found herself obsessively rereading the conversation, scanning each word, trying to decipher what was unfolding between them—or more precisely, what was stirring inside her. Just as she grew frustrated with herself and was about to toss her phone on the desk, her eyes widened as realization slammed into her like a sudden shockwave, the force of it causing her heart to catapult in her chest.

What? No way. Could it be? Is this what it feels like? No, no, no. It must just be a side effect of missing her.

Lane shot up from her chair as her mind revealed more and more truths about her feelings for Miranda. Lane's fortress of solitude, standing alone on a robust and tempered precipice of who she was and who she became, began to crumble amidst the hurricane that was Miranda Hayes. Lane's defenses could no longer withstand the crashing surges and swells of joy, contentment, vulnerability, security, and longing Miranda left in her wake. It left her breathless as if she were on the precipice of something life-altering. She rushed from her office to find one of the few people in her life who could probably help her understand or make sense of what she was feeling. A few minutes later, she pushed Alexandra's office door open after being given the green light from Melanie to enter.

Alexandra looked up from her laptop, her initial smile quickly replaced by concern as she probably noticed the distress on Lane's face. "Lane, are you okay? You seem a bit frightened."

Lane nodded as she sat in the chair across from Alexandra. Without preamble, she blurted out, "What does being in love feel like? How do you know that it's love and not just intense lust? You and Blake started off casual and then became more. How did you know your feelings for her were more than just a desire for sexual release?"

A wide, knowing smile stretched across Alexandra's face, and Lane furrowed her brows, wondering what she had said that was funny. "Ah, so you've finally realized you're in love—or falling in love—with Miranda?"

Lane's eyebrows shot up to her hairline, eyes widening in confusion. "What do you mean, 'finally realized'? I wasn't aware until maybe a few minutes ago that I might have developed feelings beyond casual." Her mind raced, baffled by Alexandra's assessment. How could Alexandra have seen something that had only become apparent to her moments ago? Or perhaps she had been blind to the signs all along, because of the intense desire she had always felt for Miranda? Had she been confusing love with intense lust all this time?

Alexandra leaned back in her chair, a gentle smile

playing on her lips. "It's in the way you look at her, Lane. I first saw it when you came over for dinner last month. When you first got here, you used to look at her like you wanted to devour her whole. You still do." Alexandra let out a quiet chuckle. "But now there is something more. You look at her like you're in awe of her, with a tenderness in your eyes that's reserved just for her. The moment she walks into a room, you smile and your gaze never leaves her."

Alexandra paused as if giving Lane a minute to let her words sink in. "Overall, you're much softer in your interactions with her, and it's like you lower your guard around her. You also went against many of your principles in dating her. I personally think your relationship has never been truly casual from the start. And I'm speaking from experience." Alexandra shook her head, chuckling softly. "Blake and I thought what we were doing was casual but our actions were the opposite of two people who only wanted sex from each other. I saw the same signs in your relationship with Miranda."

Lane frowned, struggling to process Alexandra's words. She crossed her arms and uncrossed them, her gaze dropping briefly to her lap as she tried to reconcile her feelings. *What, now I'm fidgeting? God. Love. I might be in love? Christ.*

Alexandra continued, her voice warm and understanding. "You've gone above and beyond to make Miranda happy. If it were just sex, regardless of your staunch principles of treating every woman you date with respect, you wouldn't have shared so much of yourself with Miranda. You've been to multiple Broadway shows with her, even though you're not a fan.

The fact that you were willing to do that just to spend time with her says a lot. You've also donated your time to Found Family, because you know how much it means to Miranda."

Lane's heart pounded as she absorbed Alexandra's words. Images of her and Miranda flashed through her mind—their quiet evenings together, the way Miranda's laughter lit up her world, the comfort she felt in Miranda's presence. How she had never been afraid to share details about her life with Miranda. And how safe she had always felt with her. She realized that Alexandra was right. Miranda was different, and her feelings for her were like honey mesquite trees, running deeper than anything she had ever felt.

Alexandra tilted her head, her eyes brightening with what Lane could only describe as love. "As for your questions, Lane, I can only tell you what love feels like for me, but I believe it can be different for others. When I merely think about Blake, sometimes I feel like I can't breathe. I think about her constantly when we're apart, and even though we've been together for over two years now, I still crave her the same way I did when we first got together." Lane's gaze never moved from Alexandra's, but she didn't miss the subconscious way Alexandra's thumb twirled Blake's engagement ring around her finger. "With every decision I have to make, I always think about how it affects her, and if she hurts, I hurt. Then there's this constant longing to be close to her, an insatiable need that can't seem to be filled. Sometimes it's overwhelming and scary, but at the same time, it makes me feel so utterly complete."

Alexandra glanced at the wedding photo on her desk, eyes growing even more tender. "It's just the most amazing feeling ever. It makes me feel like I'm freefalling with no end in sight. It's the greatest high I've ever experienced outside of my love for our daughter."

Alexandra's words struck Lane like a barrage of stones, each one heavy with undeniable truth. They hit her hard, unraveling emotions that had probably been there all along, which she had confused with the intense desire she had always felt for Miranda. Thoughts of Miranda flooded her mind, and her chest tightened, as though the very act of breathing had become impossible. The sensation mirrored what Alexandra had just described—a relentless, gnawing ache for the other person's presence, as if nothing else mattered. And yes, throughout their relationship, Lane often found herself bending to Miranda's needs, sometimes placing them even above her own, without a second thought.

Lane shook her head, attempting to gather her scattered thoughts, which raced like a wild stallion. She prided herself on her honesty, both with others and more so with herself. She wasn't one of those people who chose to live in denial, even when the truth was staring them right in the face. If she was indeed falling in love, or already in love with Miranda, she needed to confront it head-on. But she couldn't afford to be reckless, given their circumstances, and she couldn't bear the thought of hurting Miranda. She needed certainty. But how could she be sure without revealing her feelings to Miranda? And what would it mean for them if she did?

"Lane, I can see your mind racing," Alexandra said, grounding Lane in the present moment. "But don't overthink it. Let your heart guide you. Love has a way of leading us down the right path, even when our minds and hearts are at odds. Especially when we're trying not to hurt someone." That ever-empathetic smile that was the epitome of Alexandra Westmore Edison Devereaux materialized, further anchoring Lane's riotous thoughts. "Ultimately, you have to prioritize your own happiness. If you're not content with yourself, you can't truly make someone else happy. So, take your time. Don't rush into any decisions until you're sure."

Lane grasped the hidden message behind Alexandra's words. She didn't want Lane hastily declaring her feelings to Miranda unless she was absolutely certain, because she could end up hurting Miranda if she wasn't. The idea of unintentionally hurting Miranda sent a sharp pang through Lane's heart, like a needle pricking at her core.

Jesus Christ. How the hell did this happen? Oh, how the mighty has fallen. And for a woman who is still figuring out her sexuality. Would Miranda even want to pursue more with me? Can I just walk away from her and allow her to find herself without me? Fuck!

Lane refocused her attention on Alexandra's compassionate visage. "Thanks for your time and advice, Alexandra. I'll definitely need some time to process my feelings. Fortunately, with Miranda being away it will give me a few days to deal with my revelation." She gently massaged her temples, sensing a headache looming ominously. "Do you mind not sharing any of this with Blake? She and Miranda share this incredible bond and I don't want to put her in a situation where she has to keep anything from her."

"Of course, I wouldn't betray your trust like that," Alexandra assured. "I'd like to think that we have developed a friendship that implies a girl code, demanding that I don't share your secrets with my wife. I don't expect Blake to tell me everything Miranda shares with her. Their conversations are private and I respect that." Alexandra paused, her gaze probing. "But you do eventually intend to discuss your feelings with Miranda?"

"Of course. I just need to be sure of what I'll be discussing with her. I don't want to be rash in my decision on how we move forward." That was the big question. How would they move forward if Lane was in fact in love with Miranda?

"Would you be open to a relationship with her? I recall you mentioning once that you weren't opposed to the idea of love, but you hadn't met someone who inspired you to explore more than casual dating. Now that it seems that you have, would you be willing to try?"

Trust Alexandra to remember that conversation. Lane's answer flowed effortlessly, borne from a place of certainty. "Yes, I would be. However, there are numerous factors to consider given the nature of our relationship."

Understanding flickered in Alexandra's eyes. "I know. You're one of the most honest people I've ever met, so I have no doubt you'll be honest with Miranda when the time comes. Until then, I'm here to talk whenever you need to."

"Thanks. I appreciate it." Lane wanted to laugh at the irony, that of all the people in the world, Alexandra was the one she ran to for advice given their history.

But who could blame her when she had never met two people more in love than Blake and Alexandra?

And the more significant question was, could she dare to dream about sharing the same love and devotion with Miranda? Was she capable of loving someone so intensely that she would sacrifice her life for them? To be that selfless. Miranda deserved to be with someone who could give her the kind of relationship that Blake and Alexandra shared. And if Lane couldn't provide her with that, then she only had one choice.

Chapter 15

The unexpected sound of her doorbell momentarily confused Miranda. She had told Lane to come right in when she arrived, and she wasn't expecting anyone else. After not seeing Lane for six days, she had eagerly requested they spend her first day back together. Her longing for Lane had been almost unbearable. Even though she enjoyed her time with her family in Italy, she had been counting down the days until her return, all because of Lane. Hastily pulling her tank top over her head, Miranda rushed down the stairs, her body vibrating with anticipation. She pictured Lane pushing her up against the door as soon as it closed behind her, giving Miranda the orgasm she had been craving since she left. Not even their steamy phone calls had been enough to quell her desire to feel Lane move inside her. Miranda shook her head and laughed at her thoughts. Maybe Lane was right in calling her a pillow princess, given how much she loved it when Lane dominated her in bed. But she knew, in her soul, what she felt for Lane went far beyond physical satisfaction. It was an exhilarating connection—one that made her heart race just as much as her body.

Arriving at the door, Miranda couldn't help the wide smile that stretched across her face as she turned the knob, eager to pull Lane into her arms. But as the door swung open, her smile vanished, replaced by shock. Her eyes widened as they landed on the last person she expected to see.

Trevor's lips curved into that teasing smile that always made him seem younger—the one Miranda used to love being the recipient of. "Hi, Miranda. I can see that me showing up unannounced was the last thing you expected."

For a moment, Miranda struggled to find her words. She stared at the man who had ended their relationship and had gone completely no contact. A fact that still stung, even though he had the right to pursue his own happiness. Trevor, the man she once thought she might marry, stood before her. His hair, though still above his shoulders, was much shorter than she remembered him ever wearing it. He seemed buffer, the black T-shirt straining against his muscled chest. But it was his crystal blue eyes that gave Miranda pause. They stared back at her with a look she could only describe as love, reminiscent of the way he looked at her when he first told her he loved her. That broke Miranda out of her momentary muteness.

"Hi. Yes, your appearance is quite a surprise," Miranda said, her voice tinged with unexpected anger. "Months ago, you broke up with me out of nowhere, left Seattle without a goodbye, and I haven't heard from you since."

Miranda's anger startled her, because she had moved on from the breakup. Had she thought about Trevor over the months since then? Yes, she had. Of all her relationships, he was the only one she had ever considered giving a second chance, had he asked for it, and she was at a place in her life where she could offer the commitment he once wanted. Miranda had always been fair, owning up to her part in the failure of their relationship. Trevor had just wanted something she couldn't give at the time. And while he wasn't perfect—no one was—he had been an amazing boyfriend in all the areas that mattered most to her.

Despite her obvious dig, Trevor's eyes remained tender, filled with a longing that made her heart twinge with compassion. "I guess I deserved that. Can I come in? I really want us to talk." Noticing the refusal forming on her lips, he quickly added, "Please. I won't take up much of your time. I know my visit is unannounced, but I just really need to tell you why I'm here. We can always make plans to meet up after you hear what I have to say."

The pleading in his voice melted her defenses, and with a reluctant sigh, she stepped aside to let him in. Regardless of how things had ended, she knew she still cared about him. She followed Trevor into the living room, her mind spiraling with questions about what he could possibly want to discuss after months of silence. She also hoped fervently that Lane wouldn't arrive while he was there, knowing how Lane felt about him—a sentiment rooted in the simple fact that, back then, Trevor had what Lane wanted: her. The thought made her smile slightly, despite the tension in the air.

"Would you like something to drink?" Miranda asked as Trevor settled on the sofa.

"No, I'm fine, thanks." He glanced around the living room, his eyes eventually returning to lock with Miranda's.

Miranda lowered herself onto the opposite end of the sofa. Despite her initial shock and brief anger, she realized she was genuinely happy to see Trevor. She wished him well, and from his appearance, he seemed to be doing fine. "So, what's up?" she asked, breaking the silence that had settled around them.

Trevor drew in a long breath, his eyes reflecting a tumult of emotions that Miranda tried to ignore until she knew why he was there. "First, I just want you to know how sorry I am about the way I ended our relationship." The sincerity in his voice was unmistakable, and she could see it in his eyes. "I was selfish in my desire to have a future with you, instead of being patient. I guess love really does cloud our judgment at times. I was also afraid that maybe you would never feel the same way about me, and to spare myself further heartache, I made a rash decision. It's something I regret enormously."

Miranda's mind spun. Of all the things she expected, an admission of regret wasn't one of them. "Why now? It's been months." Some people might have felt some satisfaction in his regret, but all Miranda felt was an immense sense of sadness for him.

"Because even though we haven't spoken in months, I'm still deeply in love with you." Trevor swallowed hard and ran his hand through his hair—a nervous gesture. "As for why it took me this long to show up here, I had some family matters in New York that required me to relocate temporarily. My father was diagnosed with colon cancer, and I chose to stay in New York to support my parents."

Miranda gasped, her mind skimming over the first part of Trevor's statement and focusing on the news about his father. "I'm so sorry. How has his treatment been? Is he in remission?"

A new form of sadness overshadowed Trevor's

features. "He's in remission, but the whole ordeal wasn't easy. The treatment was rigorous, and it took a toll on him, not just physically but also mentally. He's in a much better place now. Hopefully, it won't return."

Miranda instinctively moved closer to Trevor and reached for his hand. "I know how hard that must have been for you. How are you feeling now that it's over?"

Trevor shrugged. "I'm just grateful that he's alive. It was difficult to witness such a formidable man slowly withering away before my eyes. Now that he's healing, I'm just grateful to have more time with him."

Realizing she was still holding Trevor's hand, Miranda slowly withdrew it. Trevor's fingers tightened around hers, holding her hand in place. He stared at their entwined fingers before reluctantly letting go. His hand was just as soft as she remembered, but now she had experienced the touch of hands much softer. Hands that made her feel so much just from a simple caress.

"I'm glad to hear that." While Miranda's empathy went out to him, she still didn't understand his behavior. "But still, regardless of your father's illness, why did it take you this long to contact me? I was just a phone call away."

Trevor looked away, then brought his eyes back to hers. "At first, I was hoping you'd come after me once we had some time apart, and you'd realize you wanted the same things I did," he said, letting out a humorless laugh. "But that backfired spectacularly since you didn't reach out to me at all after I left."

Miranda bit the inside of her cheek to hold back a sarcastic retort. Why would he play such games with their lives? This was why she appreciated Lane's straightforward attitude. With Lane, she always knew where they stood. But at the same time, she couldn't help sympathizing with Trevor. She knew how much he loved her and how much he had wanted a life together. "Trevor, you gave me an ultimatum and walked out of my life. I didn't see the point in contacting you when I still wasn't ready to move in with you. And then you left Seattle without even telling me."

Trevor sighed, his shoulders slumping slightly. "I know. It was a huge mistake on my part, and I'm truly sorry." He reached for Miranda's hands, enveloping them in his. "But I'm back in Seattle, and I'm really hoping you'll give us another chance. Time apart has given me perspective, and I'd much rather have you in whatever capacity you can give than not at all." Trevor's eyes were glossy and pleading as he stared at Miranda with all the love she recognized he still carried for her. "I don't expect an answer now, but I needed you to know that I'm willing to try again if you are."

Miranda opened her mouth to tell him that she was seeing someone, because while her relationship with Lane was casual, it meant something to her. But the sound of the door opening cut off her words. She looked over her shoulder to find Lane stepping over the threshold, her eyes locked on Trevor's hands holding Miranda's. Lane's expression was an impenetrable iron mask, giving no clue as to what she was thinking. But Miranda had come to know Lane well enough to pick up on certain tells even when her expression was neutral. The firm set of her jaw and the coldness in her eyes were unmistakable signs of a woman who was not happy with what she had walked in on. Miranda's heart sank, realizing how this must look to Lane.

Miranda gently withdrew her hands from Trevor's,

rising to her feet to greet Lane—the woman whose absence for six days had felt like a lifetime. A wide smile formed on her lips as she approached Lane, pulling her into a tight hug. "God, I've missed you," she whispered softly in Lane's ear.

Lane returned the hug, but it didn't feel as warm or welcoming as Miranda had expected. She eased back to meet Lane's eyes, sensing that something was off. Lane's demeanor seemed almost sad. *Was this because of Trevor? Surely she must know that nothing was going on between them.* Miranda searched Lane's face for any clues to her behavior before turning back to Trevor, who was watching them with curiosity.

"Trevor, I'm sorry to cut this short, but I have plans with Lane," Miranda said, trying to convey the importance of the moment without being dismissive of his declaration. She couldn't focus on his request now, not with Lane standing right there, their connection palpable and demanding her full attention.

Trevor rose from the sofa, his gaze scrutinizing as it bounced between Miranda and Lane. "Okay. I'll call you. Please think about what I said," he requested with a mix of hope and uncertainty. Turning to Lane, Trevor gave a curt nod. "Hello, Lane. Nice to see you again."

"Hello," Lane replied, her response short and devoid of warmth. Miranda wanted to both laugh and scold Lane for being rude. Lane had always been terse with Trevor, even from their first encounter.

"I'll walk you out," Miranda informed Trevor, eager to conclude their conversation and return to her reunion with Lane.

With a last glance at Lane, Trevor followed Miranda to the door. Before opening it, he turned back to her, his eyes affectionate and pleading. "Please think about what I said. I've missed you more than you can imagine," he whispered earnestly.

Miranda didn't know how to respond to Trevor's plea, so she simply nodded. While she had missed him initially after their breakup, those feelings faded once she became aware of her growing attraction to Lane. "Take care. Give your father my regards."

Trevor nodded in acknowledgment. "I will." He opened the door and stepped outside, pausing to look at Miranda one last time before continuing on his way.

Miranda closed the door, drew in a deep breath, and turned to find Lane's eyes fixed on her. She tried to summon a smile, but the expression on Lane's face wiped it away, leaving an unsettling sensation in Miranda's gut. Approaching Lane by the sofa, she spotted an unfamiliar emotion in Lane's eyes. Fear. What was she afraid of?

A strong urge to comfort Lane surged within Miranda, compelling her to reach out and pull Lane into an embrace, to press her lips against hers. But as she moved closer, Lane halted her attempts.

"We need to talk," Lane said softly, her voice tinged with an undertone of pain.

Chapter 16

Miranda regarded Lane with growing concern, the unease in her stomach swirling into a knot of worry. Lane had seemed a bit melancholic during their conversation the previous evening, citing a lot on her mind. Miranda had urged her to open up, and Lane had promised they would talk when Miranda returned home. Now, faced with Lane's solemn expression, Miranda couldn't shake the heavy feeling settling over her.

"Okay," she finally replied, sinking onto the sofa. Instinctively, she suspected the topic of their conversation—a realization she had subconsciously anticipated. She knew this moment would arrive eventually, though she hadn't actively prepared for it. It wouldn't be easy, but Miranda had accepted the potential outcome when she embarked on exploring her sexuality with Lane—an inevitable end.

As Lane seated herself beside Miranda, maintaining a cautious distance, Miranda's disquiet proliferated. "Does he want to get back together?"

Lane's question caught Miranda off guard, momentarily puzzled before the pieces clicked into place. "Trevor?" Lane nodded, requiring Miranda to reluctantly acknowledge the topic she had hoped to avoid. "Yes, he wants us to try again."

"I see," Lane replied, dropping her gaze to her lap

before lifting them to meet Miranda's once more. "Do you want to... try again?"

Miranda felt a surge of confusion and anxiety rise within her. "Lane, what's going on?" she asked, her voice painted with trepidation. "Last I checked, I was in a relationship with you. Yes, it's casual, but it still matters to me. I haven't even entertained the thought of being with someone else since we started seeing each other." Miranda had to clasp her hands together to keep them from trembling. She was a surgeon. Her hands never shake under pressure. But their impending reality was a mire she couldn't stitch back together. "And as for Trevor, I haven't even had a chance to process him just showing up, let alone consider trying again with him."

Miranda paused, inhaling slowly to steady her frantic heart. While she didn't want to jump to conclusions, she couldn't stop her mind from thinking the worst. She decided to rip off the band-aid. "Do you want us to stop seeing each other? Is that what this is about?" Saying the words out loud caused Miranda's heart to thunder in her chest as she waited for Lane to answer. And as the seconds ticked by, she realized that she only wanted one answer.

Lane's posture stiffened, her expression inscrutable. Miranda couldn't decipher her thoughts as Lane finally spoke, her voice measured yet decisive. "Yes," Lane said, her words landing like a cannonball on Miranda's heart. "I think it's best."

As Lane's words pierced the air, Miranda watched as the mask of composure slipped from her face, revealing the raw anguish etched in her features. Each word seemed to strain against the weight of her despair and sorrow, her voice cracking with the effort. Miranda had braced herself for this moment, but the reality of Lane's pain struck her like a physical blow, leaving her reeling. She bit the inside of her cheek to suppress the torrent of desolation and excruciation threatening to overwhelm her. She couldn't be upset at Lane for being honest about her feelings. After all, Lane had always been transparent about the nature of their relationship. If she had reached a point of exhaustion or dissatisfaction, Miranda couldn't fault her for that. Still, she wanted to know if it was her fault in some way. She thought they were fine.

"Is it because of something I did?" Miranda asked with a shaky breath, as she struggled to keep vulnerability from her voice. "I know we've been spending a lot of time together, and maybe the lines between casual and committed might have gotten a little blurry. But I know where we stand, Lane." Her hands were balled so hard into fists in her lap, she was sure she was going to make her palms bleed. "I've never expected anything more from you, other than what you've been willing to give. I would have been foolish to even think about a relationship with you, when from the start you made it clear that it was just sex and helping me explore my sexuality."

Miranda's words spilled out in a rush, desperate to reassure Lane that she didn't harbor any unrealistic expectations. "If you need us to take a step back, to spend less time together, then I'm willing to do that," Miranda continued earnestly. She wanted Lane to know that she was willing to adapt, to accommodate whatever boundaries Lane needed to set.

"That's the opposite of what I want, Miranda. It's the fact that I want to spend every second of every day with you why we need to end things," Lane replied, her voice stronger than before, but laced with frustration.

Miranda's brows furrowed in confusion, her heart pounding erratically against her ribcage. "What?" Her voice was barely a whisper, a fragile thread of disbelief weaving through the air. She lifted her hands in a futile gesture of bewilderment before letting them fall back to her lap. "How can you want to spend more time with me and yet you're here, breaking up with me?"

"Because I'm falling in love with you, Miranda," Lane confessed, her voice carrying a fragility that pierced through Miranda's defenses. "Or maybe I'm already there," she added softly, her admission hanging between them like an unspoken truth.

Miranda stared at Lane, her features stripped of any of her impenetrable masks. For the first time, she saw the vast chasm of love reflected in Lane's eyes, unclouded by desire or lust. Despite the tumult of emotions swirling within her, Miranda not for one second doubted Lane's sincerity. This was Lane, after all —guarded and cautious, yet unyielding in her honesty. If Lane had mustered the courage to bear her heart, Miranda knew there could be no doubt about the sincerity of her feelings.

Before Miranda could respond, Lane continued, her voice carrying a weight of conviction mixed with an undeniable openness. "You're still figuring out this side of your sexuality," Lane began, her words measured, but filled with an underlying turmoil. "Everything is new and exciting for you. You've only been dating me and haven't given yourself a chance to explore with anyone else to see if this is really something you want. I've had enough experience with women who aren't lesbians to know that sometimes after a while, the novelty wears off and they realize that a relationship with a woman isn't for them."

Miranda watched as Lane closed her eyes tightly, a silent struggle playing out behind the veil of her eyelids. It was clear that Lane was wrestling between the logic of her mind and the passion of her heart, trying to articulate her chaotic thoughts. "It would also be unfair of me to expect you to jump into a relationship with me when you haven't had much experience outside of what we have been doing," Lane continued, her voice betraying a hint of resignation. "And more than anything, if I'm going to risk my heart for the first time, it has to be with someone who is sure that a relationship with a woman is what they want."

The meaning of Lane's words thickened the atmosphere, casting a shadow over Miranda's thoughts. She listened intently as Lane paused, taking a cleansing breath to steady herself. "So, while it hurts to let you go, because it does," Lane admitted, her voice tight with said hurt, "I feel it is the right thing for both of us. I need to let you go so that you can fly and discover more about your sexuality. I've been selfish in not encouraging you to date anyone else." Clearly, this decision weighed heavily on Lane and came from an undeniable sense of selflessness.

Miranda's head spun as she tried to process what Lane was saying. Her fingers unfurled from their self-constriction. Her right hand coming to rub the space on her chest above her heart. "You're in love with me?" she managed to whisper with disbelief coating every syllable. Given Lane's dating history, she had never allowed herself to dream of such a thing. But now that they were here, Miranda felt like someone had just tilted her world on its axis. But it was the utter unreservedness and concession in Lane's voice, so raw and sincere, that surprised Miranda the most.

A sad smile formed on Lane's lips. "Yes, I think I am." She let out a small chuckle. "Well, you know I have no experience in that department, but what I feel for you can only be love. It's no longer just lust. Sitting here staring at you, I feel like I can't breathe, and my heart feels like someone has pierced me in it with a knife."

"I don't want us to stop seeing each other," Miranda heard herself say before she could even think about it. While Lane's confession was a shock and she needed to process it, she knew she didn't want to lose Lane.

"It's the right thing for both of us…" Lane reiterated, but Miranda cut her off, desperation clawing at her.

"No! It's not. We can still be together and figure things out. It doesn't have to be all or nothing, Lane." Miranda heard the pleading in her voice, but she didn't care because she was certain that she didn't want things to end.

"Do you love me, Miranda?" Lane asked, her eyes burning with that intensity that always left Miranda breathless. Now, however, the usual passion and lust were diminished by Lane's naked honesty and emotional surrender—and it was going to render Miranda's heart to pieces.

It was precisely because of that intensity that Miranda didn't rush to say… yes. She was certain she didn't want things to end, but Lane was right—Miranda needed to be sure about her sexuality. More than anything though, she needed to be sure about her feelings for Lane. Here was a woman who had never been in love before, declaring her love for Miranda. So, no matter how much she wanted to say "yes", she just couldn't. She didn't want to hurt Lane if she wasn't sure. She needed to be certain, for both their sakes.

Another sad smile marred Lane's beautiful face. "The fact that you have to think so hard about it, is all the answer I need." Her words were adorned with so many emotions, but the most prominent was sadness.

Why is she doing this if she is hurting?

"That's not fair, Lane. I've never allowed myself to think of a future with you because I didn't want to set myself up for heartbreak." Miranda sighed heavily, hoping she could inhale against the tightness twisting in her chest. "And you've just told me that you would want more with me. Don't you think you should at least give me time to process this change in expectations?" Yes, she needed to process this new development, but she didn't think they needed to do it apart. The fact that she was fighting for them to continue their relationship, even though she couldn't tell Lane that she loved her, spoke volumes. Not to mention the fact that the thought of not having Lane in her life felt like she would be losing something precious she had just found.

"And that's exactly why you need to take the time to think about what you want, especially with this new development." Lane reached for Miranda's hand but stopped at the last moment, hesitating as if afraid to touch her. "While I'd love to continue what we have, I don't think it's wise because I'd just keep falling deeper in love with you."

Lane clenched her jaw, her eyebrows furrowing in introspection. "I have to be honest with you, and more importantly, with myself. Being in love is new to me, and it's also terrifying." Lane flexed her hands into fists, like she was trying to maintain her composure. Her breathing appeared to be slow and constricting in the back of her throat as she persevered on. "While life offers no guarantees, I have to do what's best for both of us given all the facts. I need you to be sure, Miranda." Miranda watched the ramparts of the citadel that was Delaney Remington, crumble before her. "Because I'm so very sure that I've fallen in love with you." Her words carried such certainty that Miranda felt it resonate through every fiber of her being.

"I don't want to be with you and constantly worry if one day you might decide that being with a woman isn't for you because you rushed into a relationship with the first woman you dated." Lane shrugged, her expression a mix of susceptibility and determination. "Maybe I'm a coward for not being willing to throw caution to the wind and see where this goes. But I'm certain you would ruin me, Miranda." Her last words were a pleading whisper, as if she were begging Miranda to understand and let her go.

And you're ruining me by ending what we have, Miranda wanted to say, but she willed the words to remain in her subconscious. Instead, she asked, "Will you wait for me?" She knew the question was ridiculous and selfish, but she couldn't stop the words from spilling from her mouth.

"I don't want to put that pressure on you, Miranda, to feel as if you have to rush your journey because you have me waiting on you. This is about you and your desires and that's the most important thing—the *only* thing that matters." The selflessness of this woman was going to be the death of Miranda. "It's not selfish to put yourself first and do what truly makes you happy. Please don't think about my feelings." *How could she sound so practical,* Miranda thought.

"However, I can say that I don't see myself dating anyone anytime soon. I also need time to reflect on my life." Lane released a smile that never quite reached the corners of her face. "I've just discovered that I'm indeed capable of falling head over heels in love. I think that's something that will take some time to get used to. To see if I'm really capable of sharing my life with someone." Lane lifted her hands helplessly. "And more importantly, what if after much self-reflection you realize that you don't want a relationship with me? I would just be waiting in vain. I don't want to put such expectations on either of us. It wouldn't be fair."

Relief washed over Miranda, knowing that another woman wouldn't be touching Lane anytime soon. The notion of someone else touching Lane made Miranda feel nauseous. Lane was hers—the woman who gave her so much pleasure and had been so patient with her. Lane didn't just have sex with her—she treated her experience with respect and kindness. Maybe Lane was right, and some time apart would put things into perspective. Miranda couldn't afford to be selfish with her desires and end up hurting Lane. She felt like laughing at the irony of her day. She had one person asking her for a second chance and another breaking up with her. Given her track record with relationships, maybe Lane was right to end things now. But nothing felt right about this.

"It seems your mind is made up, and there is nothing I can do to change it," Miranda whispered, her voice cracking as the reality of their situation sank in.

Lane nodded. "I'm sorry if my decision hurts you in any way, but I just couldn't continue without telling you. It would have been a deception on my part, and you deserve the truth." Lane stood, looking down at Miranda with a mixture of sorrow and quiet resolve. "Thank you for some of the best months of my life. Regardless of where your journey takes you, I'll always cherish our time together."

The anguish in Lane's voice wrapped itself around Miranda's heart, and she wanted nothing more than to soothe her. Before she could stop herself, Miranda rose from the sofa and pulled Lane into a tight embrace. She expected Lane to resist, but Lane melted in her arms, holding Miranda close. Lane's hug was desperate, as if she was trying to hold onto parts of Miranda for safekeeping. Her heart beat so hard that Miranda wondered if she was on the verge of an anxiety attack. But she remained still, savoring the warmth of Lane's body pressed against hers, unwilling to let her go.

Moments passed with them locked in each other's arms, a fragile solace before Lane slowly released her and whispered, "I should go."

Lane stepped away, but Miranda's hand instinctively reached out, grasping Lane's wrist, holding her in place. She knew she would let Lane go, but she couldn't without making one last request. It felt selfish, knowing Lane was in love with her, but the longing was too deep, the desire to remind Lane of what they had too strong to ignore.

Miranda lifted her eyes from their joined hands to meet Lane's, the consuming desire to be close to her one last time making her desperate. "I want you to make love to me before you go," she said, her tone raw and pleading. Under different circumstances, Miranda would have been embarrassed to beg someone to have sex with her, but she realized she didn't care. She wanted Lane. She needed to feel Lane move inside of her one last time, just in case a future together wasn't in the cards.

Lane stared at her for a long moment, and Miranda saw the war in her eyes as she pondered the request. She waited with bated breath, refusing to focus on the expanding void she felt in her chest.

******

Lane dropped her gaze to Miranda's fingers, wrapped so delicately around her wrist. The touch was gentle, yet it seared Lane's skin as if being branded with fiery steel. Everything in her mind screamed at her to refuse Miranda's request. What was the point of subjecting herself to further torment? But her heart waged a war against her mind, and it was winning. All Lane wanted was to bridge the distance between them, express the magnitude of her adoration, and relinquish her soul to Miranda. Days of introspection had led her to one undeniable truth— she was undeniably, irrevocably in love with this woman who had stealthily stolen her heart like a thief in the night.

She opened her mouth to tell Miranda she didn't think it was a good idea. But Miranda's soft lips met hers before she could utter a word, her tongue sweeping inside her mouth with a desperate urgency. Lane could do nothing but surrender to the kiss, her resolve crumbling. Her hands moved of their own volition, pulling Miranda closer, needing to feel every part of her.

The kiss detonated like a minefield, each touch a silent declaration of love, each caress a plea for more time together. Lane's mind silenced, drowned by the ocean of adulation and devotion roaring through every fiber of being, and all she could do was lose herself in the woman she loved. To experience what it was like to make love to someone she knew she was in love with.

She allowed Miranda a few more swipes of her tongue, savoring the taste of desire lingering on her lips, before reluctantly pulling back from lips that followed hers. She found herself lost in Miranda's mesmerizing eyes, darkened with longing—her own weakness for Miranda decimating her. It was a weakness, this inability to resist when she knew she should. "Let's go to bed."

Miranda's body relaxed against hers, a silent exhale of relief. They ascended the stairs in silence, fingers intertwined, both seemingly afraid that a single word might shatter the fragile moment and force them to confront the reality they were skirting. At the foot of the bed, Miranda turned to face Lane, her gaze unwavering as she began to undress Lane—each garment removed, revealing layers of vulnerability that extended far beyond mere physical exposure. Still, neither spoke, the cloud of unspoken words hanging heavy in the air. As Lane reciprocated, carefully removing Miranda's clothes, the silence between them grew more pronounced. It was a palpable presence, amplifying the sound of their racing hearts and heightening Lane's awareness of the intimacy shared between them. With a gentle push, Lane guided Miranda down onto the bed, her hand resting on Miranda's racing heart.

Miranda slid up the bed, her legs parting slowly, revealing her heated core to Lane's ravenous gaze. Lane drank in the sight unabashedly, committing every curve of Miranda's naked form to memory. The thought of not tasting Miranda again threatened to bring tears to Lane's eyes. Miranda's intense gaze felt like a tangible caress, drawing Lane closer as she placed a knee on the bed. With deliberate tenderness, Lane kissed the inside of Miranda's thigh, trailing soft, wet kisses along every inch of exposed skin. Though she was the one walking away, Lane was determined to leave her mark on every inch of Miranda's body.

Despite her bewitching desire to ravish Miranda, Lane restrained herself, determined to honor Miranda's request for lovemaking. She kissed her way up Miranda's body, smiling at the whiny complaint that escaped Miranda's lips when Lane deviated from where she longed to be kissed most. From hip bones to navel to stomach, Lane lavished every inch of Miranda's skin with feather-light kisses. And when her lips finally closed around Miranda's tight nipples, sucking with a delicate but firm pressure, the cry of pleasure that escaped Miranda's lips made it worth going against her better judgment. She allowed her heart to guide her movements, moving from one breast to the next, rolling her tongue around each taut bud. With each tender caress, Lane felt as though her heart might explode with the vehemence of her love for this incredible woman who had melted her heart.

Strong fingers entwined in her hair, urging her upwards. "Kiss me, please," Miranda pleaded, her grip tightening on Lane's hair.

Lane slithered further up Miranda's body until they

were face to face. At that moment, staring into Miranda's eyes, Lane felt as though she was submerged in a sea of emotions, and Miranda was the lifeline she desperately needed to keep from drowning. Without hesitation, Lane surged forward, capturing lips that held a taste she knew would linger in her memory forever, in a searing, ardent kiss. Miranda responded with equal fervor, parting her lips to welcome each sweep of Lane's tongue. With every passing moment, their passion swelled like a gathering storm, threatening to obliterate them both. Yet, amidst the cathexis, Lane couldn't shake the fear that the only casualty of this passionate farewell would be her own heart. Still, she couldn't bring herself to pull away, pouring every ounce of her love, longing, and vulnerability into that single kiss. Miranda clung to her, legs wrapped around Lane's waist as if Lane were her anchor amid a tempest that could tear them apart.

They lost track of time in the haven of their kiss, an immortal moment suspended in the atmosphere around them. Lane was enraptured in the sensation, her arousal building with each passing minute. She marveled at how something as simple as kissing Miranda could ignite such a fiery passion within her. It was a revelation, one that left her breathless and trembling with desire. For the first time in her life, she felt like she was going to orgasm from just kissing a woman. But as she felt the wetness coating her thigh, Lane knew she couldn't ignore the urgent call of Miranda's desire any longer. Reluctantly breaking the kiss, she trailed kisses down Miranda's body, each one a testament to her compulsion and need. When she finally reached her destination, Lane paused, her gaze fixed on Miranda's glistening center. Every detail was tattooed into her memory, a treasure to be revisited during moments of self-induced orgasms. Lane knew she would carry this image with her, a vivid reminder of the intoxicating allure of Miranda's passion. It was a memory she would cherish, one that would probably haunt her in the days to come and make her constantly aroused.

Lane glanced up to find Miranda watching her, chest heaving and waiting patiently for Lane to give her what she wanted. She had always loved how Miranda always just so naturally submitted to her in bed and always allowed Lane to fuck her at her own pace. It was like she trusted Lane to give her all the pleasure her body craved. But it was the emotions in Miranda's eyes that tugged at Lane's heartstrings. In those depths, Lane saw longing, a yearning for connection that transcended the physical—it was as if she was telling Lane that she missed her even though Lane was right there. To distract herself from the maelstrom of emotions threatening to vanquish her, Lane leaned in, her lips grazing Miranda's sex. The taste of Miranda, the familiar scent of her arousal, sent a shudder down Lane's spine. With a guttural moan of pleasure, she surrendered herself to the act, allowing herself to be consumed by the intoxicating sensation of giving Miranda the release she craved.

Lane made love to Miranda's sensitive flesh, savoring each moment knowing it might be the last time she would ever taste her. It was as though Miranda's vagina was a sacred temple, and Lane knelt before it, reverent and adoring. With slow, purposeful strokes of her tongue, she worshipped every inch of Miranda's entrance. There was a purity to Miranda's taste, a freshness that was uniquely hers, and Lane drank it in, craving more with each passing second. Her tongue slid slowly, but firmly into Miranda's core, flicking against the rough spot on the roof of her vagina before sliding out and finding her clit. She relished the way Miranda's body responded to her touch, the way she quivered and gasped with pleasure. Though she knew it was slow torture for Miranda who much preferred when Lane fucked her hard and fast, Lane needed this moment to be different. She needed to express her love in every gentle caress, in every lingering kiss—to make slow, sweet love to the first woman she ever loved. The woman whose touch made Lane's skin burn, made her ache with unquenchable lust, made her want things she had never dared to dream of before, made her vulnerable, and more than anything, made her feel safe.

She added two fingers, filling Miranda with long, slow thrusts as her lips wrapped around Miranda's clit, sucking in perfect precision with her fingers. An abundance of moisture coated her fingers as she licked and sucked on the taut, warm, wet flesh. With each action, Lane felt like she was falling more in love with Miranda—her heart swelling with the longing, the exhilaration, the fear, and the vulnerability that came with being in love. She could one thousand percent say having sex with someone she loved was way better than all her previous experiences. She questioned if she really wanted to feel this way forever. So defenseless. To give someone so much power over her. And the irrefutable truth was, yes. She wanted to give Miranda every part of her—mind, body and soul.

"Lane... baby... please fuck me harder. I'm so very

close," Miranda moaned out as the telltale signs of her orgasm made themselves known.

Lane wanted to prolong the moment and savor every second of this last encounter. To feel every shiver. To feel Miranda's pussy tighten around her fingers. To hear her breathy moans and soft whimpers—just everything that she had never felt while fucking another woman. But as usual, her desire to fulfill Miranda's needs overruled her impulses. With her fingers still buried deep within Miranda's dripping center, Lane ascended Miranda's body, positioning herself between trembling thighs. Using her own hips to apply pressure, she drove her fingers deeper into Miranda's quivering flesh. Though the inescapable temptation to lower her lips to Miranda's consumed her, Lane forced herself to maintain eye contact, wanting to witness Miranda's unadulterated beauty as she surrendered to Lane's ministrations.

Miranda seemed to sense Lane's unspoken need, meeting her gaze with unwavering ardency as her orgasm crashed over her, causing her to arch further into Lane's touch. Throughout the climax, Miranda never faltered, holding Lane's gaze, even if it took all of her willpower to do so. Lane maintained her rhythm until Miranda sagged onto the mattress, spent and satisfied. Miranda pulled her into a tender, affectionate kiss that elicited the most profound sentiments more than anything she had experienced in the past half hour. Lane slipped to the side, her fingers still nestled within Miranda's warm, wet heat. Miranda shifted to face Lane, draping a leg over Lane's hip and resting her head on Lane's other arm, which was extended above her head.

They remained in a serene silence for a few precious moments until Miranda shifted, her eyes meeting Lane's with profound sadness. Tears welled up in Miranda's eyes, spilling over as she uttered softly, "I'm going to miss you so very much."

The sight of Miranda's tears was a heavy blow to Lane's heart, knowing that she was the cause of such anguish. Disregarding any concern for making a mess, Lane tenderly withdrew her hand, still moist with Miranda's essence, from between her thighs and drew Miranda closer, allowing her to bury her face in the crook of Lane's neck. She realized she couldn't bear to witness Miranda's tears, so she embraced her tightly, offering whatever comfort she could. At that moment, doubt gnawed at Lane's resolve, but it also made her realize that she too needed to be certain about whether she could truly be the partner Miranda deserved in the long run. The last thing Lane wanted was to inflict any more pain on Miranda.

"I'm going to miss you, too," Lane whispered, squeezing Miranda's ass cheek gently to stave off her own tears.

Chapter 17

Curled up in a ball in her childhood bed, Miranda fought against the sadness that threatened to consume her. The emptiness left by Lane's sudden departure was heartrending, and the sting of their abrupt ending still lingered like a festering wound. She wasn't even angry with Lane—Lane had been right, after all. She hadn't considered exploring her sexuality with anyone else. But the unequivocal truth was that she still didn't want anyone else but Lane. The powerful, overwhelming attraction she felt for Lane still blazed within her, as intense as the sun on its hottest day. She was certain now, more than ever, that she wanted Lane on a profound, almost elemental level.

Yet, as much as she longed for Lane, she knew they needed this time apart. Everything between them was still so new, and she needed to be sure that her feelings weren't just the product of novelty. She had to figure out if what she felt for Lane was truly enduring, if this immense voracity was something that wouldn't fade with time. But she was no longer confused about her feelings for Lane and she didn't need to explore with a myriad of women to understand her sexuality. Plus, the fact that as a teen Halle Berry was her biggest celebrity crush, who she never thought twice about sleeping with, said a lot. So maybe Blake was right and she had just never met a woman who awakened this side of her until Lane came along. Or maybe it wasn't about gender at all—maybe it was simply Lane, the person, who drew her in so completely with her unique personality and presence.

Everything that had transpired between them was so very unexpected, as if fate had been subtly guiding them toward each other all along. Miranda had always believed that every event in life happened for a reason, that some unseen thread connected seemingly random occurrences, weaving them into a larger tapestry. And it was an individual's response to these unexpected turns that determined whether or not they found happiness. They had crossed paths years ago, and while she didn't remember the details of that early encounter, there had always been a sense of familiarity, a magnetic pull toward Lane that she couldn't quite explain. Even on that night at Josephine's, there was an inexplicable connection that drew her to Lane, one that had only strengthened over time. Since then, they had been unable to stay away from each other, as if some omniscient force was at work.

So, yes, she had never anticipated being in a relationship with a woman, but perhaps a woman was exactly who she was meant to find her happily ever after with. After all, sexuality was fluid, and sometimes, it wasn't about gender but about the person who captured your heart. Still, given her track record with relationships, was this truly what she wanted for the long haul? A soft knock on her bedroom door interrupted her spiraling thoughts. Miranda looked up to see her mother entering the room. She met Caroline's gaze as she approached, and when her mother sat beside her, placing a comforting hand on her back, Miranda felt a sense of solace amidst her turmoil.

"Are you feeling any better? You've been locked away in here since arriving yesterday." Caroline leaned over to place a soft kiss on Miranda's temple. "I know when you're sad you tend to isolate yourself so you can think things through. Normally, I'd give you the space you need, but I can't help but worry. I've never seen you this heartbroken over a relationship ending, and that speaks volumes about what Lane means to you," Caroline said with motherly concern as her fingers gently traced soothing patterns along Miranda's back.

Miranda shook her head slightly. "I just need some time to figure out how to move forward."

Caroline's expression grew contemplative as her gaze softened, studying Miranda's face. "As much as it pains me to see you hurting, I can understand why Lane made the choice she did."

Miranda turned fully to face her mother, remaining silent, knowing that Caroline's insight would likely offer some much-needed clarity on the situation that had left her feeling so adrift.

"Because of her upbringing, she's incredibly guarded. She endured experiences no child should ever face, especially at such a tender age. The very people who were supposed to protect her were the ones who caused her pain, which made it difficult for her to trust others or let anyone into her heart." Miranda cringed at the thought of Lane, her Lane, having to endure and battle on her own until she found Anita. "She wasn't raised in an environment that modeled love or vulnerability. She learned, from a young age, how to survive on her own and protect herself from further hurt.

"She might not even be fully aware of how deeply

her childhood has impacted her ability to open up to love. The idea of being in love is foreign to her, and she's probably scared out of her mind. Her survival instincts likely kicked in, and she did what she believed was necessary to shield herself from the potential hurt, given the circumstances that led to your relationship.

"Her focus has always been on escaping poverty, not on seeking companionship. Her primary need was financial stability, surviving a world that has often been harsh and unforgiving to her—not finding love. She understands survival and knows how to fight for it, but being in love is something she's never been taught to comprehend. So when faced with it, she chose flight over fight. She's strong and has created her own happiness, but she may not even realize that her childhood trauma still lingers. People cope with trauma in different ways, and sometimes they're unaware of its impact because they've used it as a tool to survive and remain resilient."

"The last thing I'd ever want to do is hurt her," Miranda said softly.

Caroline's gaze softened with a tender, motherly warmth. "I know, sweetheart. I think Lane fell in love with you because you're the opposite of what she expects from most people—and everything she's not when it comes to being open with your heart. You've never shied away from expressing your emotions, and you're very nurturing, kind, and compassionate. These qualities likely captivated Lane, because even if she didn't realize it, maybe all along she just needed a partner to care for her the way you did." Caroline ran a hand through Miranda's curls, easing the tension building in her head. "Plus, while you're soft-hearted, you're also very strong and not a pushover. Your personality is an appealing combination for someone like Lane, who probably doesn't understand weakness because she has had to be strong all her life.

"You brought her happiness simply by being yourself. Perhaps she never imagined wanting more than the life she crafted for herself until you came along and showed her that life can be richer, more fulfilling, with someone who truly cares for her and accepts her as she is. That's why I think it's wise for you to take the time to reflect on what you truly want—for both your sakes. I loved seeing you two together because she made you happy. In fact, I've never seen you as happy in a relationship as you were with Lane. But I don't want either of you to get hurt in the long run if a relationship with her isn't what you truly desire."

"I know. I guess everything will work itself out in time." Miranda replied, swallowing the knot of emotions in her throat. Her mother's words rang so true. She had never felt more at ease in a relationship than she did with Lane. But she couldn't help wondering if the initial euphoria of a new relationship might eventually give way to unmet expectations.

Caroline gently tucked a stray curl behind Miranda's ear. "Maybe some time apart will give you the clarity you need. A change of scenery without the chance of running into Lane might also help. You should change your vacation plans and go to Barbados. Damian returned home yesterday, so the house will be all yours."

"Thanks, Mom. I'll think about it," Miranda replied, sitting up and folding herself into her mother's embrace, seeking the comfort she so desperately needed.

She felt fortunate to have parents who had always been her unwavering support. Reflecting on Lane's past, she could agree that her mother was right in deducing that Lane might be afraid of risking her heart because she was scared. Therefore, she couldn't afford to be rash or careless in whatever she decided to do.

Chapter 18

Lane stared out the window, the relentless rain pelting against the glass mirroring the storm of thoughts assaulting her mind. It had been a week since she had ended her relationship with Miranda and she was far from feeling confident in her decision. Every time she saw Miranda at Parkwood, the desire to pull her into her arms and never let go was a battle Lane's heart barely escaped, retreating with casualties that left the Somme stained red. The sadness in Miranda's eyes was a constant tug at Lane's heart, a poignant reminder of the pain she had caused. Knowing she was the source of that sorrow made her heart ache so severely as if it were being pummeled from within. She kept reminding herself that it was the right choice for both of them, but the days apart had only made her realize how much she loved Miranda—a love that refused to wane regardless of the distance she had created between them.

Lane had always been practical. Her rapid ascent in her career was proof of her ability to analyze situations realistically. She never let emotions hinder her, even when it meant making tough decisions, such as firing employees to save a hospital from imminent bankruptcy. People often resented her for those choices, but Lane valued the long-term survival of the institution over immediate, short-sighted concerns. Though often unpopular, her strategic vision always focused on the greater good.

She had analyzed her relationship with Miranda with the same pragmatic mindset. Dating women was new to Miranda, and their intense connection from the start hadn't given Miranda the chance to explore other possibilities. Lane couldn't in good conscience allow their relationship to continue without considering this. It would have been a recipe for heartbreak if months from now the excitement faded and Miranda realized she no longer wanted Lane to fuck her brains out. Irrespective of her own entrenching feelings, Lane couldn't ignore the facts in favor of wishful thinking. She needed to make the tough decision now to prevent greater heartache later. This adherence to facts over emotions had always served her well, even if it meant breaking her own heart to protect both of their futures.

Even though deep down she wished she could just throw caution to the wind and leave everything to fate, logic had never failed her in the past—logic was the most consistent thing she had and what had been her greatest means of endurance. She hadn't applied the same rules of her past affairs to her relationship with Miranda. But even if she had, Lane knew the overwhelming answer would be the same—she would have still fallen in love with Miranda. There was a magnetism about Miranda that pulled Lane in, making her want to jump off a cliff to save her life—making her crave Miranda in a way she never had with anyone else.

Then there was the underlying truth that little Randi Hayes was the girl who first made Lane's young heart flutter. The day young Miranda gave Lane her shoes was the day she experienced her first crush. Initially, Lane had attributed it to the kindness Miranda showed during a time when she mostly knew cruelty. But years later, when she saw Miranda lying in that hospital bed—by then, knowing she liked girls—Lane felt that same undeniable attraction.

That was why she had accommodated Miranda more than she had ever accommodated anyone else, because she had always remembered how special Miranda made her feel during a time when all she knew was sadness. And yes, over the years on her visits to Seattle, she sporadically thought about the little girl from the park, wondering if she had indeed become a surgeon and was still kind and caring. Maybe all that mumbo jumbo about fated love was real after all. Because years later, she felt the same pull toward Miranda that night at Josephine's, and now she was undeniably in love with her.

Christ. My life now sounds like some cliché Hallmark romance movie. I don't even watch romance movies for crying out loud. Oh, wait yes you do, because once again, you had relented to Miranda's desires by subjecting yourself to several sappy romance movies because Miranda insisted you cuddle up and watch them together.

"Why are you sad, my child?" Anita's voice floated softly from behind.

Lane turned to face the only person who could offer her any semblance of comfort. Seeing Anita almost back to her vibrant self before the heart attack filled her with immense gratitude. Anita's dark brown skin glowed, her cheeks were filling out, and she radiated a strength Lane had always admired. Lane moved from the window to join Anita on the sofa, lying on her side, curling her legs at the knees, and resting her head in Anita's lap. As expected, gentle fingers began to move through her hair, providing the maternal comfort she so desperately needed. This was why she wasn't ready to lose Anita. After enduring fifteen years without any form of maternal love, just a few months of living with Anita had made Lane feel as though she had never been without a mother's care. Even years later, whenever she felt sad, Lane always sought Anita out for comfort. But this time, Anita's touch didn't provide the solace she sought. Lane realized, in that moment, that only Miranda's touch could heal her wounded spirit.

"I've fallen in love for the first time with the most amazing woman, and I had to let her go," Lane admitted, her voice faltering under the weight of her despair and heartsickness.

"Ah. So, you've finally realized you're in love with Dr. Hayes. I was hoping that once you did, you would give yourself a chance to be in a committed relationship with her."

Anita's tone was so matter-of-fact that Lane was taken aback. How had she come to that conclusion? Yes, Miranda had accompanied Lane on a few visits since Anita's heart attack, but Lane couldn't see why Anita would have assumed she was falling in love with her, or why she hadn't said anything before.

Tilting her head to meet Anita's gaze, Lane asked, "How did you know I was in love with her, and why didn't you say anything?"

All-knowing eyes filled with love bore into her. "You've always shared small details about your dating escapades, mostly when those women fell in love with you and you had to end it. But you hardly spoke of any of them except Gabriella. Maybe you didn't realize it, but you've spoken a lot about Miranda over the last few months when you came to visit. Your eyes always lit up when you mentioned her. It was like you were in awe of her."

Anita smiled down at Lane. "Then when she came to see you in my room while I was in the hospital, the way you looked at her confirmed my suspicions. The way you interacted with her was different from everyone else. You were carefree. Less guarded. You've always been cautious around people but with Miranda, you had this lightness about you."

The grin on her face widened as if Lane being in love was the best news she had ever heard. "I didn't say anything because I didn't want to spook you, out of fear that you would end things with her if I pointed it out. I wanted it to be something you realized on your own and I've been praying you wouldn't run away from it when you did. So, I'm very sad to hear that you did." Sadness crept into Anita's eyes. "Why did you?"

"Because it's the right thing to do. She's just discovering her attraction to women. The last thing she needs is to feel pressured into a relationship because..." Lane rolled her eyes at herself. "... I fell in love with her." She shrugged slightly. "I also can't risk my heart with a woman who isn't even sure if a relationship with a woman is what she truly wants." Lane held Anita's gaze, her voice softening. "I need her to be sure of her feelings. My emotions are so raw and being away from her feels like a part of me is missing. It's such an unsettling feeling, missing her so much that it hurts and I fear the void that has been consuming me since I walked away from her will never be filled. How would I feel months from now if she decides this isn't something she wants?" Her voice sounded so vulnerable to her own ears, but this was Anita, with whom Lane had always allowed herself to be vulnerable.

"Sweetheart, life offers no guarantees, and love is one of the riskiest ventures we can embark on. Still, the most rewarding things in life are always the riskiest. Yes, you're the first woman Miranda has been involved with, but that doesn't mean she needs to be with fifty others to know you're the one she wants. Experience is valuable, but it's not always necessary, especially when you find someone who is just *it* for you."

Anita traced Lane's eyebrow with her index finger, her touch gentle and comforting. "And you've never been afraid to take risks, Delaney. Why are you afraid to take a risk on a woman who made you fall in love with her simply by being herself? Someone who sees you for who you are and accepts you as you are." Anita continued to trace Lane's opposite eyebrow, while her free hand cradled Lane's as she began rubbing her thumb over Lane's knuckles. "You have a strong personality, intimidating at times, and not many people today appreciate someone who doesn't sugar coat their words and refuses to dance to the tune of the masses. Worse when it's a woman as strong-willed as you are."

Lane pondered Anita's words, recognizing she hadn't fully considered her reluctance to risk her heart with Miranda as fear. This was precisely why she'd valued Anita's counsel over the years—she had a knack for forcing Lane to see things from a different perspective. Perhaps she was more apprehensive about risking her heart due to the uncertainty surrounding Miranda than doing the right thing by giving Miranda a chance to explore her sexuality.

"Maybe I am afraid," Lane conceded, her voice filled with vulnerability. "But this isn't like making a risky business deal or transitioning between hospitals. This is my heart we're talking about, and the intensity of my feelings for her is overwhelming."

Lane closed her eyes, and tried to inhale as deep as she could, attempting to break through the constriction in her chest. "Sometimes, it feels like I can't even breathe when she's near. Walking away from her hurts so very much and it feels like I've been struggling to live since then. I find no joy in being alone anymore. Everything just seems dark—like she was my light and without her, my life is now a dark pit of sadness and emptiness."

Lane let out a rueful chuckle. "Why do people willingly subject themselves to falling in love? To grant someone such power over their emotional well-being? Because what I've experienced in the past week has been nothing short of torture. It's as if I have no control over my feelings." Her voice wavered as she continued, "I can't even stop myself from thinking about her, from missing her. So, can you blame me for wanting to proceed cautiously when I'm on the brink of giving someone this much control over me for the first time?"

Anita shook her head, her expression a blend of maternal love and gentle admonishment. "Oh, my sweet child. The point of being in love lies not in controlling your emotions, but in surrendering to them with someone you trust implicitly. It's about finding happiness with someone, where vulnerability is met with understanding and compassion, not exploitation." Her words carried a weight of sadness, underscoring her deep empathy for Lane's turmoil. "You don't always have to be strong, Delaney. It's okay to let yourself feel, to cry if you need to. While it pains me to witness your distress, I'm also grateful you're experiencing what falling in love feels like. You deserve to both receive and give love, to allow another soul to care for you in ways you have never allowed anyone but me to."

Lane couldn't control the emotional torrent unleashed by Anita's words. Try as she might, tears betrayed her stoicism, streaming silently down her cheeks. It was a peculiar sensation, this vulnerability, foreign yet liberating, as she surrendered to the tumult of emotions surrounding her love for Miranda and the pain of their separation. The love, the heartbreak, the gnawing ache within her—all surged forth, overwhelming her senses. At that moment, enveloped in Anita's comforting embrace, Lane allowed herself to purge the pent-up anguish, her tears mingling with the consolation of her surrogate mother's arms.

Though doubt plagued her decision not to dive headlong into a relationship with Miranda, Lane recognized the wisdom in ensuring her beloved was truly ready. For as the agony in her chest intensified, and tears continued to flow, she understood that committing to Miranda without certainty could shatter her heart irreparably in the future. Uncertainty was a part of life, but she knew Miranda wouldn't engage in a relationship with her unless she was absolutely sure she wanted Lane outside of the bedroom. Furthermore, it reassured Lane that she was investing her heart with a woman who was steadfast in her commitment to being in a relationship with another woman.

Lost in the sanctuary of Anita's arms, Lane lost track of time, her tears gradually yielding to a sense of catharsis. With a gentle touch, Anita tenderly wiped Lane's tear-stained cheeks.

Lane tilted her head to face Anita, her eyes reflecting a depth of gratitude and love. "Thank you," Lane murmured, her voice hoarse with emotions. "For always being my pillar of strength, for giving me a home when I needed it most, for simply being you. I hope you truly know how much I love and appreciate you."

Anita's response was immediate, her own eyes shimmering with unshed tears. "No, my dear, I'm the one who should be thanking you for not neglecting me when you could have," she whispered thickly. "You're everything I could have hoped for in a daughter, and more. I am immensely proud of the woman you've become." A bittersweet smile graced Anita's lips as she continued, "And if I should die tomorrow, I would die happy because you're a part of my life and have brought me so much joy. I would die even happier knowing you have found someone to love you after I'm gone."

Lane's voice trembled slightly as she addressed Anita, the weight of their shared history floating around them. "No talking about death," she insisted with a mixture of determination and vulnerability. "You're stuck with me for many more years to come. After all, the universe owes me for giving me a shitty birth mother. It can make up for it by giving me many more years with you."

Anita's laughter rang out in the room, a soothing melody amidst the poignant tumult. "I'm relieved she hasn't tried contacting you again," Anita admitted, her expression hardening. "If she had returned and asked for forgiveness, I might have encouraged you to forgive her. But the gall of that woman to try and blackmail you." Disgust colored Anita's words, her protective motherly instincts kicking in.

"I know, but let's not talk about her." Lane paused wondering if now was the right time to broach the next topic on her mind. They had to discuss a potentially life-changing decision, and the sooner they discussed it, the better.

"I know you've been steadfast in your decision not to move with me wherever my career takes me," Lane started, her tone gentle yet earnest. "But I'd like you to consider something. Mason Ridge in New York has been courting me for a while now. Initially, I didn't give it much thought because of Miranda and my desire to stay close to her. However, circumstances have changed, and over the last few days, I've been contemplating this opportunity more seriously."

Lane paused, allowing her words to sink in before continuing. "I know you love Seattle. But it would mean a great deal to me if you would consider moving with me if I decide to take this offer. And please don't feel like you'd be a burden. You've never been."

Anita studied Lane for a long moment, her gaze very introspective with years of wisdom that had weathered many experiences. "Delaney, before you make any hasty decisions, give Miranda the time she needs to process everything that's happened between you two," she advised, gently yet firmly. "Running away won't solve anything. True love requires patience and understanding, even in the face of challenges. When you truly love someone, distance may physically separate you, but it won't erase the love you share."

With a reassuring pat on Lane's cheek, Anita

continued, her expression softening. "As for moving to New York, you know I can't fathom leaving Seattle. This city, with its rainy skies and vibrant greenery, holds a piece of my heart. I need nature, Delaney, not the hustle and bustle of a concrete jungle. Don't worry about me. I'll be fine." Anita twirled a finger around the room. "The price tag of this place is worth every penny. I'm happy here. You go and be even greater."

Why did this woman have to know her so well? Lane couldn't deny the truth in Anita's words regarding her contemplation of leaving. While she had initially felt a sense of restlessness upon returning to Seattle, she had found solace in being home again—especially in the comforting presence of Anita. *And even more with Miranda.* "All right, I won't rush into anything. Besides, it's been nice being closer to you," Lane admitted, a small smile tugging at her lips.

"Good," Anita replied with a smile of her own. "Now, how about you treat me to dinner from that vegetarian restaurant you're so fond of? Since you insist on keeping me on the healthier side of the menu."

"Doctor's orders," Lane quipped, a bittersweet reminder of Miranda's insistence on Anita's strict diet to reduce the risk of another heart attack. Rising from the sofa, Lane reached for her phone, determined to honor her promise to Anita while also considering her own professional future. While she wouldn't rush into any decisions, she knew she would discuss terms with Mason Ridge. The prospect of working alongside Miranda, given their complicated history, weighed heavily on her mind. Could she endure the weekly encounters, the longing, without being able to touch her? Lane prided herself on her resilience, but this challenge tested even her strength when from the beginning, she had always found it hard to stay away from Miranda. But she had never been weak, so perhaps with time, she would be able to cope and eventually get over Miranda if they weren't meant to be together.

Chapter 19

Miranda's heart slammed against her ribs as she stepped off the elevator, suddenly face-to-face with the woman who had haunted her dreams for the past week. The woman who, with just one look, made her blood sing and ignited an ache deep inside her. Those captivating, greenish-gold eyes bore into her, but Miranda saw no hint of emotion. After a week apart, she was once again relegated to the category of everyone else—an outsider to the thoughts of this woman with one of the best poker faces she had ever encountered.

"Hi, Miranda. I was just on my way from your office," Lane said softly. The unexpected tenderness in her voice threw Miranda off guard, considering that a moment ago, Lane's eyes had revealed nothing. But as Miranda looked closer, she noticed a shift. Lane's defenses had lowered, and now her eyes brimmed with longing and sadness, evoking a powerful surge of raw, visceral ache that struck Miranda like a punch to the gut.

Miranda forced her hands to stay at her side, resisting the overwhelming desire to pull Lane into her arms and comfort her. "Hi, Lane. We can go back to my office, or I can follow you to yours." She didn't waste time speculating about the reason for Lane's visit. As her boss, it was likely work-related, and given their current status, Lane wouldn't discuss anything personal during work hours.

"No, that's not necessary." Lane lifted her hand, holding a pair of sunglasses. "I found these while cleaning yesterday. Seems you left them at my place the last time you were there. I know they're one of your favorite pairs, so I was just returning them." Her lips curved into a half smile. "I know how particular you are about matching your sunglasses to your outfits."

Miranda wanted to smile, but the chaotic whirlwind of conflicting thoughts and memories swirling within her made it impossible. Being so thoroughly understood and seen by Lane was disarming. This was one of the many things she loved about her—Lane noticed the smallest details about who Miranda was without needing them pointed out. It was why dating Lane had been so effortless—she paid attention to everything and often showed Miranda through her actions that she knew her better than anyone ever had. Since their separation, these revelations had only intensified as Miranda reflected on their time together. Though it had been excruciating to be apart, she had come to accept that perhaps it was the right course of action for now.

"Thank you. I didn't even realize they were missing," she finally said, reaching to take the glasses from Lane.

Their fingers touched, and an electric jolt shot from Miranda's fingertips straight to her core, quickening her heartbeat. She knew Lane felt it too—her eyes darkened as she glanced down at their still-connected hands, each holding opposite ends of the glasses. The magnetism that had always drawn them together intensified, pulling Miranda into Lane's orbit as they both stepped closer. The air thickened around them, crackling with desire, and Miranda's breathing grew ragged as she stared into Lane's eyes.

She saw the visceral, animalistic want that always made her knees weak. But this time, there was something more—love. In many ways, Miranda still couldn't believe that this woman, who had bedded so many with more experience, had fallen in love with her. But she never doubted Lane's declaration because Lane was the most honest person she had ever dated. This truth, combined with the piercing depth of Lane's gaze, left Miranda both humbled and aching with a need that bordered on being painful.

Simultaneously, their eyes dropped to each other's lips. Although Miranda had accepted Lane's decision, she knew what was about to happen and welcomed it—longing to feel Lane's lips against hers once more. The magnetic pull between them was undeniable, and she felt herself surrendering to it. Just as they began to close the few inches separating them, the elevator doors dinged open, shattering the emotionally charged moment.

Lane stepped back, and they both turned to see Blake stepping off the elevator, her eyes darting between them. Blake, like Lane, had a masterful poker face, her expression betraying nothing. But Miranda knew her well enough to sense that Blake suspected what would have transpired if she hadn't interrupted. The atmosphere was thick with unspoken words and the aching tension of what could have been.

Lane was the first to recover, a genuine smile forming on her lips as she turned to Blake. "Hi Blake, it's so good to see you. How's Amara doing? Last I heard she was still the perfect angel who sleeps through the night."

Blake smiled, eyes lighting up with motherly love. "Yes, she indeed is. She's growing too fast for my liking, but given that she was born prematurely, I'm extremely grateful for her development."

"I'm glad to hear that." Lane's smile widened, though Miranda noticed a fleeting shadow in her eyes. "I'll leave you to your visit. Take care, Blake" She directed her attention to Miranda. "Dr. Hayes, have a good day."

"See you around, Lane," Blake replied, her eyes flickering between Lane and Miranda.

"Bye, Lane," Miranda said, her voice thick with a sadness she couldn't quite hide, each word trembling with the weight of their current dynamic. Lane must have heard it because, for a long moment, she stared at Miranda, and the same sadness was visible in her eyes.

"I'll meet you in your office, Miranda," Blake said, cutting into the wordless exchange. She stepped closer to Miranda, subtly placing a hand on her shoulder, grounding her in the present.

Lane gave a small nod, her lips twitching into a bittersweet smile before she turned and walked away, the distance between them growing with each step. Miranda watched her go, the ache in her chest deepening into a sharp, gnawing pain as the urge to chase after her became almost unbearable. But she knew she couldn't move, not until she had taken the time to fully understand her feelings for Lane. Was it just intense lust borne from the thrill of being with a woman for the first time, or was it something deeper?

Sensing Blake's watchful gaze, Miranda headed toward her office. Arriving before her desk, Miranda frowned at the sight of a bouquet of red tulips sitting on it. Excitement surged through her as she reached for them, wondering if Lane had left them. However, the excitement vanished just as quickly as it had appeared when she read the accompanying note. The flowers were from Trevor, expressing that he was thinking about her. Miranda let out a heavy sigh and dropped unceremoniously into her chair, feeling the burden of her emotions settle over her once again.

"Red tulips—flowers that symbolize romance," Blake observed, lowering herself into the chair across from Miranda. "I assume they're not from Lane, given that you don't seem particularly pleased to receive them."

Miranda handed Blake the note, slumping further into her chair—the exhaustion from the previous week's hectic schedule of surgeries kicking in—and as usual, seeing Lane only heightened the inner turmoil she struggled to contain.

Blake hummed thoughtfully, placing the note back on Miranda's desk. "Have you given any more thought to Trevor asking for a second chance?"

Miranda sighed deeply. "If I weren't so fucking depressed by the current state of my love life, I'd probably laugh at the irony. One person is begging for a second chance, while the one I truly want is pushing me away." She shook her head, a rueful smile tugging at her lips but never quite forming. "Honestly, I haven't given Trevor much thought since he left my house. Any spare moment I've had, my mind was occupied with thoughts of Lane. If the last week hadn't been so busy, I probably would have lost my mind thinking about her."

Blake nodded empathetically, leaning forward with a concerned expression. "Have you tried talking to Lane again?"

Miranda ran a hand through her hair, her fingers

trembling slightly. "No, I haven't. I wish it were that simple and every time I see her, the misery inside me grows." Her voice cracked, and she blinked back tears.

Blake regarded Miranda with a searching gaze, her concern palpable in the furrow of her brow and the earnestness of her expression. "If you feel this way about Lane, why not take the leap and tell her you want to give a relationship a chance?" Her voice was gentle but insistent, cutting through the layers of uncertainty. "I've seen you two together, and you make each other happy. I don't see why either of you think you need to explore with other women to know if a relationship with Lane is what you want?"

Miranda listened intently, hoping that Blake's advice would provide some much-needed insight. "I know Lane is the first woman you've been sexually attracted to, but that doesn't mean your attraction to her will fade in a few months. Yes, it's possible, but the same uncertainty exists in any relationship, regardless of gender. As I've mentioned before, you don't have to confine yourself to labels or constraints. At this point in your life, you're attracted to a woman and want to be with her. It's really that simple."

Blake's words resonated deeply with Miranda, but she found herself grappling with the complexities of love. Because when love was involved, nothing was ever that simple. "It's not solely about labeling myself, Blake, or questioning my attraction to Lane because she's a woman. I'm fully aware of my feelings for her. But seeing that it's my first experience with a woman, I need to ensure it's more than just intense lust that won't fade away after a few months of mind-blowing sex. Lane's love for me adds another layer of responsibility.

I didn't envision a relationship with her because of her dating history. So, maybe some time apart, free from the influence of sex, is necessary for clarity."

Miranda paused, swallowing hard. "I've only been with men all my life, Blake, and out of nowhere I found myself attracted to a woman. It's definitely something that requires careful consideration in deciding how to move forward." A pang of guilt tugged at Miranda's heart as she voiced her concerns. "I can't risk hurting Lane without being absolutely certain about what I want. She's never been in a relationship before. I refuse to be the cause of her first heartbreak because I didn't take the time to truly understand my feelings for her. While life offers no guarantees, approaching this with clarity ensures that whatever the outcome, I can move forward with a clear conscience. Lane deserves nothing less than my unwavering certainty."

"Okay, so from all that you've said it comes down to the fact that you don't want to hurt Lane," Blake summarized.

"Yes, precisely. Considering my track record with relationships, can you blame me for wanting to be sure?" She shrugged with her hands up in surrender. "Even with Trevor, who loved me and treated me well, I couldn't give him the commitment he wanted after over a year of dating. All my other relationships failed because they wanted more than I could give at the time. I can't risk entering into a relationship with Lane only to realize later that I can't fulfill her needs." She closed her eyes and kneaded the sides of her temple with the pads of her fingers. "What then? Apologize for not taking the time to understand myself? I refuse to ignore these simple truths based on my relationship history."

Having reflected on her situation with Lane, Miranda realized that her main concern wasn't Lane's gender, but rather her own doubts about her ability to meet Lane's expectations in a committed relationship.

"I understand. But you also have to consider that maybe Trevor and the others just weren't the ones you were meant to have your 'happily ever after' with," Blake suggested. "Maybe you were just destined to have your 'happily ever after' with the superior gender," she added with a devilish grin.

Miranda couldn't help but chuckle despite her somber mood. "Leave it to you to see it that way when it comes to men versus women. But I can admit, based on my experiences with both, Lane is superior in every aspect of a relationship. She embodies everything I could ever want in a partner, and then some." The briefest of radiant smiles flashed across Miranda's face, before returning to her despondent state. "That's why I can't afford to be callous with our situation. She deserves nothing but the best, Blake. Beneath her confident demeanor lies a woman who is incredibly thoughtful, loving, and possesses the most generous heart when it comes to the few people she holds dear."

"Well, I guess only time can offer clarity on what to do next. Sometimes, it's the only guide we have to navigate our path forward," Blake mused.

"I know. Mom suggested that I go to my grandparents' house in Barbados for a few weeks and take the time to really think about what I want. I was already scheduled to be on vacation for the next two weeks, so I might just do that. I didn't have any other plans to travel, other than going to Atlanta to spend some time with my grandparents." Miranda exhaled the weighted breath she wasn't aware she was retaining. "Maybe not seeing Lane will help me to better put things into perspective, because each time that I see her, all I want to do is pull her into my arms and never let go."

"Speaking from experience, I know sometimes being away from someone can show us how much that person means to us and force us to fight for them. I didn't realize I was in love with Alexandra until she left for L.A. I also thought I was doing the right thing by letting her go without putting up a fight and it was one of the most painful periods of my life." Miranda saw the pain in Blake's eyes as she reflected on that moment in her history. "I hope by the time you return, you will find the answers you're searching for."

"Me too." While Lane didn't plan on dating anyone soon, Miranda knew it wouldn't be the norm for long. Lane was a very attractive woman who enjoyed having sex and she selfishly didn't want Lane to move on before she had the chance to seriously consider how to move forward. She could only hope that amidst this pause, she would unearth the answers she sought before Lane slipped through her fingers.

Chapter 20

Sitting at the same table where she had first met Miranda over a year ago at Josephine's, Lane stared into a glass of bourbon, her whirlwind thoughts drowning out the soulful music playing in the background. She had planned to go directly home after work, but the idea of spending another Friday evening confined to her penthouse, surrounded by memories of their intimate moments, was too disheartening. The place was haunted by Miranda's presence, from the lingering scent of her perfume, to the ghost of her laughter echoing off the walls. Lane had even entertained the idea of bringing a woman home with her, hoping a fleeting connection might distract her from the aching void Miranda's absence left behind. But since arriving at Josephine's, three women had approached her, and she felt absolutely no attraction to any of them. Even worse, she felt as though she would be cheating on Miranda—a ridiculous notion given their separation. Even when they were together, Lane had been free to sleep with whomever she wanted, yet now the very thought felt like a betrayal and made her nauseous. Her mind was a turbulent sea of longing and confusion. She swirled the bourbon in her glass, its amber depths reflecting her inner unrest. The irony wasn't lost on her—here she was, in the very place where it all began, still tethered to a connection that was as intoxicating as it was painful.

Two weeks had passed and Lane was just as miserable as the day she left Miranda's house. Her feelings for Miranda confounded her on so many levels that she was becoming scared of them. Though she didn't have many friends and was usually good at making herself happy, no matter how hard she tried, she couldn't recapture the internal happiness she had before Miranda. God, she was so lonely—it was a loneliness that stemmed primarily from no longer having Miranda in her life. It was the small things Lane missed the most—the way Miranda would curl herself around Lane's body when they watched TV, the nightly texts wishing her a good night when they were apart, their daily conversations about their work, and Miranda always checking if she had eaten lunch because she knew Lane tended to forget to eat while in the office. She simply just missed Miranda and wondered if she would ever be able to go back to life as it was before her. While she remained firm in her belief that she did the right thing for both of them, the thought of someone else touching Miranda made her want to murder them.

"Penny for your thoughts?" The voice Lane hadn't heard in months pulled her gaze from her drink.

She looked up and met the eyes of a woman who once ignited a fierce primal desire within her. Now, staring at her, Lane felt absolutely nothing. Despite how their relationship had ended, Lane had long moved past it and saw no need for indifference, even though she wasn't in the mood for company.

"Hello, Gabriella," Lane greeted, unable to muster any enthusiasm into her voice.

A tentative smile formed on Gabriella's lips. "May I join you?" Lane could see the nervousness in her eyes and understood why, given how things ended between them.

"I'm not really in the mood for company," Lane replied, knowing that Gabriella wouldn't be offended by her honesty as their history was built on straightforwardness.

Gabriella chuckled. "I see you're as blunt as ever. One of the many things I love about you." Her features softened, eyes earnest and pleading. "Please, Delaney, I just need a few minutes of your time."

Lane studied Gabriella for a brief moment, recalling the friendship they once shared and how much she had cared deeply for Gabriella. On those grounds alone, she decided the least she could do was give Gabriella a minute of her time. "Okay."

Relief washed over Gabriella's features as she pulled out the chair and sat across from Lane. She stared, her eyes doing a slow, deliberate perusal of Lane's body, darkening with familiar desire as they met hers again.

Lane arched a questioning eyebrow. "I'm sure you didn't invite yourself to my table just to ogle me?"

Gabriella laughed, and to her own surprise, Lane also found herself chuckling. The enduring bond they had shared was rooted in the deep comfort and understanding they had found in each other's presence over the years. "Can you blame me for ogling you, Delaney? You're still the most beautiful woman in the room."

"And you still have a smooth tongue," Lane replied, wondering what Gabriella was doing in Seattle. "What are you doing on this side of the map?"

"Would you be surprised if I said I came here to see you?" Gabriella's expression was inscrutable, leaving

Lane unsure of her sincerity.

"Yes, considering we haven't spoken in months, and given how things ended, you have no reason to travel over a thousand miles just to see me. For all you know, I could have relocated," Lane answered confidently, knowing Gabriella well enough to suspect that she would have tried to contact her first before showing up.

"Fair enough. I haven't forgotten that you know me so very well." Gabriella paused, a fond smile dancing on her lips. "I'm currently shooting a movie here. But I've thought about reaching out to you many times. I was just afraid of being sent to voicemail again."

"I see. All the best with your new movie," Lane replied, deliberately sidestepping the subtext of Gabriella's sentiments.

"Thanks." Gabriella held Lane's gaze for a moment, then sighed. "We're not one for pointless small talk, so I'm going to get straight to the point. I risked coming over here, knowing you might reject me, because I miss you, Delaney." Lane was acutely aware that the sincerity of Gabriella's words still didn't bombard her heart like the melancholy she found in Miranda's eyes lately. "I'm still hoping you can find it in your heart to forgive me. I destroyed one of the most important relationships I've ever had, and the void of not having you in my life still lingers. I have few regrets in this life, but using you like that is the biggest one. I'm truly sorry."

Lane, emotionally drained from her situation with Miranda, found herself devoid of the anger she once harbored toward Gabriella for the deception that tore them apart. Staring at the woman across from her, she felt only a profound sadness for both of them. "It's fine. Don't worry about the past. I hope coming out has been everything you hoped it would be."

Gabriella shook her head, a mixture of relief and sorrow evident in her features. "No, because I don't have you, Delaney. I was serious when I said part of the reason I came out was to pursue an open relationship with you. And I meant it when I said I love you." Gabriella reached across the table, taking Lane's hand in hers, her touch both familiar and foreign. "I still do."

Before Lane could react to Gabriella's touch, she felt a shift in the atmosphere, as if an invisible force was pulling her in. She looked over Gabriella's shoulder and her heart sank—Miranda stood there, watching them, her face a picture of heartbreak. Lane couldn't blame Miranda for whatever she might be thinking, seeing Gabriella holding her hand so intimately. Panic surged through Lane as she retracted her hand from Gabriella's grasp just as Miranda spun on her heels and headed swiftly toward the exit. *Shit.*

"I have to go," Lane said to Gabriella, almost knocking over her chair in her haste to stand.

"Lane, what's wrong?" Gabriella asked with concern.

"Nothing. Take care, Gabriella," Lane replied as she rushed to the exit. She couldn't let Miranda leave thinking the worst. The look on Miranda's face haunted her—a mix of hurt and betrayal that Lane couldn't bear to let linger. Regardless of their current situation, she had to explain, to make sure Miranda knew the truth.

Bursting through the door, Lane spotted Miranda heading in the direction of the parking lot, her pace quick and determined. "Miranda, wait!" Lane called, her voice echoing in the night. She quickened her steps, desperation fueling her as she tried to close the distance. Miranda kept walking, her shoulders stiffening, but Lane was certain she had heard her. *I swear when it comes to this woman, I have lost my goddamn sanity. Now she has me running after her.*

Once close enough, Lane's fingers wrapped around Miranda's elbow, her touch firm yet gentle, coaxing Miranda to stop and face her. As their eyes met, Lane noticed the beginnings of rain, the droplets painting Miranda's features with a delicate sheen. A primal urge surged within Lane—the desire to taste the rain-kissed skin on Miranda's face smothering her senses. With each step closer, the space between them seemed to evaporate, their bodies drawn together as if by an invisible force. Their breath mingled in the cool night air, forming misty clouds between them, their chests rising and falling in perfect synchrony.

Lane was entranced by Miranda's arresting hazel eyes, their depths stirring emotions she couldn't contain. At that moment, Lane felt that undeniable unique pull, her heartstrings tethered to Miranda's presence. It was as if she had no control over her own body, subjugated by an insatiable need for the woman before her, a longing that left her feeling utterly vulnerable and powerless.

"It's not what you think," Lane whispered, the rain drumming down around them, adding a dramatic backdrop to their tense exchange.

"You don't owe me an explanation, Lane. As per *your* request, we're not together anymore, and you're free to go back to sleeping with whomever you want," Miranda retorted sharply with an underlying anger, despite her attempt at nonchalance.

Lane couldn't suppress a smile, the familiar thrill of interacting with Miranda coursing through her veins.

But the smile faded as she caught the hurt in Miranda's eyes. "Come on, Miranda. You and I both know that you don't have a poker face. Your beautiful face tends to reveal everything you're thinking."

"And what exactly is it that I'm thinking, Delaney?" Miranda's voice was barely above a whisper, her gaze flitting between Lane's lips and eyes, a subtle hint of vulnerability betraying her bravado.

Lane couldn't restrain the involuntary shudder that rippled through her body at the sound of Miranda saying 'Delaney' in that particular tone. Each time Miranda addressed her as such, it ignited a reverential urge within Lane—a desire to drop to her knees and worship her. Despite the warning bells ringing in her mind, Lane dared to take a step closer, fully aware of the perilous game she was playing. The proximity to Miranda was unraveling her already frayed resolve to stay away from her.

"You were thinking I ended things with you to go back to my Casanova ways and would be going home with Gabriella. Or that despite telling you I won't be dating anyone anytime soon, I've already moved on. How close am I?" Lane's voice wavered slightly, betraying the impact of having Miranda so close to her, but she held Miranda's gaze steadily, awaiting her response.

Miranda met Lane's gaze steadfastly before finally speaking. "Were you going to go home with her? I know sex is an escape for you, which always helps you to relax." Her words cut through the charged air, revealing the clairvoyance of her understanding of Lane's coping mechanisms.

"No," Lane replied resolutely, leaving no room for

doubt. Against her better judgment, she closed the remaining gap between them and enveloped Miranda in a tight embrace, drinking in the familiar scent of shea butter, vanilla, and coconut that clung to her skin. Miranda melted into the hug, her arms encircling Lane's waist—they fit together perfectly. And for the first time in weeks, Lane felt whole, even as the aching longing inside of her expanded.

"I don't want to have sex with anyone but you, Miranda." Lane breathed into the crook of Miranda's neck—like an addict in withdrawal finally getting a high from the fragrance that was Miranda Hayes. "I think it's safe to say you've ruined sex for me with anyone else. Please, never doubt that my reasons for ending things with you are anything other than what I've said. It's agonizing to stay away from you, but I truly believe it's the right thing for both of us." As the final words left her mouth, Lane drew Miranda even closer, her heart heavy with the weight of her decision and the uncertainty that gnawed at her. She found herself increasingly questioning whether she had made the right decision for them. The doubts eddied in her mind, growing louder with each passing moment as she also contemplated her ability to give Miranda the grand romance she had always dreamed of.

"I know," Miranda whispered in response, her voice carrying an intimate understanding that resonated with Lane, yet offered little consolation to her conflicted heart.

They remained locked in each other's arms, oblivious to the torrential rain pouring down around them, their embrace a refuge amidst the storm. In Miranda's arms, Lane found a sense of belonging she had never longed for and a feeling of completeness she had never known she needed until Miranda showed her another way to live. It was as if every moment before this had been leading her to this exact breaking point—back to Miranda. The blaring horn of a car shattered the moment, jolting them back to reality. Startled, they reluctantly untangled themselves from each other's arms, realizing they were standing in the middle of the entrance to the parking lot. Stepping aside, they watched in silence as the car maneuvered past them, its headlights piercing through the rain-soaked darkness, a stark reminder of the world beyond their private cocoon of emotions.

"I guess we should get out of the rain," Miranda murmured, looking down at her soaked jacket. Lane noticed the way her hair clung to her face, raindrops trailing down her skin like glistening tears.

"Yes, we should," Lane replied, resisting the urge to brush the wet strands away from Miranda's face. "Do you want to go back inside?"

"No, I think I'll just call it a night." Miranda's voice held a hint of weariness, her shoulders slumping slightly.

"Okay. I'll walk you to your car," Lane offered, her words a veil for the longing that simmered beneath. Her heart ached with the desire to accompany Miranda home, to linger in her presence a little longer, to chase away the shadows that haunted her. She yearned to share the quiet intimacy of the night with Miranda cuddled up in bed, to bridge the distance between them.

Miranda's lips curved into a soft smile. "Whoever said chivalry was lost?"

Lane returned the smile, a warm feeling spreading

through her chest. "What can I say other than that I haven't been tainted by a society hellbent on destroying common decency to the point where basic acts of kindness are labeled as offensive." She extended her arm, gesturing for Miranda to walk ahead.

Miranda shook her head, and shot Lane an exasperated look, her eyes dancing with a mixture of amusement and fondness. With a sigh, she started walking in the direction of her car. Lane fell into step beside her, the rhythm of their footsteps echoing in the silent streets.

"Well, I'm glad you've maintained your gentlelady mannerisms," Miranda remarked with a teasing edge in her voice. "It's one of your most appealing qualities."

"Good to know," Lane replied with a wistful smile, her gaze fixed on the ground as she fought against the despondency that threatened to engulf her at the thought of going home alone. And this in itself was unsettling because, before Miranda, she relished her solitude at home.

Chapter 21

"If you weren't so utterly depressed, I'd laugh over the fact that out of all the women you've bedded over the years, you've fallen in love with one who has never been in a relationship with a woman before you. I've always known you like a challenge, but seeing as you're here in your glass tower, miserable and pining away for her, I think it's safe to say that this is one challenge you're not winning and love is kicking you in the ass. Cupid's arrow has finally struck and it seems to have hit very deep," Nia said, her tone laced with humor, though Lane could sense the genuine worry beneath it.

Lane lifted her head from her glass of wine to meet Nia's gaze. After Lane had canceled their dinner plans twice last week and once this week, Nia took it upon herself to show up at Lane's home with dinner on a Tuesday night. Lane wasn't in the mood for company, but this was Nia, and she wouldn't allow Lane to kick her out before they at least talked. Even though talking was the last thing Lane wanted to do because ever since Miranda went on vacation over a week ago, Lane's mood had been darker than anything she had ever experienced.

The void left by Miranda's absence grew more expansive each day, her longing intensifying with each passing moment. While encountering Miranda at the hospital had been torturous, the agony of not seeing her at all was even more excruciating. Learning from Alexandra that Miranda was in Barbados only amplified the ache of her absence. Lane had been tempted to call her so many times but fortunately, she had a little self-control remaining. Her inability to move on—to not think about Miranda every second of every goddamn day—was becoming a source of extreme frustration. This whole falling in love business was rather stressful and again she didn't understand why people so willingly subjected themselves to it. As Lane's despondent thoughts threatened to annihilate her, the sudden vibration of her phone on the kitchen island jolted her back to the present.

She reached for it, grateful for the distraction, but frowned when she saw Blake's name on the screen. She can't recall Blake ever calling her cell. She quickly answered, thinking something must be wrong. "Hi, Blake."

"Hi, Lane. Have you heard from Miranda since yesterday?" Blake's voice carried traces of worry.

"No. Why? Is something wrong?" Lane's own apprehension instantly cascaded over her like a sudden downpour.

"She was supposed to come home yesterday because a hurricane was heading straight for the island. She was booked on one of the last flights out before the airport closed. She had a layover in Miami, and her mom became worried when she didn't hear from her then." Lane's heart began pounding against her chest, like a battering ram about to breach a gate. "She called the property caretaker, who confirmed that Miranda had left for the airport as scheduled. She should have been home by midnight last night but never made it onto the plane. Her phone keeps going to voicemail. The hurricane made landfall this morning, and from what we've seen on the news, it's devastating." The phone went silent, and Lane thought the call had disconnected. Then Blake's voice came through again, cracking with emotion. "Miranda is missing. And there's nothing we can do but wait until the hurricane passes and we can get in touch with the authorities there."

As each word escaped Blake's lips, Lane felt a numbness enveloping her, like a suffocating embrace threatening to crush her bones. Summoning the resilience of a survivor, she managed to maintain her composure and asked, "Aside from waiting for the hurricane to pass, what other measures are being taken to locate her?"

Blake's response was steady, but not strong enough to hide her fears. "Her family is mobilizing all available resources. Once travel is feasible, her parents and grandparents will head to Barbados. We're currently at her parents' house, going over the details."

Lane absorbed Blake's words, the weight of the situation pressing down on her like a heavy stone. Despite the turmoil raging within her, she forced herself to focus on the task at hand. There was no time for panic—only action. She nodded silently acknowledging the gravity of the situation before preparing to join Miranda's family in their collective efforts to bring her home.

"I'm on my way," Lane informed Blake. She couldn't bear the thought of sitting idle while Miranda's whereabouts remained unknown.

"Okay. I'll see you soon," Blake replied and

disconnected the call.

"Miranda is missing?" Nia's voice wavered with concern as she rose from her seat, mirroring Lane's sense of urgency.

"Yes. It seems she didn't board her flight from Barbados yesterday. I'm heading to her parents to gather more information," Lane explained, her attempt to remain composed crumbling under the weight of trepidation.

"Keep me posted. I'll clean up and leave after. Drive safe." Nia offered a quick hug as Lane passed her out of the kitchen.

Lane's footsteps reverberated against the hardwood floor as she dashed toward the elevators. She wasn't one to pray, but with each hurried step, she whispered a silent plea to any higher power listening to let Miranda be safe. The drive from her penthouse to Miranda's parents' home passed in a blur, every second stretching into an eternity of uncertainty.

Thirty agonizing minutes later, when Blake swung open the door to let her in, Lane's worry had reached a fever pitch, a knot of anxiety tightening in her chest. Blake must have sensed her distress because she reached out a hand, gripping Lane's shoulder in a reassuring squeeze.

"We have to stay positive," Blake urged, her voice a lifeline in the sea of fear.

Lane could only offer a silent nod as she trailed behind Blake into the living room, settling into a seat across from Miranda's grandparents. The atmosphere felt heavy, akin to a war room where the weight of life-and-death decisions saturated the air. Miranda's mother paced in front of the flat-screen TV, her movements restless, though she managed a feeble smile in Lane's direction before resuming her anxious pacing. Colin's parents greeted Lane with their own strained smiles. On the screen, Caroline's parents appeared, and Lane's gaze locked onto Corey Carter, a figure she recognized from numerous financial articles, noting the striking resemblance between him and Caroline. Miranda's grandmother sat beside him, her eyes red-rimmed from tears.

If she hadn't ended things with Miranda, Lane would have been meeting them in person in just a few days. Miranda had invited Lane to join her for a long weekend visit while she was on vacation. Lane had initially hesitated, but ultimately relented, unable to resist the allure of spending time with Miranda and wanting to share in new experiences together. It struck Lane then that her decision to end things with Miranda had led them to this moment. Miranda had shared her vacation plans with Lane, which had seemed simple enough—rest, tend to her greenhouse, assist with a fundraising event for Found Family, and spend time with loved ones. But now, faced with the gravity of the situation, Lane's heart felt heavy with regret.

"Even if there are no active networks and the cell towers are down, there's a satellite phone at the house for exactly those situations. If Miranda was there, she would have called," Corey's voice cut through the tense silence, grounding Lane in the present moment.

"She also knows the island very well. Something bad must have happened for her not to have been in contact with us," Caroline added, her voice trembling with each word.

Colin rose from the sofa and wrapped his arms

around his wife, offering her a comforting hug. "We can't think the worst, sweetheart. Our baby girl is strong and resourceful."

Lane couldn't fathom the magnitude of worry gripping Miranda's parents. She understood the immense love they had for Miranda, their only child—a path not chosen but embraced wholeheartedly. Miranda had confided in Lane about her mother's three miscarriages before Miranda was born and the lingering impact they had on her family. Caroline had decided not to attempt to have another child because of those reproductive struggles that left many scars on her mental health. The side effects of that history only added to the gravity of the current situation. Sitting there, a sense of helplessness consumed Lane, a feeling she knew Miranda's parents must be grappling with tenfold. Despite her efforts to remain composed, Lane found herself inundated with a relentless stream of worst-case scenarios, each more agonizing than the last. *Was she in an accident? Could she have been kidnapped? Murdered?*

Caroline's voice quivered with anguish as she voiced her worst fears to Colin, her eyes reflecting the abyss of her dread. "If something terrible has happened to her, I won't survive it, Colin. I won't survive losing my baby," she insisted, her words laden with desperation as she pulled away from his embrace to search his face for reassurance. Colin gently grasped her trembling hands, his eyes mirroring her pain but determined to instill hope.

"Sweetheart, as Colin said, we need to remain positive," Corey urged his daughter, sounding like the formidable businessman who had built a multi-billion-dollar empire from the ground up.

"The hurricane was a category two when it passed over the island. With luck, the airport should reopen in a day or two. The jet is on standby, ready to go as soon as we get clearance."

Caroline's resolve hardened as she nodded, a glimmer of determination flickering in her eyes. "I'll be on the earliest flight home. This way, there'll be no delays once we get the go-ahead."

Lane listened with rapt attention, observing the palpable love and resilient bond that permeated Miranda's family dynamic.

"Hey, how are you feeling?" Hearing Alexandra's voice, Lane redirected her attention from Miranda's parents, noticing Alexandra's presence beside her. "Let's go into the kitchen to talk," Alexandra suggested gently.

Lane acquiesced with a nod, rising from her seat and following Alexandra into the kitchen. Once they were alone, Lane couldn't help asking, "Why didn't you tell me earlier at work that Miranda was missing?"

"I only found out after I left the hospital. I had surgeries all day, and Blake didn't want me worrying until they were certain she was missing," Alexandra explained, her expression painted with concern. Lane recognized that beyond her worry for Miranda, Alexandra also fretted for Blake. The bond between Miranda and Blake was one of the strongest friendships Lane had ever witnessed, and she knew any harm to Miranda would deeply affect Blake, who was still recovering from her own traumatic ordeal. "I told her to contact you to check if you had heard from Miranda and to brief you on the situation. I would have reached out myself, but Blake could provide a more detailed account of the events."

Since joining Parkwood, Lane had come to tremendously admire Alexandra for her many remarkable qualities. Genuine goodness and kindness were rare traits, and Alexandra possessed them in abundance. Her warm and considerate demeanor naturally drew people toward her.

"Thanks for filling me in," Lane expressed her gratitude, pulling out a chair from the counter and sinking into it, her head dipping into her hands. She sensed Alexandra settling beside her and lifted her head to meet her concerned gaze. "I can't shake this feeling of responsibility for whatever has happened to her," she confessed, the heaviness of the admission pressing heavily upon her chest.

Alexandra's brow furrowed. "What do you mean?"

"If I hadn't insisted on her taking time to think about what she wanted, she wouldn't have felt compelled to travel thousands of miles away from me," Lane professed, her voice strained as her chest tightened, making each breath a struggle. "I've always believed that our actions shape our path in life. Not destiny or some unseen force. It's the choices we make as humans." She absent-mindedly rubbed the spot on her chest over her heart, as if to massage the constricting muscles that seemed to be proverbially suffocating her. "And here we are, uncertain of Miranda's fate, because I chose to end our relationship. That one decision set us on this path."

"Please don't think like that. It won't do you any good," Alexandra interjected, her voice soothing yet firm. "You're right in many ways, but at the end of the day, everything in life happens for a reason and unfolds as it should. Maybe something positive will come from this ordeal." Alexandra's counsel didn't surprise Lane. Alexandra had once shared that despite her heartache with Taylor, she wouldn't change a thing because it ultimately led her to Blake. "Until we have more information, it's best not to speculate. I know waiting is hard, but given the circumstances, it's all we can do and pray for the best."

"Regardless, if the worst has happened, I won't be able to not feel responsible." This time Lane's voice betrayed her inner turmoil, cracking with the burden of it. Lane gripped the edge of the counter to steady herself, her knuckles turning white. The reality of Miranda's disappearance crashed over her like a relentless tidal wave, threatening to engulf her. She closed her eyes, trying to hold back tears, and took a deep, shaky breath. And when Alexandra pulled her into an unexpected embrace—an act they had never shared before nor one she easily allowed from people—Lane found she didn't have the strength to refuse the gesture. The fear gripping her felt like a vice around her heart, draining her strength, and she desperately needed something, or someone, to anchor her in the storm.

Please let her be okay.

Chapter 22

Lane felt every bit of her sleepless night as she trudged down the stairs at Miranda's parents' house. Exhaustion clung to her, making each step feel like a monumental effort. After hours of discussing every possible scenario and hoping against hope that Miranda would call, they finally decided to try and get some rest. Caroline had insisted Lane stay in one of the guestrooms—an offer that surprised her. She knew Miranda must have told her mother about their breakup, and she had expected some form of resentment or anger.

At the guest room doorway, Caroline had paused, looking at Lane with a mixture of worry and kindness. "Miranda would have been happy to know you're here," she said softly. Lane had only been able to nod, unable to find the right words. Her emotions were a tangled mess, and anything she might have said would have offered no comfort to Caroline, or herself.

When she finally laid down on the unfamiliar bed, Lane's mind raced with thoughts of Miranda. The cataclysm of her absence was a constant, gnawing pain. She stared at the ceiling, feeling a profound sense of helplessness. Nothing seemed to make sense. Worry seethed like an ocean storm, sending unrelenting waves to bludgeon the foundation she built her fortress of strength upon.

Then there were the what-ifs that plagued her mind. What if she had just agreed to let them figure things out together, as Miranda had suggested? Would it have been so bad if she had followed her heart instead of her overly logical mind? In deciding to end things, it was her mind she obeyed and not her bleeding heart. If she had listened to her heart, she would have confessed her love to Miranda and asked for the chance to give her the grand romance she had always dreamed of. She wished she could return to that moment when Miranda had begged her to let them continue seeing each other and figure out the future together. *If she had followed her heart instead of her very logical mind*, she would have chosen Miranda over the fear of uncertainty.

In the silence of the guest room, Lane was exposed to every missed chance for what could have been with Miranda—the blows like the knives of Brutus, plunging and twisting into her heart. The regret was almost unbearable as she realized she had betrayed herself—her own heart.

Those thoughts forced her to scrutinize why she had never had a serious relationship before. What did she truly know about being selflessly in love? About being the partner Miranda deserved? After much reflection, Lane came to the same conclusion that she had always believed: before Miranda, she simply hadn't met anyone for whom she was willing to change her lifestyle. Her lack of relationships wasn't due to some deep-rooted trauma or her background, even though that was arguable since it was her childhood that pushed her to be ambitious and aspirational with a single-minded focus to achieve wealth.

Still, early in her career, she realized she didn't

have time for relationships while climbing the corporate ladder, but she loved sex and enjoyed the company of women when she had time. So, instead of dating women who wanted relationships, she chose like-minded, enterprising women, who wanted nothing more than sexual fulfillment and occasional companionship.

Yes, some women developed feelings and wanted to try for a relationship, but until Miranda, Lane had never felt the desire for more. She had never wondered what it would be like to come home every night to someone. To wake up every morning with a warm body on top of her. To have someone who took care of her when she was sick. Someone who called just to find out how her day was going and to tell her that she was missed. Someone who forced her to watch sappy romance movies while cuddled up on the sofa. These were all things Miranda did. And these were the things Lane had missed immensely since they separated. The things she wanted to experience again with Miranda. And she knew herself well enough to know that she could achieve anything she put her mind to, even if that meant being the best partner Miranda could have asked for.

Reaching the bottom of the stairs, Lane heard voices in the living room and decided to say goodbye before leaving. She wasn't surprised to find Miranda's parents awake, given their early flight to Atlanta, where they would wait to fly to Barbados with Caroline's father and two of her brothers, one of whom was Miranda's favorite uncle. Just as Lane entered the room, Caroline's phone rang on the coffee table.

Lane watched as Caroline rushed to pick it up, her

forehead creasing in concern. "It's a number I don't recognize," she said, her voice trembling. Her eyes then widened in alarm. "Maybe it's Miranda."

In the next breath, Caroline answered the phone, and Lane noticed she had stopped breathing, frozen in place, as she waited. What must have been seconds felt like an eternity. Lane finally gasped for air when Caroline collapsed onto the sofa, tears streaming down her face as she clutched the phone to her ear. Paralysis wrapped around Lane, fear gripping her heart, as she braced herself for the worst possible news, seeing Miranda's mom breaking down in such a way. And as she waited for the news that would obliterate her heart into a million pieces, the room seemed to close in around her, and she had to steady herself against the wall, her mind racing with dread.

Oh god, no. No, no, no.

"Sweetheart, who is it?" Colin asked, kneeling in front of his wife, his voice cracking.

"It's..." Caroline's voice cracked as she covered her mouth to restrain a sob "It's..." Lane's heart was on the verge of imploding. "It's our baby," Caroline stammered, tears of joy streaming down her face as she struggled to speak.

Colin took the phone from his wife's trembling hands, placing the call on speakerphone. "Miranda, honey, are you there?"

"Hi, Dad. Are you hearing me clearly?" Miranda's voice echoed through the room, causing Lane's heart to start beating once again.

Lane didn't know that just hearing the voice of someone could make her feel so many emotions simultaneously. She tried to steady herself, focusing on the conversation between Miranda and her parents instead of the erratic beating of her heart.

"Yes, honey, we're hearing you. Are you okay? Where are you? What happened?" Colin fired off, his concern still evident despite the relief of hearing Miranda's voice.

Lane moved closer, eager to hear every word Miranda relayed to her parents. As she listened, she learned that Miranda had been on her way to the airport when the car in front of her swerved off the road and into a ditch. Miranda had pulled over to check on the driver, discovering a woman suffering from what turned out to be a heart attack. With the help of other passersby, they had managed to remove the woman from the car and rush her to the hospital in Miranda's SUV, knowing that waiting for an ambulance would take too long.

At the hospital, there hadn't been a surgeon immediately available to perform the necessary surgery, so Miranda had volunteered. She was well-known and respected at the hospital, licensed with BAMP, and had a history of volunteering as part of a team of specialists who performed surgeries in developing countries. The hospital's head, who had welcomed Miranda when she performed her first surgery there years ago, quickly approved her request to operate. By the time the surgery was completed, the airport had already closed. Miranda had decided to stay at the hospital, anticipating the hurricane would bring in a surge of patients needing medical attention.

With her focus on helping the woman, Miranda had left her bag, containing her cell phone, in her SUV and was only able to retrieve it after the hurricane had passed. By then, the cell towers had been damaged, leaving her without a signal. However, she saw the dozens of frantic messages from her parents. Fortunately, the roads to her grandparents' house were passable, and she remembered that they had a satellite phone there.

Listening to Miranda recount the events of the last forty-eight hours, a mixture of awe and admiration swelled within Lane. She wasn't surprised Miranda had missed her flight because she chose to save a stranger's life. That was quintessentially Miranda—selfless, kind, and inherently good. Miranda's stanch commitment to helping others, even at great personal cost, highlighted the depth of her character. Lane's heart swelled with both relief and a renewed appreciation for the woman she loved, who never hesitated to lend a helping hand.

"Mom, the high school on our way to the house suffered significant damage. I want us to donate funds for the repairs. Could you also ask Granddad to consider donating to help rebuild homes in the poorer parts of the country? Many families have been displaced in those communities."

Lane smiled, feeling herself fall even more deeply in love with the woman on the phone.

"Of course, sweetheart. Dad has the jet ready to pick you up as soon as the airport reopens. They've been so worried," Caroline replied, her voice still trembling with emotion.

"I'm so sorry for making you worry. In the heat of the moment, I forgot to send you a message to inform you of my change of plans. Totally forgetting I'd lose phone signal during the hurricane. No need to send the plane though, I'm going to return as originally planned. I'm staying to assist at one of the clinics to help with the increase in patients due to the hurricane," Miranda informed them.

"Would you think terribly of me if I want you home today?" Caroline interjected.

Miranda chuckled softly. "No, Mom, I won't. I understand you've been scared, but they could use the help. I'll fly back on Sunday. As soon as I have cell signal, I'll video call so you can see that I'm fine. I'll let you go now so you can call Granddad and let them know I'm okay. I can only imagine how worried Grandma has been. I'll call them later."

"Okay, sweetheart. We love you. Please call us later and keep us updated on what's happening there," Caroline replied.

"Bye, Dad, I love you both. Talk soon."

"Bye honey, love you more," Colin added, and the call ended. Miranda's parents wrapped their arms around each other, sharing a moment of relief knowing their daughter was safe and the unthinkable had not come to pass.

Before Lane could process her next thought, her phone buzzed in her pocket with an incoming call. With trembling fingers, she retrieved it, her heart pounding with anticipation as she glanced at the unknown number flashing on the screen. A surge of happiness swept through her, hoping it was Miranda reaching out to her. Silently but swiftly, Lane slipped away from the living room and into the kitchen.

Taking a moment to steady herself, Lane drew in a deep breath to calm her racing heart before swiping her index finger over the green call icon. "Hello."

"Hi." Miranda's soft, affectionate voice whispered through the phone, warming Lane's body and causing her heart to flutter even faster.

"Hi." Returning Miranda's greeting, Lane matched her tone, feeling like someone waking up from a long torturous nightmare. She made her way to the patio door with measured steps and stepped outside into the crisp morning air.

"I'm not sure if you heard, but I was stranded in Barbados during a hurricane. I thought I'd call and let you know I'm okay. I didn't want you to worry any more than you had to," Miranda said softly as if they were lying in bed sharing an intimate moment after making love.

Lane rubbed the spot where her heart was, feeling so utterly overwhelmed with joy. "Thanks for thinking of my mental health and not wanting to cause me any unnecessary stress. I'm getting old and since you're the esteemed heart surgeon, you know this level of stress isn't good for my poor old heart."

Miranda's laughter danced through the phone, and even though Miranda couldn't see her, Lane couldn't help but grin like a love-struck fool. The line became silent, the steady rhythm of their breathing the only thing filling the void. Then Miranda whispered, so very softly, "I miss you so much."

Those five unvarnished words hit Lane square in the chest, the precise blow to the Achilles' heel of the impenetrable rampart around her heart. And though she had no intention of denying her feelings she was surprised at how powerless she was to control herself as she matched Miranda's cadence and replied, "I miss you more." The silence that followed wasn't uncomfortable —it was filled with unspoken longing. With her eyes closed, Lane wished she could see Miranda's face, to hold her close and never let go.

"I want us to talk when I get back," Miranda requested, breaking the silence.

Lane suspected Miranda meant to talk about their relationship and she found herself not wanting to wait. "We're talking now."

"This is a conversation I'd much rather have in person. I'll come see you Sunday night if you don't have plans."

Lane knew Miranda well enough to know she couldn't get her to change her mind. "Okay, Sunday."

"Okay. I'll call you. I have to call Blake now. Have a great day."

"You too…" She drew in the fullest breath she could marshal in weeks, as if her lungs suddenly woke up. "Bye," Lane replied softly, reluctantly not wanting to let Miranda go. As soon as the call disconnected, Lane felt that void from not having Miranda close descend upon her. Suddenly, Sunday felt like an eternity away, and the thought of waiting that long to see Miranda felt unbearable.

Chapter 23

Standing on the deck, Miranda took in the picturesque view of houses scattered among lush palm trees, a few meters from the Caribbean Sea. She inhaled deeply, savoring the air saturated with salt water carried by the sea breeze. The last few days had been a whirlwind of activity, assisting with the aftermath of the hurricane, and this was the first moment in seventy-two hours she could simply relax. There was still so much she wanted to do before leaving, but she knew that without taking a moment to rest, she would be unable to offer her services effectively. Miranda wished she could stay longer, but her obligations in Seattle wouldn't allow it. She resolved to continue her efforts from afar, working with her family's organization to help rebuild homes that were destroyed. This was her first experience with a hurricane, and during those tense moments, as she listened to Mother Nature's furious onslaught, Miranda had asked herself if she would have any regrets if she were to perish in the storm. Her mind had wandered to that introspective place unbidden, and she had found no regrets—except one.

As with most near-death epiphanies—and her innate and professional nature to objectively debrief events she experienced—Miranda had felt compelled to delve deeper into the comparison between her past relationships and the enthralling anomaly she had been living the past few months. Like the fragile hearts she analyzed and toiled to save, Miranda dissected the evolution of her own heart and feelings. Her core personality made her a great cardiothoracic surgeon, pouring everything she had into saving a life. That tenacious energy and devotion mirrored itself in her relationships. She was self-assured enough to know that her inability to maintain a relationship wasn't because she lacked something or wasn't good enough. In fact, it was this very self-assurance—the fact that she knew who she was as a person and would never allow anyone to control her or push her into something she wasn't ready to do—that perhaps led to their demise.

But she also inherently knew that sometimes despite giving everything her all, she couldn't save every patient…and she couldn't save every relationship. She had treated every partner with respect and care, showing up for big and small moments. She compromised when it was necessary, remembered birthdays, and gave thoughtful gifts. And despite her hectic schedule at the hospital, she always tried to make time for her relationships. Yet, her partners had always wanted more of her and from her—more of her time, more of her emotional investment. They were often the first to fall in love, expecting her to reciprocate on their timeline and wanting to put the shackles of girlfriend— or wifey—criteria on her.

But Miranda knew love didn't work like that. She undoubtedly believed that love was accepting who a person was in that moment, not the infinite potential they could become or the person that they were in the past. She had always been the one to accept her partners for who they were. But it had slightly hurt that despite the plethora of qualities she brought to the table, her partners still wanted her to become what they wanted, not taking into consideration who she wanted to become.

But Miranda was resilient and full of self-confidence and self-love, and she refused to sacrifice her own expectations for a partner's. Reflecting on this, she recognized that her past decisions had been about self-preservation, ensuring that she didn't lose herself in trying to fulfill someone else's expectations. This clarity, borne from recent introspection and experiences, reaffirmed her belief in the importance of being true to herself.

And in remaining true to herself when those relationships ended, she had just accepted their demise and moved on with her life. With each of these revelations, Miranda had come to realize one simple truth. A simple truth that while she hadn't been willing to give more of herself to those who demanded it, she was willing to give it to the one person who hadn't asked her for more. The one person, who—unlike her previous lovers who had expected her to sacrifice her happiness for them—had let her go, prioritizing Miranda's happiness over own. The one person Miranda ever begged not to end their relationship, even if they weren't technically in a relationship. The one person she wouldn't, or couldn't, just walk away from. The one person who probably wouldn't give Miranda a second glance if she wasn't anything but confident in who she was. The one person she wanted to make happy because it made her happy to do so.

Yes, leave it to time, distance, and Mother Nature to

bring about the paradigm shift she was about to embark on when she returned to Seattle.

Her stomach grumbled, reminding her that she hadn't eaten all day and interrupting her rumination. It was nearly midday, and having woken up just an hour ago, she had decided to forego breakfast for a late-morning swim, planning to have lunch instead. As she turned to head back inside, she heard a knock on the door. Smiling, she assumed it must be Althea— the property caretaker—likely bringing her some delicious home-cooked lunch. Although her family had a catering contract with a restaurant to supply them with authentic Bajan dishes whenever they visited, Miranda had realized years ago that home-cooked food tasted different—better. So, whenever she was on the island, she never refused Althea's offer to feed her.

Opening the door, the welcoming smile she had ready for Althea was wiped away by shock as her eyes landed on the last person she expected to see. Her heart somersaulted in her chest as she stared at the familiar teasing smile she adored. Miranda smiled indulgently as her initial shock transformed into pure happiness. She stared at the gorgeous specimen standing before her, soaking in every detail of those goddess-like features.

"I see my unannounced appearance has the desired effect." Miranda almost rolled her eyes teasingly at the unapologetic smirk she received. "You seemed absolutely stunned when you opened the door. Am I to assume that smile means you're happy to see me?"

Miranda knew she had missed Lane, but having her standing right in front of her after not seeing her for almost two weeks, made the feeling even more pronounced. "What are you doing here?" she managed to ask, her mind still reeling from the shock.

Lane hesitated for a moment, a flicker of self-doubt crossing her features before vanishing just as quickly. "You said we needed to talk. And since you insist on doing it in person, I decided to grant your wish." Lane opened her arms offering herself to Miranda. "So, here I am."

Miranda shook her head, grinning like a teenager whose teenage crush had just done something grand for her. "Sunday is just three days away."

Lane's gaze swept over Miranda's body, igniting that familiar heat within her. It reminded her of what one look from this woman could do to her. "I'm not always a patient woman. I'm also a problem solver. Hence, I decided to remove the barrier preventing us from communicating in your preferred format." Lane leaned against the doorframe, her signature scent enveloping Miranda like a warm cloak. "So, Dr. Hayes...are you going to invite me in?"

Miranda stepped aside to allow Lane to enter. As Lane's shoulder brushed hers, the smoldering desire that hadn't dimmed during their weeks apart ignited into a blazing inferno. The longing and want surged through Miranda's body with the intensity of Zeus unleashing his lightning bolts from Mount Olympus, and she was powerless to restrain herself. She grabbed Lane's hand before she could fully step past, slammed the door shut, pushed Lane against it, and joined their lips in a rough, passionate kiss. Lane gasped at the sudden onslaught but soon responded with equal hunger. Their moans blended, rising and falling in sync as their hands explored feverishly, gripping, caressing, and kneading every inch of flesh with a hunger too intense to restrain. The heat between them built, electrifying the air as they gave in to the desperate yearning that had consumed them for far too long.

Driven by an insatiable need to touch Lane and feel her skin, Miranda reached up and slid Lane's white shirt off her shoulders, grateful that Lane hadn't bothered with the buttons. Her hands dropped to Lane's breasts, squeezing them through her camisole. Her arousal spiked as Lane's nipples hardened beneath her touch. They moaned in harmony when Miranda pinched Lane's nipples, the pressure rough enough to be felt through the layers of clothing. But these barriers were unbearable, and Miranda needed them gone. Her desire was a coiled spring in her belly, winding tighter and tighter, making her delirious. She had never wanted anyone to fuck her as much as she wanted Lane to. This was something she had never once questioned. And she doubted she ever would.

******

Miranda's tongue slid against Lane's, demanding and taking everything she wanted with a kiss that made Lane's skin burn and her core clenched with an almost unbearable ache. She knew they should stop, but she felt powerless as her tongue tangled with Miranda's, and moisture pooled between her thighs. She could only call her feelings for Miranda a weakness she couldn't control, a force that had driven her to buy a ticket to Barbados the moment the airports opened —even enduring a connecting flight, something that was among the list of top ten things she detested. But her need for Miranda overshadowed her aversion to wasting time in airports.

Miranda's hands lowered to the hem of Lane's camisole, starting to remove it. As much as it pained her—and god did it pain her—Lane found the strength to grip Miranda's wandering hands and sever the kiss. She reluctantly eased back, reveling in the petulant whimper that escaped Miranda's swollen lips. They stared at each other, chests rising and falling in tandem, trying to catch their breaths. Miranda's eyes blazed with the same longing that Lane felt, their unspoken desire creating an electric tension between them.

"We should talk," Lane said with more conviction than she felt. Talking was the last thing she wanted to do, but she knew it was the right thing.

Miranda shook her head in refusal, her hands sliding under and up Lane's camisole, cupping her breasts, and rolling her nipples. Lane groaned and was unable to prevent her body from leaning into Miranda's touch. "We can talk later. Right now, I need you to fuck me and make me come so hard that I can't feel my legs." Despite the brashness of Miranda's words, there was a pleading edge in her voice. She rolled Lane's nipples harder, causing her to moan deep in her throat, breaking her resolve. Holding Lane's gaze, she continued, "Forget about everything we need to discuss. Pretend this was when you first saw me at Josephine's and I had said 'yes' to your advances and went back to your hotel with you. I want you to fuck me the way your eyes had told me you wanted to that night."

Miranda's hands slowly retreated from Lane's breasts, lingering at her side. Lane saw the act for what it was —Miranda relinquishing control to her. Well now, Lane had only so much self-control and she had never been the type to deny herself life pleasures that made her happy. And that night at Josephine's she had wanted to fuck Miranda raw and dirty. She also didn't believe in denying a woman's request for an orgasm. And more than anything, she was simply unable to deny Miranda anything that was in Lane's power to give her.

Yes, a weakness indeed.

With this final thought, she spun them around and pushed Miranda roughly against the door. She wasted no time—capturing Miranda's lips in a fierce kiss, her tongue demanding entrance which Miranda eagerly granted—giving Miranda exactly what she requested. Lane pulled back, biting Miranda's bottom lip before soothing it with her tongue, all the while deftly removing Miranda's tank top and tossing it aside. With a single-minded focus, Lane swiftly stripped off Miranda's shorts and underwear, her hands tracing the most glorious curves that she'd ever had the pleasure of caressing. She always thought of Miranda's body as a work of art that deserved to be worshipped.

Miranda wrapped her leg around Lane's hip, inviting her deeper, a throaty moan escaping her lips as Lane's fingers glided through her soaked folds. With deliberate intent, Lane slid two fingers inside Miranda's slick heat, thrusting forcefully. Miranda cried out, dragging her lips from Lane's, her head falling back against the door. Taking advantage, Lane captured Miranda's pulse point between her lips, biting hard before soothing the marks with languid strokes of her tongue. Miranda writhed against Lane, meeting each of Lane's thrusts fervently. Her urgent pleas for more only fueled Lane's desire, urging her to increase the tempo, driving harder and faster until the door shook behind them with each passionate thrust.

She feared she might hurt Miranda but that thought quickly vanished with Miranda pleading for more, pulling Lane even closer and digging her nails into Lane's flesh. With every movement of her fingers, Miranda begged for more and Lane gave it to her. Still, it wasn't enough. *Jesus help her.* Lane gave in to her desperation. It felt like no matter how many times she fucked Miranda it was never enough. This carnal need that had consumed her since that night at Josephine's had only grown more intense each time, she wrapped her lips around Miranda's clit or filled her with her fingers.

"Oh... fuck. Don't stop!" Miranda panted with every stroke, her mouth now opened against Lane's neck—warm breath teasing Lane's skin, spiking her already nuclear lust.

Lane had no intention of stopping until Miranda was a quivering mess—unraveling under her touch. She wanted to drag out Miranda's pleasure, savor the sensation of her pussy pulling Lane in and fucking ruining her for every other woman.

As Miranda's walls spasmed and tightened around her fingers, Lane wondered how the hell she had found the strength to walk away from this woman, who she could—quite literally—say had her wrapped around her clit. And after weeks of not being able to touch Miranda, each stroke of her fingers felt like coming home. A home she knew so very well to recognize the telltale signs of Miranda's impending orgasm—the breathy gasp, trembling thighs, the frantic movement of hips—but Lane wasn't ready for it to end. She withdrew her hand, hissing when Miranda's walls clenched around her fingers, trying to keep her inside.

"No, no, no! What are you doing? I'm so very close." Miranda groaned in frustration as she eased back to meet Lane's gaze, her eyes wild and pained. "Lane please, I really need to come. It's been weeks. *Please*... I need you."

"Don't you want me to lick your pussy, Miranda?" Her thumb flicked Miranda's clit. "Don't you want me to fuck you with my tongue the way I know you love it?" Her index finger circled Miranda's entrance. "Don't you want me to clean up the mess you've made down there with my mouth?" Lane seductively ran her tongue over her bottom lip, before biting her lip into her mouth. "Don't you want to come in my mouth?" Another swirl in the increasing wetness. "Hmm?"

Lane stared at Miranda, awestruck by the profound effect she had on her with just her words. That night at Josephine's, Lane had hoped they would be compatible in bed, but Miranda exceeded all expectations. Miranda was Lane's perfect match when it came to sex—a mesmerizing blend of submission and command. Fearlessly demanding Lane to take her one moment, then yielding to Lane's every desire in the next.

Miranda seized Lane by the back of her neck, drawing her into a bruising, passionate kiss that left Lane momentarily breathless. Before Lane could fully respond to the rough claiming, Miranda abruptly broke the kiss and pushed Lane to her knees. Even before Lane's knees touched the floor, Miranda deftly hooked a leg over Lane's shoulder, offering herself eagerly to Lane's salivating mouth.

Chuckling softly, Lane lifted her eyes to meet

Miranda's gaze. "Impatient, aren't we?" She playfully nipped at the sensitive spot on Miranda's hip bone that she knew would make her even more aroused.

Miranda responded by threading her fingers through Lane's hair, gripping tight, and guiding her toward her waiting pussy. Though tempted to tease Miranda further, Lane couldn't resist the igneous desire to taste her. Yielding to Miranda's wishes, Lane ran her tongue along Miranda's drenched folds, emitting a low growl of satisfaction as Miranda's sweet essence coated her tongue, making her ravenous for more.

"You taste incredible," Lane moaned appreciatively, her passion intensifying with each lap of her tongue as Miranda grew wetter and wetter.

She swirled her tongue around Miranda's clit, relishing in the taste and feel of her arousal, before sucking the hard nub between her lips. Miranda's hands tightened in Lane's hair, a mixture of pleasure and urgency coursing through her touch, igniting a savage hunger within Lane.

Lost in the intoxicating moment of pleasuring Miranda, Lane felt the vice-like grip of arousal tighten around her, threatening to overwhelm her senses. The intense desire she felt for this woman was palpable, consuming her thoughts and actions as she explored every inch of quivering flesh with her tongue. She wouldn't be surprised if she came simply from sucking Miranda's pussy.

"I need your fingers, baby. Three. I need three, please," Miranda pleaded, her voice thick with desperation.

At that moment, there was nothing Lane wouldn't have given her, but she knew Miranda's body well enough to know that she couldn't immediately take three fingers, given that she hadn't had sex in weeks. Instead, she slid her hand between them and slipped two fingers inside Miranda's warm, wet core that welcomed her with little resistance. She curled her fingers, hitting Miranda in that sweet spot that had her riding Lane's face with reckless abandon.

Lane continued to work her magic, alternating between thrusting her fingers and skillfully teasing Miranda's clit with her lips and tongue. With each motion, she drove Miranda closer and closer to climax, delighting in the sounds of pleasure and curses escaping Miranda's lips and the way her body responded eagerly to her touch.

"Fuck me. Do it harder," Miranda gasped. Lane responded by thrusting harder, each movement eliciting a fervent chant of affirmation from above her. "Yes, that's it. Right there. Oh god, yes," Miranda cried out, her walls quivering around Lane's fingers as moisture gushed from her. "I'm coming, please don't stop! Fuck... Fuck... Fuck!"

Miranda's scream echoed in the room as her orgasm slammed into her, her hips bucking uncontrollably against Lane's face. Her grip on Lane's hair tightened as she pulled Lane closer, pressing her heated flesh against Lane's lips and tongue. Lane, though her own core throbbed with need, continued her ministrations until she had extracted every last drop of pleasure from Miranda's body until she begged Lane to stop.

The only sound that filled the air was their ragged breathing, both struggling to regain composure. Lane nestled her head against Miranda's stomach, trying to steady her racing heart, but before she could acclimate, Miranda swiftly disentangled her leg from Lane's shoulder and dropped to her knees. Pushing Lane onto her back, Miranda yanked off her cotton pants and underwear in one fluid motion. Lane's sex-addled brain struggled to keep up with Miranda's swift movements, and when Miranda's hot, wet mouth descended on her clit without preamble, Lane's back arched involuntarily off the floor. A torrent of pleasure, like a dormant volcano come to life, erupted through her, causing blinding flashes of ecstasy behind her closed eyes.

Weeks of pent-up sexual frustration and fucking Miranda heightened Lane's arousal to an unbearable peak. She surrendered to the overwhelming sensations, knowing she wouldn't last long. Miranda's skilled tongue flicked and teased, driving her relentlessly toward the precipice of release. Lane welcomed the rush of an embarrassingly quick orgasm, unable and unwilling to resist the euphoria that flooded her senses as Miranda's tongue expertly explored her, taking her to the brink and beyond.

After months of being together, Lane still marveled at Miranda's skill in bringing her pleasure, especially since Lane was the first woman she had slept with. Miranda possessed a natural talent for satisfying Lane, never failing to bring her to climax. It was as if she instinctively understood Lane's desires, effortlessly adapting her touch to match Lane's unspoken needs. Whether it was rough and urgent or slow and tender, Miranda seemed to intuitively know exactly what Lane craved.

Right now, Lane needed rough, and Miranda's eager mouth met her needs with a passionate resolve that mirrored Lane's own desire. Miranda devoured Lane with a hunger that left her breathless, driving Lane towards an orgasm that swept through her like a storm, engulfing her with its power. Surrendering to the wave of emotions crashing over her, Lane could only succumb to the annihilation as she dissolved into a trembling mess at the skillful tongue of the only woman she had ever loved.

As Lane's climax subsided, Miranda's touch gentled, her lips trailing tender kisses along Lane's heated skin as she moved up her body. Meeting Lane's lips, Miranda kissed her deeply, their mingling essences creating an intoxicating concoction that Lane wanted to drink every day for the rest of her life.

Miranda slowed the kiss, her breath warm against Lane's lips. "I think round two should be in the bedroom."

"What about talking?" Lane asked, knowing they should discuss their situation to clarify what their falling back into fucking each other's brains out meant.

"We have all afternoon to talk," Miranda countered, her voice laced with desire. "Right now, you need to make me come again. We're still pretending it's our first time together and I know you wouldn't have stopped after just one round that night."

Miranda posed a very strong defense. Lane knew that if their first encounter had led Miranda to her hotel room that night at Josephine's, she probably would have fucked Miranda into the early morning hours. Even then, it didn't escape her that once again, she found herself unable to defy Miranda's demands. But then again, she did believe in delayed gratification. "As usual, I'm here to serve at your pleasure, Miranda darling. Lead the way."

Chapter 24

Lane's eyes fluttered open from her most restful sleep in weeks. Daylight still streamed through the bedroom's floor-to-ceiling windows, suggesting only a few hours had passed. Despite the short rest, she felt remarkably rejuvenated, her body deliciously sore from the marathon sex they had indulged in. Miranda had been insatiable, and once they reached the bedroom, she had explored Lane's body with an exhilarating blend of roughness and tenderness, culminating in slow, sweet lovemaking in the end. Miranda, as usual, lay practically on top of Lane, her warm breath a gentle caress against Lane's neck. God, how she had missed this—the simple pleasure of waking up beside Miranda, feeling her presence, and all the comfort and joy it brought.

She smiled, marveling at how one woman could shift her perspective on so many things without even trying. A year ago, the idea of enjoying a night spent cuddling would have seemed absurd to her, yet here she was, savoring every moment. She didn't regret them sleeping together, but she wished they had talked about their future before giving in to their desires. After everything that had transpired since their breakup, Lane knew the path she hoped they would take. However, the future hinged not only on her wishes, but more so on what Miranda wanted.

Miranda stirred, her leg nestled between Lane's

thighs, the subtle friction sending a delicious shiver through Lane as it grazed her clit. She bit the inside of her cheek, struggling to stifle the moan threatening to escape. Soft lips brushed against her neck, leaving a trail of feather-light kisses that sent heat coursing through her. The kisses moved upward, finally capturing her lips in a tender, sweet caress that melted her insides with every lingering touch.

"Hi," Miranda whispered against Lane's lips, her eyes slowly opening as a beautiful smile formed on her lips.

Lane's weak heart did a little dance in her chest. Miranda was so very beautiful, but there was something extraordinary about her when she woke up—a youthful and ethereal charm that was simply captivating. "Hi," Lane replied, mirroring Miranda's smile. God, she was a goner for this woman—which was why they needed to talk sooner rather than later.

Just as Lane opened her mouth to voice her concerns, Miranda gave her a chaste kiss and rolled off her. "I really need to pee," she said, hopping off the bed and rushing into the bathroom.

Lane shook her head, chuckling softly, her eyes fixed on Miranda's ample backside as she disappeared into the bathroom. Once the door closed, Lane turned toward the windows, the breathtaking view calling to her. Getting out of bed, she walked slowly to the glass, stretching her well-used muscles, reveling in the laxness resulting from a well-pleasured body. She wasn't concerned about her nudity. Miranda had assured her that transparency was one-sided when Lane asked if she was worried about being so exposed to their neighbors.

Standing by the floor-to-ceiling windows, she

marveled at the sunset casting its golden hue over the crystal blue water. Mansions of various sizes dotted the landscape, all within walking distance of the beach. Once Miranda's mom had provided the location details, Lane had done her own research on the island. However, the scene was even more spectacular than she had imagined—the reality far surpassing any photos she had seen online. Sometimes she forgot how wealthy Miranda's family was because they were such down-to-earth people who didn't place undue importance on their affluence.

"Beautiful, isn't it?" Miranda's voice was soft as she came up behind Lane, wrapping her arms around her waist. She pointed to a house in the distance. "That's Rihanna's house." The hard press of nipples bored into Lane's back sending shivers through her as Miranda's hands wandered, cupping her breasts and capturing her nipples between a thumb and forefinger.

Lane's body reacted instantly, but she found the strength she needed to wrap her hands around Miranda's, halting her ministrations. Turning in Miranda's arms, she held her gaze. "We should talk before any more orgasms."

Miranda sighed dramatically. "I know." She closed her eyes briefly, and when she opened them, Lane saw a flicker of uncertainty and fear. "I just wanted to stay in this bubble with you a little longer. Let's go back to bed." Lane lifted a questioning eyebrow. "To talk."

"Don't you think that's playing with temptation," Lane pointed out, knowing that once they were in bed, she might not be able to resist Miranda's advances.

Miranda grinned mischievously. "I'll keep my hands to myself if you can."

Though it might be difficult, they needed to have this conversation, so Lane would summon the self-control required to resist temptation. "Okay, as you wish."

They returned to the bed, and Miranda sat in the middle, folding her legs at the knee, exposing herself to Lane. Lane followed, mirroring her position, but her eyes inevitably landed on Miranda's bare sex—a distraction she didn't need. She reached for the sheet and spread it over their laps.

Miranda chuckled. "Delaney," Miranda purred, teasingly. "I thought you had more self-control."

"Not when it comes to you, it seems." One of the many truths Lane had discovered during their time apart was that she had never been afraid to lose control with Miranda.

"I'm glad." Miranda's features grew serious, and once again Lane saw signs of uncertainty and nervousness. Miranda took a deep breath, her eyes searching Lane's for reassurance. "I've used my time here to really think about my life, my unexpected attraction to you, and what it means in terms of my sexual orientation. I'm absolutely certain of my feelings for you, but I'm also still sexually attracted to men. Maybe I'm bisexual or maybe it's just you, the person, I'm attracted to regardless of your gender."

"I can guarantee it's me. Even though, back in the day, you claimed that I was insufferable." Lane mock sighed, shooting Miranda that grin she couldn't refute. "Yet, here you are, naked in bed with me." Lane teased, hoping to lighten the mood and dispel Miranda's nervousness.

Miranda managed a small smile. "You were rather persistent in your pursuit. Who could blame me for falling for temptation? And you're rather charming…" Miranda rolled her eyes, playfully, "even when you're being insufferable."

Lane laughed, feeling a rush of affection. This was another thing she had missed. Their interactions were never boring. She gestured for Miranda to continue.

"I don't know why of the many women I've met over the years, you're the only one I've ever been sexually attracted to. But while I've never been attracted to another woman before, I'm absolutely certain I want to be with you—to have more than just a casual relationship. My feelings for you aren't fleeting or just some moment I'm having because I'm going through a mid-life crisis and it's thrilling to be with a woman." Miranda's voice wavered slightly, her eyes pleading for understanding. Lane's heart swelled with empathy as she looked at Miranda, recognizing the depth of her vulnerability.

Hearing Miranda declare that she wanted more than just sex from Lane stirred a whirlwind of emotions within her. Relief washed over her, a balm to her hopes that in time Miranda would eventually reach this conclusion. Yet, fear also coursed through her veins — the reality of falling in love and committing to one woman was still so very daunting. There thought of falling short and hurting Miranda was even more utterly unbearable.

Miranda glanced toward the windows, her features introspective as if she was thinking how best to voice her next words. When her eyes met Lane's again, what Lane saw in them stole her breath away. "In my past relationships, one of the many reasons they failed was because something was always missing. I've never been able to identify what it was I was looking for, but now I can, because I felt it with you." The conviction in Miranda's voice sped up the heartbeats in Lane's chest. "I still can't clearly define it, but it's close to feeling like I'm incomplete without you. Like I burn from the inside out with desire and I ache for you in a way I've never done before. There's this longing that is so palpable that it makes me feel paralyzed and I can only move if you touch me. This feeling where I want to spend every second of every day with you and it's still not enough." Lane wanted to reach out and touch Miranda in reassurance and to steady her racing heart. "Burning passion, Lane, that's what I've never felt with anyone before. This primal, animalistic need to have you, combined with an overwhelming desire to make you happy and give you every part of me."

Lane understood all too well what Miranda described as those same feelings blazed inside of her for Miranda, and she was willing to do everything in her power to make Miranda happy.

"During the hurricane, I asked myself, if I should die, would I have any regrets about the choices I've made in my life. And the only thing I would have regretted was not telling you that I love you. I wouldn't have wanted to die without letting you know your feelings for the first woman you ever loved were returned." Lane thought her heart stopped and she couldn't remember if she knew how to breathe.

"Before our separation, I didn't allow myself to analyze my feelings for you, because I knew you didn't want a relationship and I didn't want to set myself up for heartbreak. But being apart the last few weeks has been agonizing and when I really think about what I feel for you—outside of all the constant lust—it's pure love." Tears pricked behind Lane's eyes, but she bit the inside of her cheek to keep them at bay.

Miranda lifted Lane's hand and placed it over her rapidly beating heart, betraying how nervous she was despite her composure. "I can't guarantee you a happily ever after. I can't guarantee I won't hurt you. Because sometimes despite our best intentions, we end up hurting the people we love the most."

Miranda's eyes glistened with unshed tears, and Lane felt the overwhelming urge to pull Miranda into her arms and comfort her, but she held back, knowing she needed to allow Miranda to finish. "But what I can guarantee is that I'll try my best to make you happy. To support you and love you as best as I can. Because while I can't predict the future, at this moment, right here, right now, I'm absolutely certain I'm in love with you—even if you're arrogant and insufferable. And I wouldn't want you any other way, with your complexity, confidence, and very high standards."

Miranda paused, her gaze staunchly fixed on Lane, burning with what she recognized as love. "I love you, Delaney, and I'm asking you to take a chance on me. Trust me with your heart because I'll handle it with care and cherish it. I know being in love is new and frightening for you, but I'm asking you to risk your heart with me. Let me love you."

Tears rarely came easily to Lane, which perhaps explained why the tears pricking behind her eyes refused to fall down her cheeks. When Lane decided to go to Barbados, she did so without knowing what to expect from Miranda. To protect herself from potential disappointment in case Miranda didn't want the same future, Lane had consciously kept her hopes from soaring. No expectations meant no further heartache. Just like Miranda, their time apart had led Lane to realize one undeniable truth.

She took their hands from Miranda's chest and placed them over her own pounding heart. "I've always been a risk-taker—fearless in my pursuit to achieve everything I've wanted from this life. But falling in love with you has brought a fear I've never known—the vulnerability of giving someone so much power over me. It's such a turbulent and disquieting feeling."

She inhaled a deep cleansing breath, causing their hands to rise and fall with the expansion of her chest. "Still, it's the most beautiful thing to feel what I feel for you. This overwhelming paradox that makes me feel both powerless and powerful at the same time. To want you with such intensity that being apart from you was the most unbearable thing I've ever had to endure. I'm still not used to the overwhelming emotions that come with loving you—the constant longing, the ache, the missing you even when you're near, being breathless in your presence, and feeling like I would die if you don't touch me when we're making love. But I want to feel all those things even if it's scary because it's everything that comes with loving you."

She reached out her other hand, cupping Miranda's cheek. "Being in love is probably the biggest risk anyone can take because you're risking your heart and so much more. And if I'm going to take the greatest risk of my life, there's no one else I'd rather take it with." A solitary tear trickled down Miranda's cheek and Lane brushed it away with her thumb. "You're everything to me, Miranda. And just as I've always worked hard to achieve everything I wanted from this life, I promise to work just as hard to make you the happiest person alive."

Miranda launched herself at Lane, their bodies tumbling onto the bed in a tangle of limbs. Her mouth claimed Lane's with a demanding kiss that was consuming and slow, brimming with passion and tenderness. At that moment, Lane felt the vastness of Miranda's love, and she surrendered herself completely to it, allowing herself to be cherished.

Time seemed to stand still as they kissed, enveloped in each other's warmth. When Miranda finally pulled back, her eyes met Lane's with a vulnerability that mirrored Lane's own. "I love you," Miranda whispered, her voice carrying the weight of her emotions.

Lane felt her heart skip multiple beats with overwhelming joy. How could three simple words hold such power over her? Regardless, she undeniably knew that she wanted to feel this way for the rest of her life. "I love you too," Lane replied, her voice filled with sincerity and warmth.

Their lips met again in a tender reunion, and Lane gently rolled Miranda onto her back. They made love with a slow and passionate rhythm, savoring every touch and kiss until the sun dipped below the horizon and hunger pulled them from their intimate cocoon.

Later, as they sat on the beach sharing dinner, Lane felt a profound sense of contentment envelope her. Falling in love had never been part of her plans, but now, she couldn't imagine life without Miranda. Her journey had led her to experience unconditional love, bringing her back to the woman who had shown her kindness many years ago and who had made her young heart flutter. Maybe some things were just meant to happen even when they were the last things one could have expected.

Chapter 25

"Oh honey, I'm so glad you're finally home," Caroline said, enveloping Miranda in the maternal warmth of a woman who had faced one of a mother's deepest fears.

Lane watched, feeling her own heart swell with the love Caroline must be experiencing, having her daughter back safely after days of worrying about the unthinkable. Colin followed, embracing Miranda in a bear hug that almost lifted her off the ground. Then came her grandparents, who had flown in from Atlanta to be there when Miranda arrived home. Observing the outpouring of love from Miranda's family, Lane couldn't help but reflect on the stark contrast between their upbringings. From birth, Miranda had been surrounded by the nurturing care of a loving family, shaping her into the kind, compassionate woman who had captured Lane's heart. Miranda had confided in Lane about her experiences as a biracial person—sharing how she had never felt the weight of not belonging or the pressure to conform to societal norms that often burdened those of mixed heritage.

Embraced wholeheartedly by both sides of her family, Miranda found solace and acceptance in their unwavering love. To her, what truly mattered was not her skin color but the values her parents instilled in her and the authentic identity she cultivated for herself. She refused to be defined by racial labels, choosing instead to embody the essence of who she was as a person embracing her individuality and forging connections based on shared humanity rather than superficial differences.

Lane, on the other hand, had known none of that until she was fifteen. In spite of this, she had not allowed her challenging childhood to turn her into an angry, sad human who hated the world because she didn't have a model upbringing. All of this proved what she had always believed—that people were in control of their destinies, capable of becoming anything they wanted, regardless of their upbringing. Through sheer hard work and determination, she had overcome every obstacle life had thrown at her, resisting the path that could have led her to become like her neglectful mother. Now, she was in love with the most amazing woman she had ever met.

Though she hadn't experienced the same familial love growing up until her mid-teens, Lane had no doubt in her ability to love Miranda deeply and make her happy. She would simply apply the same relentless effort and determination that had made her a formidable CEO to her relationship with Miranda.

"Sweetheart," Miranda said, breaking into Lane's thoughts as she came to stand beside her, linking her arm through Lane's. "I'd like you to meet my grandparents, Corey and Analise Carter." Miranda smiled up at Lane, her eyes glowing with so much love it made Lane's heart race. She fought the urge to rub the spot where her heart sprinted in her chest, overwhelmed by the emotion she saw in Miranda's eyes. Miranda turned back to her grandparents who had come over to meet Lane. "Grandma, Granddad, this is my girlfriend, Lane Remington." Lane's heart hammered even faster hearing the certainty and confidence in Miranda's voice as she introduced her to the people who meant the most to her. *God, will I ever get used to feeling like butterflies are dancing in my stomach? Jesus.*

"Hi, Lane. It's nice to finally meet you in person. I was quite shocked when my blabber-mouth grandson snitched and told us that Miranda was dating a woman," Analise said with amusement in her voice. Miranda and her grandfather chuckled. "But I can see why she was captivated by you. You're absolutely stunning."

Lane cringed inwardly, remembering how Miranda's favorite cousin had visited from Atlanta a day earlier than planned and walked in on them making out on Miranda's sofa. He was a little drama queen, who had made it a whole scene, and insisted that he got all the details of how his favorite cousin went from being railed by men to being worshipped by God's finest creation. "Thank you. It's nice to finally meet you both. And well, Damian does know how to make an entrance. I can only imagine the tails he spun when informing you about our relationship."

"Oh, yes, he was rather detailed in regaling how he caught you with your tongue down my grandbaby's throat," Analise jested. Then, her expression shifted to one of stern protectiveness. "We don't care who our grandbaby dates, as long as they treat her well. So, don't take this personally, but if you break her heart, you'll have one angry grandmother to deal with."

Miranda groaned beside Lane. "Oh my god, Grandma. You promised you would stop threatening my partners when you meet them."

Lane laughed. It was always so refreshing to witness the carefree way Miranda interacted with her family. "I have no intentions of hurting your grandbaby. My plan is to make her the happiest woman alive."

"Well, you shall have no problems from me then," Analise replied, smiling at Lane—a smile so very similar to Miranda's.

"Sweetheart, stop trying to intimidate Lane. For someone to have risen so quickly to the top in her profession, I can guarantee she isn't easily intimidated," Corey interjected. Lane glanced at him questioningly—a bit surprised that he had researched her. He smiled at her. "I have a few connections in the business world."

Lane returned his smile, knowing that a man of his stature likely knew many people she had worked with over the years. "I'm sure you do."

"You arrived just in time for dinner. We should continue getting to know Lane while we eat," Analise suggested.

"Okay, we'll be right there," Miranda replied.

Once her grandparents were out of earshot, Miranda wrapped her arms around Lane's neck and kissed her softly. "I know you didn't plan on staying the night, but I want to spend some time with my grandparents and I also want to sleep in your arms. Could you please stay here with me tonight?"

"Why, Dr. Hayes, after spending every second together for the past three days, it seems you still can't get enough of me," Lane teased, though she was secretly thrilled Miranda felt the same way about spending the night apart. Yes, they had spent the last three days together, but it seemed like no matter how much time they spent together, it just wasn't enough.

"No, it seems I can't." Miranda's gaze bore into Lane, holding her completely mesmerized. God, she loved this woman. "Being around you makes me happy."

"Well, then, I guess I have no choice but to agree, since I did promise your grandmama that I'd do everything in my power to make you happy."

"Thank you." Miranda gave her another tender kiss before lowering her hands from Lane's neck to intertwine their fingers. They walked hand in hand to the patio, and while Lane didn't know what the future held, she fervently hoped they would never get tired of wanting to be around each other.

Later that night, after leaving Miranda with her family to call Anita, Lane was drifting into a deep sleep when she felt warm hands slip under her tank top, gently massaging her breasts. She slowly opened her eyes to find Miranda staring at her with unbridled desire. Miranda pushed her onto her back, following and settling between Lane's thighs. Even though she was so very exhausted, Lane's body instantly reacted to Miranda's touch, her skin tingling and core throbbing as Miranda's hands continued to torture her nipples. Lane's sex clenched even more, realizing that Miranda was completely naked, her bare skin radiating heat and wanton need.

"I know you're tired, but I really want to make love to you," Miranda whispered, rotating her hips against Lane's pelvis.

With what little agency Lane had remaining, she managed to say, "I don't think it's a good idea to have sex with your parents and grandparents a few doors down the hall."

Miranda chuckled softly. "We'll just have to be very quiet." She momentarily pressed a finger to Lane's lips, as she continued to whisper, "Plus, I know you love being adventurous. So, let's pretend we're in high school, I snuck you into my room and we need to be very quiet so that my parents don't hear us."

"I thought you'd need a night to rest after three days of marathon sex," Lane moaned out as Miranda lowered her hand and slipped it into her underwear.

"It's your fault for being utterly irresistible," Miranda whispered seductively, dipping a finger inside Lane's wetness and circling her clit. "I can't get enough of you." She nipped Lane's bottom lip, using her tongue to trace away the sting.

Lane had always believed in the transformative power of words. Depending on their wielder, they possessed the ability to slice through the heart with a pain that lingered, leaving wounds that never truly healed. Conversely, in the tender care of someone like Miranda, words could weave a tapestry of joy and affirmation, wrapping around her soul like a warm embrace. When Miranda expressed how much she wanted her, each syllable was a brushstroke painting a portrait of happiness in Lane's heart. It was overwhelming, this love she felt. It made Lane tremble with fear of the unknown, yet soar with a newfound courage to embrace vulnerability. For all its uncertainties, she knew deep within that this love was worth every moment of fear.

Raising a trembling hand, Lane gently cupped Miranda's cheek, her touch a silent declaration of devotion. "I love you so much," she whispered, her voice rough with raw adulation. At that moment, all she yearned for was to convey the depth of her feelings—to show Miranda how she was the anchor in her chaotic sea of emotions. Vulnerability wasn't Lane's forte, but it was a gift she willingly offered to Miranda. She knew that being with Miranda meant baring her soul, so that Miranda could feel how much she loved her.

Miranda's eyes shimmered in the soft, muted light, mirroring the vulnerability Lane felt. "I love you too, my love," Miranda whispered, her voice filled with a longing that echoed Lane's own. She rolled over, pulling Lane on top of her. "Now..." she gently commanded, widening her legs to allow Lane to settle between them. "Please show me how much you love me."

Lane's response was instinctive—driven by her desire to always give Miranda whatever she requested—as she joined their lips in a slow, deep, passionate kiss. And even though it was hard, they managed to contain their ardor as Lane moved with deliberate gentleness—each touch a testament to the depth of her love for Miranda. As they moved together in a rhythm of love and connection, Lane marveled at how Miranda had become her everything—her confidante, her lover, her home. Miranda had opened Lane's heart to a love she never dreamt of, but now hoped she would never have to live without.

Chapter 26

Reading her messages, Miranda couldn't contain the wide smile that spread across her lips as she absorbed each word, reveling in the cascade of emotions they evoked. Nor could she suppress the flutter in her stomach or the way her heart skipped a beat. God, she was so helplessly in love with this woman. Who would have thought that after everything they had been through, she would have ended up with Lane—a woman? This chapter of her life was so unexpected, but so far it had been the happiest chapter when it came to love and relationships.

> *Lane: I miss you so much. I spent most of my life comfortable with solitude and now not seeing you for four days feels like a part of me is missing. What have you done to me, Miranda darling? Did you put a spell on me? Sometimes, I think I've been in love with you since the day you gave me your shoes. The day when for the first time in my life I felt cared for. I can't wait to be home to show you just how much I love and appreciate you.*

Whenever Lane expressed her love so openly and freely, it still surprised Miranda. Because to be honest, she never expected Lane to be so expressive with her feelings, since it was her first time being in love. Though to be fair, Lane had always been open and honest with Miranda, showing a gentleness and softness she reserved for no one else, even when she was relentlessly flirting with Miranda.

Miranda: I miss you too, sweetheart. I think you're the one who put a spell on me since despite thinking I could resist your charms, I ended up falling in love with you. I know you don't believe in fate, but just maybe, our paths crossed that day because we were meant to find happiness with each other. I'm leaving here in ten minutes. I'll call you on my way home. I love you too.

Lane: Okay, love. I have a few things to finalize in the next twenty minutes. Let's talk when you're home.

Miranda continued to grin like a lovesick puppy as her eyes soaked up Lane's words. Lane was in London on a business trip and Miranda hated every second of being apart from her. She wondered if the newness of their love was why everything felt so intense and perfect with Lane. Since returning from Barbados a month ago, they had spent almost every day together, and for the first time in her life, Miranda didn't feel suffocated by a partner who wanted to be with her constantly. Instead, she was the one who had been worried about being too clingy and wanting to be with Lane all the time. But knowing Lane valued communication and honesty, Miranda had expressed her concerns to her. Lane assuaged her worries by confirming that she felt the same as Miranda and also hated being away from her. Miranda lowered her phone, closed her eyes, and envisioned Lane's beautiful face and intense gaze. She rubbed the spot where her heart was, savoring the feeling that had always been missing from her previous relationships. A soft knock on her office door shattered her daydream.

Miranda's eyes snapped open. She took a deep breath to calm her thudding heart and said, "Come in."

The door opened and Ava entered, looking less like her usual jovial self. Miranda, knowing her staff well, immediately became concerned. "There's a man and woman here to see you. They claim they're your partner's parents. They stopped by a few days ago and wanted to know when you would be in and I told them today. I thought they would ask to make an appointment, but they just left. Now, they're here again. It's none of my business, but I just find it odd that they didn't just call you or visit you at home."

The hair on Miranda's neck stood at attention. The only two people who came to mind were individuals she wanted nothing to do with. She opened her mouth to tell Ava to send them away and to call the police if they refused, but stopped herself just as the words were about to leave her mouth. Because how had they found her and how did they know about her relationship with Lane? Miranda's protective instincts kicked in, because to keep them away from Lane, and prevent them from hurting her any more than they already did, she needed the answers to those questions.

"You can send them in, but please stay close by until they leave," Miranda requested, knowing that based on everything Lane told her about her birth mother and stepfather, she had to be careful around them.

Ava nodded and went to retrieve her unwanted guests. A minute later, the woman who had given birth to Lane entered her office, still exuding the same desperation and meanness similar to the day Lane kicked them out of her office. Looking at Barbara,

Miranda couldn't believe this woman had given birth to Lane. They looked nothing alike, but Miranda could see that if Barbara had taken better care of herself and wasn't so mean-spirited, she might have been pleasant to look at. Miranda's eyes drifted to Dick and instantly she felt a surge of red-hot rage shoot through her. The thought of how he could have destroyed Lane's life, and even worse done the unthinkable to her, made Miranda want to castrate him. Both of them were trouble and she wanted them nowhere near *her* Lane. Because Lane was now hers and Miranda was fiercely protective of the people she loved.

They didn't even wait for an invitation to sit. *Such insolence.* As soon as they sat down, Miranda asked sharply, "How may I help you?" She had no patience for pleasantries with people who had harmed an innocent child.

Dick looked at Barbara, a clear sign he was waiting on her to respond. Barbara cleared her throat, her eyes scanning Miranda's office like a vulture in search of carcasses to pick apart before finally meeting Miranda's gaze. Miranda held her stare doing everything in her power to ensure her features didn't betray the disgust she felt for them. Her heart ached as she thought about how frightened Lane must have been in their presence, with no one to turn to. But Lane had survived and blossomed into a remarkable woman who loved fiercely and gave so much of herself to the few people she cherished, and secretly donated to charities that helped young girls who walked a path similar to hers.

"You're in a relationship with my daughter, Sarah. She goes by Lane now," Barbara began, studying Miranda as if she expected some sort of reaction to that revelation. Miranda kept her expression impassive. Realizing that Miranda wasn't going to respond, Barbara pressed on, "I need my daughter's help, but she has refused to assist me. You seem more reasonable and kind-hearted, doing so much for strangers in need." Miranda's poker face almost slipped as she restrained an eye roll. It was clear that Barbara had absolutely no idea who Lane was or how charitable she could be, and she was just trying to hoodwink Miranda. "So, I was wondering if you could persuade her to help me, or maybe *you* could assist your potential future mother-in-law."

Miranda stifled a laugh at the use of the term "mother-in-law." Lane was right—Barbara was delusional and manipulative. Lane had mentioned that her mother would have made a brilliant actress, and the performance she was putting on now proved it. This woman sitting in front of her was far calmer than the one who had been forcibly ejected from Lane's office, frothing at the mouth.

"How do you know about my relationship with *Lane*?" Miranda asked, emphasizing Lane's chosen name as a reminder to her egg donor that Lane had chosen a different path, one that included rejecting the name given to her by a woman she despised.

Barbara glanced at Dick and then back at Miranda. "One of our friends saw you two in a magazine where you were honored for your work here."

Ah. Miranda knew exactly which article Barbara was referring to. She had received a key to the city for her work with Found Family, and a local magazine featured her success with the center, touching on her personal life as well. She had spoken candidly about her relationship with Lane and finding love unexpectedly. She had seen it as an opportunity to inspire other women who realized later in life that they might be bisexual or simply just met a woman who made them happy. She wanted to encourage them to venture into the unknown and not be afraid to take a leap of faith. Lane had also been her date to the gala and the magazine included photos of them together at the event. So, that explained why these two opportunists knew where to find her and more than likely concocted some plan to extort her by appealing to her sense of humanity.

"How much do you need?" Miranda asked, cutting to the chase regarding this unwelcome intrusion.

Surprise flickered on their faces as if they were taken aback by how easily they were getting what they wanted. "Well, I don't want to be too much of a burden, but two hundred thousand would solve my problems and help me to get on my feet after a few setbacks." Seriously, Miranda was going to give herself a medal for holding her composure this long. "You know how difficult life can be at times. Family has to stick together in trying times, which is why it breaks my heart that Sarah abandoned me when I needed her the most." Barbara divulged, finishing in a tone that would make someone with a weak heart feel sorry for her.

Miranda stared at the woman across from her, still incredulous that such a vile person had brought someone as wonderful as Lane into the world. Here was a woman spinning tales to get what she wanted, rather than making any effort to be a better person. It was clear that Barbara felt no remorse for the harm she had caused Lane. Miranda considered giving her the money with the stipulation that she stay away from Lane. She had witnessed firsthand how much Barbara's presence upset Lane. That had been the only time she had ever seen Lane visibly enraged, and Miranda wanted to protect her from experiencing that pain again. Two hundred thousand was nothing for her to lose for Lane's safety. However, she knew that giving them the money would likely hurt Lane even more. And people like Barbara would always come back for more.

Miranda focused all her attention on Barbara, her eyes no longer masking the disgust she had tried to contain. "You won't be getting any money from me or Lane. Maybe if you had taken a moment to reflect on the kind of mother you were to her, tried to be a better person, and asked for forgiveness, she might have considered helping you. Lane is incredibly generous and treats the woman who has been more of a mother to her than you ever were, like a queen. But here you are, devoid of any remorse for your cruelty and neglect, failing to protect the person you should have loved above all else.

"Please leave my office and stay the hell away from Lane. If you come near us again, I'll obtain a restraining order. My family has enough connections to judges to ensure it happens or to see you end up in jail for harassment." Miranda typically refrained from leveraging her family's connections in such an unscrupulous manner, but desperate times called for desperate measures, and she would do anything to protect the woman she loved.

A nasty scowl twisted Barbara's features, and Miranda braced herself for an even more venomous remark. But before Barbara could speak, Dick jumped up from his chair and said, "Let's go. They're not worth getting into trouble with the law."

Barbara glanced up at him, and Dick shot her a look that seemed to persuade her to reconsider whatever she was about to say. She huffed, glared at Miranda one last time, and then rose from her seat. As Miranda watched them leave, a sense of relief swept over her the second they stepped out the door.

She contemplated calling Lane immediately but recalled that Lane had mentioned needing to wrap up a few things before their call. For a moment, she considered not telling Lane about the encounter to protect her, but she knew Lane valued honesty and wouldn't appreciate that kind of shielding. With a sigh, Miranda began packing up her things. She needed to get home and call Lane, especially since it was almost midnight in London, and she knew Lane would want to get some rest before her flight the next day. *Just one more night apart*, Miranda thought as she rose from her chair and headed home, her heart full of love and longing for the woman who meant everything to her.

Chapter 27

Opening her front door, Miranda froze when she heard music playing upstairs. Frowning, she wondered if she had forgotten to turn off the radio before leaving for Found Family earlier. Closing the door behind her, she decided to call Lane while preparing her jacuzzi. A proper soak in her hot tub on weekends was a ritual for de-stressing after a long week. Climbing the stairs to her bedroom, she video-called Lane, a wide smile already forming on her lips in anticipation of seeing Lane's beautiful face. When the call went unanswered, Miranda decided not to try again, knowing that Lane would call her back before bed. These were some of the small things she cherished about being with Lane—she felt none of the pressure she had experienced in her previous relationships regarding communication and expectations. She knew Lane would have called or sent a text to let her know if she was going to bed before Miranda got home. She never had to wonder where they stood on any plans they made.

Entering her bedroom, Miranda was greeted by the smooth, seductive notes of Marvin Gaye's "Sexual Healing." She froze, her breath catching in her throat, as she saw Lane standing in the bathroom doorway, gazing at her with that heated intensity that still made Miranda's blood sprint through her veins. Lane stood there in just her black dress pants and lace bra, her mahogany tresses gloriously mussed, exuding an air of cool, calm, and devastating sexiness. Miranda wanted to rush to her, but she was rooted to the spot, her eyes drinking in the sight of the magnificent woman who was all hers. Lane began to stalk towards her, and though Miranda longed to meet her halfway, she found herself unable to move, spellbound by Lane's penetrating stare. God, the way Lane looked at her had always had a profound impact, but now, with all that lust intertwined with so much love, it made Miranda's knees weak and her heart swell to the point of bursting.

The things Lane made her feel were what she had always dreamed of experiencing in a relationship. Miranda was blessed to have known what it meant to have love and support all her life. She even found a sister in Blake. But Delaney Remington, was the unexpected half of Miranda's heart she didn't even know she needed. She was the perfect melodic counterpoint in their polyphonic composition. Lane was her eyes to see the best in herself when Miranda had an ounce of self-doubt. Lane revered Miranda's compassionate heart and assertive soul, never asking anything more of her. Lane's belief in their love solidified Miranda's belief in fate. And all these qualities made her willing to submit to Lane's every desire, knowing she could trust Lane to take care of her.

When Lane reached her, she stopped and gazed into Miranda's eyes, communicating everything she seemed unable to put into words. Before Miranda could speak, Lane's lips were on hers, kissing her deeply and passionately. The kiss wasn't rough, but Miranda could feel the hunger in Lane's movements as her lips claimed Miranda's with a ravenous appetency.

Four days—only four days apart, yet it felt like a lifetime, and as they kissed, Miranda felt a missing piece of herself falling back into place. She kissed Lane back just as eagerly, needing to show her how much she had been missed. Their tongues slid against each other, and they moaned in unison, pulling each other closer, erasing every single inch of space between them. Miranda's heart pounded as she melted into Lane's embrace, the potency of their union vanquishing her. Every touch, every breath, every movement was a declaration of the love and longing they felt. In that moment, all the words left unsaid were conveyed through their kiss, through the way their bodies pressed together, desperate to make up for lost time.

Miranda lost track of time as they kissed. Was it five, ten, fifteen minutes? She didn't know and she didn't care because she was in Lane's arms. When Lane slowly pulled back, her breathing just as ragged as Miranda's, she whispered, "I missed you so very much," her voice emitting every ounce of meaning behind those words.

A wide smile spread across Miranda's lips as she looped her arms around Lane's neck. "I think the fact that you're here a day earlier than expected is proof of how much I was missed."

Lane's hands slid down to Miranda's ass, cupping and pulling her closer. "I convinced the Zantos team there was no reason for me to be there in person for the final meeting, just so I could come home to you." Leaning in, Lane rubbed her nose along Miranda's and whispered, "What are you doing to me, Miranda? Four days without having you in my arms was torture."

Miranda's heart expanded at Lane's words, feeling the profundity of her love and the longing that had driven her back sooner than planned. Miranda eased back slightly to stare into Lane's eyes, which were filled with that rare vulnerability that only Miranda was privy to. A vulnerability that made Miranda fiercely protective of Lane, wanting to shield her from anything that could ever hurt her. Because yes, Lane was strong, having survived a horrific childhood that had demanded she constantly rely on her own strength. But Miranda wanted to show Lane that she loved her perfect imperfections—the good, the bad, and the ugly of her past. She wanted to go through Lane's heaven and hell side by side, being Lane's strength when she was fragile.

Miranda held Lane's gaze with all the conviction and love she could muster, and said, "All I'm doing..." She languidly ran her fingertips up and down the nape of Lane's neck. "And want to do..." Her fingers now tenderly massaging soothing circles on either side of Lane's spine. "Is to love you the best way possible, to always be here for you and be a constant source of support." Miranda's fingers wrapped delicately around Lane's neck as if to hold her in place, as she drove home her final point. "To take care of you."

Lane's eyes burned with so much love causing Miranda's heart to somersault in her chest. "Thank you. To be loved by you is truly special and I don't ever want to know what it would be like to not have you in my life."

Miranda pressed a soft kiss to Lane's temple. "You don't have to thank me. Loving you, taking care of you—it's what I want to do."

Lane closed the sliver of space between them and kissed her slowly and softly. Though the kiss was gentle, the impact was profound as Miranda felt all the love she saw in Lane's eyes in the movement of her lips against hers. Lips still lingering against hers, Lane whispered, "I really want to take you to bed and lose myself in showing you how much I missed you, but I need to wash away over nine hours of traveling. Let's go have a bath."

Feeling overwhelmed by their shared moment, Miranda could only nod, allowing Lane to lead her into the bathroom while simultaneously undressing her. As they crossed the threshold, Miranda gasped, her breath catching at the sight before her. The bathroom was bathed in the soft, flickering glow of countless small candles, their warm light casting a serene and intimate ambiance. The bath was already prepared, the water invitingly steaming and infused with lavender. The soothing, aromatic scent filled the air, mingling with the fragrance of the candles, creating an atmosphere of pure relaxation and romance. Lane's hands moved with reverence, slipping Miranda's shirt off her shoulders, their touch sending shivers down her spine. Miranda's eyes were drawn to the bath, marveling at the thoughtfulness and effort Lane had put into creating this perfect setting.

"How long have you been home?" Miranda asked as Lane unhooked her bra and let it fall to the ground.

"Maybe thirty minutes. I arrived while we were texting. I knew you'd be coming home to have your bath and wanted to save you the trouble of preparing it. That's why I told you to call when you got home and not on the way. I wanted to surprise you," Lane explained, kneeling before Miranda and pulling down her underwear. Her hot breath caressed Miranda's skin, making her core throb with anticipation.

Miranda looked down at Lane, bracing herself for the familiar sensation of Lane's tongue on her heated flesh. But instead, Lane only placed a soft kiss on her mound before rising to her feet. She chuckled at the look of disappointment on Miranda's face.

"Such impatience. Who would have thought, Dr. Hayes, that you'd come to crave my very wicked tongue so much that you can't even wait an hour to have it do very wicked things to you. Hmm?" Lane teased.

Miranda reached for Lane's pants, unbuttoning them as a means of occupying her hands instead of pushing Lane against the wall and demanding that she fucked her. "No one would blame me for being impatient when you do the things you do to me with that mouth of yours."

Lane's pants and the thin strip of silk she wore pooled at her ankle. Her bra dropped to the floor next, and Miranda couldn't resist lowering her head and wrapping her lips around a nipple. Lane hissed, arching into Miranda's hungry mouth. God, she loved Lane's breasts. She could spend hours just kissing them, feeling Lane's body shudder beneath her, making Miranda wonder if she could make her orgasm like that. She loved how responsive Lane was to her touch, how every sigh and shiver spoke volumes about their connection. After months of really, really amazing sex and lovemaking that melted her insides, Miranda was one hundred percent sure she was a breast person.

She attempted to move to the other nipple but Lane stepped away from her eager mouth, her breathing ragged and pupils dilated. "Bath first," she breathed out, linking her fingers with Miranda's as she stepped into the tub.

Miranda followed, settling between Lane's thighs and resting against her chest. She sighed as the warm water infused with bath bombs soaked her skin, immediately loosening her muscles. Lane wrapped her arms around her middle, and Miranda snuggled even closer against her chest, enjoying the sensation of Lane's stiff nipples caressing her back. They sat in silence for a few minutes, each savoring the quiet, a needed reprieve from their typically busy lives. Miranda closed her eyes, her body relaxing completely in Lane's embrace. She felt Lane's heartbeat against her back, steady and reassuring. This was her safe haven now, her sanctuary. Every touch, every breath, every beat of Lane's heart was a reminder of the love they shared, a love that had grown deeper and more life-changing with each passing day.

"I told Alexandra to fire James. I wish I could do it myself, but since he reports directly to her, I have to leave the beheading to her. She was actually planning to demote him, but I told her to go straight for termination," Lane said, breaking the comfortable silence.

Miranda wasn't surprised that Lane was sharing this upcoming update with her. Although Lane was her boss and had to maintain certain boundaries regarding confidential matters, they often discussed their work lives openly and respected the limits that came with their respective roles.

"I'm surprised it took you so long," Miranda replied teasingly. "I thought you would have done it months ago when I was chief of surgery. I would have fired him myself, but since my assignment was temporary, I wanted to leave it for when Alexandra returned."

The memory of all the times James had been passive-aggressive toward Lane when she first started at Parkwood resurfaced, igniting a flicker of anger within her.

"I wanted to ensure I had enough evidence to fire him without risking a lawsuit. He's more than likely going to think it's personal, but my decision was based solely on his professional shortcomings. He's a crap human with a nasty attitude and an even crappier doctor. His bedside manners sucked and he made the nurses uncomfortable. His misogyny and inflated ego were his downfall." Lane's hands glided down to Miranda's inner thighs, massaging gently and inching dangerously close to where Miranda craved her touch the most. "But enough with such an unpleasant topic. How were things at the center today?"

Miranda's muscles tensed at Lane's question, the reminder of the obnoxious visitors she had dealt with casting a shadow on her thoughts. She knew she had to share the details with Lane, even though she hesitated to do so, as she didn't want to burden her with any discomfort.

Lane peered over Miranda's shoulder, using a finger to tilt Miranda's face toward her. "What's wrong? Did something bad happen there today? I felt your muscles tense as soon as I asked my question."

This was another one of the many things that made Miranda fall deeper for Lane—the way she was attuned to every nuance, sensing when something troubled Miranda before she told her. Miranda inhaled sharply, steeling herself. "Barbara and Dick stopped by Found Family today."

This time it was Lane who stiffened behind her and

Miranda watched as the concern in her eyes morphed into fierce rage. "They did what?" Lane whispered in that chillingly composed manner she adopted when she was struggling to maintain her calm in situations that threatened to ignite her anger.

Miranda reached into the water, intertwining her fingers with Lane's in a gesture of comfort. "They wanted me to give them two hundred thousand dollars because you refuse to help. They assumed I must be very generous and soft-hearted since I own Found Family. Apparently, they learned about our relationship from that magazine article detailing my journey with the center. I kicked them out and warned them that if they ever come near you again, I'd seek a restraining order."

Lane closed her eyes, her expression clouded with what Miranda could only describe as anguish. "I'm so sorry for bringing people like that into your life. It pains me to know that, by association with me, you've been exposed to individuals I consider monsters—people who wouldn't hesitate to hurt you."

Seeing the agony etched on Lane's face, Miranda rose from the water and turned around to straddle Lane's thighs. She had anticipated that the news would upset Lane, but witnessing her so visibly distraught —blaming herself for exposing Miranda to people she deemed dangerous—made Miranda's heart ache. Given the trauma Lane had endured with her birth mother, Miranda understood all too well why Lane feared for her safety.

Miranda cradled Lane's face in her hands, her gaze steady and brimming with love. "You're not responsible for their actions. As much as I loathe your mother for what she did to you, I'm still grateful she brought you into this world. But know that you don't have to face them alone if they refuse to stay away from us. I'll always be by your side, loving and supporting you through everything." She understood how accustomed Lane was to shouldering her burdens alone, and it was essential for Miranda to convey that she was there to help carry life's challenges whenever they arose.

As Miranda spoke, she watched Lane's eyes soften, the affliction within them transforming into warmth and affection. "I love you. Thank you for taking a chance on me and giving me the most unexpected gift of knowing what it feels like to be truly loved and cared for by a partner."

"I love you, too," Miranda whispered, drawing Lane into a slow, deep kiss. An overwhelming need to show Lane just how cherished she was consumed her, wrapping them both in the warmth of their unexpected love.

Lane kissed her back with an intensity that magnified the connection between them. Miranda instinctively ground against Lane's pelvis, seeking friction against her pulsing clit, her body acutely aware of the days that had passed without Lane's fingers or mouth between her thighs. It never ceased to amaze her how attuned her body was to Lane's touch, as if it had been waiting for Lane her entire life. No one could compare to Delaney Remington when it came to giving Miranda the best sex of her life. There was something magical about how Lane made her feel when she fucked her—every encounter was like a rebirth, as if Miranda were discovering the world of intimacy for the first time. When Lane adjusted their bodies without breaking the kiss and slipped two fingers inside Miranda's throbbing core, a gasp escaped her lips. At that moment, she realized that no matter what the future held, she would never be the same. Lane had awakened an unfathomable sense of completeness within her, something no one else could ever replicate.

Chapter 28

"I hope the traffic from here to your parents isn't terrible. I hate being late," Lane muttered as they stepped out of the gallery. "This is exactly why I don't do things last minute."

Miranda grasped Lane's elbow, halting her steps. "I told you, you didn't have to get my mom anything," she said gently.

Lane turned to face her, her expression a mix of mild frustration and anxiety. Miranda couldn't help but find her irresistibly endearing in these moments of vulnerability. "It's your mom's birthday," Lane insisted. "I can't just show up empty-handed. I have to make a good impression on the woman whose daughter I'm helplessly in love with. This is your mom, who you adore. What type of girlfriend would I be if I didn't get her a gift."

Miranda stepped closer to Lane, wrapping her arms around her neck. Her heart overflowed with an all-consuming love for this woman who had brought her more happiness than she ever thought possible. Lane had been wonderful in their casual relationship, but as a girlfriend, she was extraordinary. Lane's perfectionism extended to every aspect of her life, including being an incredible partner. With every new facet Miranda discovered about her, her desire to know Lane more deeply increased.

Miranda's voice softened as she looked into Lane's eyes, kissing her on the tip of her nose. "You've already won her over, sweetheart. Your thoughtfulness speaks volumes." Miranda brought one hand down to rest over Lane's heart for a moment. "But it's your heart and the way you love me that has truly made the impression. And it's the only one you need to make. Getting her a rather expensive gift isn't necessary to achieve that."

Lane pouted like an adorably petulant child. "I have expensive taste. But the price tag isn't why I commissioned the piece. It's the significance behind the painting that matters. Knowing it's something your mom will truly appreciate makes it worth every penny."

Miranda could certainly attest to Lane's very expensive taste. Through further conversations about Lane's childhood, she had learned that some aspects of Lane's current lifestyle were a side effect of her difficult upbringing. Lane had confessed that because she was deprived of nice things growing up, she now indulged in the finest of everything she desired. This resulted in a closet brimming with designer clothes and shoes, the cost of which could probably feed a small nation. However, what Miranda cherished most was Lane's approach to gift-giving. Despite her willingness to spare no expense, Lane's gifts were always thoughtfully chosen, often carrying deep sentimental value for the recipient. This same attentiveness and consideration permeated their relationship, making Lane an extraordinarily thoughtful and considerate partner.

"Yes, she will. But she would have appreciated something from even the Dollar Store. So, stop worrying about it." Miranda closed the distance between them, sealing her words with a soft, sweet kiss. Although she loved spending time with her family, she was already counting down the seconds until they could return home, eager for Lane to finish what she had begun while they got dressed.

"Miranda?" a familiar voice called from behind, causing her to reluctantly break the kiss with Lane. She turned to find Trevor staring at them, his expression a mix of hurt and confusion.

"Hi, Trevor," Miranda replied, smiling internally as Lane intertwined their fingers possessively. Apparently, Lane was still not a fan of Trevor.

Trevor's gaze dropped to their joined hands before meeting Miranda's eyes again. He gestured between them. "Is this why you didn't want to give us a second chance?" His eyebrows knitted together further. "You never once mentioned you're attracted to women when we were together."

If it had been anyone else, Miranda might have felt annoyed by the question. As far as she was concerned, she didn't owe anyone an explanation about her relationships, regardless of her partner's gender. But this was Trevor, and she knew his confusion was genuine—not malicious. She had simply told him she wasn't interested in trying again without much explanation because, in her eyes, she didn't owe him one—especially since he was the one who initially ended their relationship.

"No, my relationship with Lane isn't why I didn't give us a second chance," Miranda answered, her tone carefully neutral to convey that she wasn't being unkind. "As for your statement, now isn't the time or place to discuss it."

Trevor nodded slowly. "I see." He glanced at Lane,

then returned his attention to Miranda. "I guess I'll see you around. Take care."

"You too, Trevor," Miranda replied, noticing the sadness in his eyes. She sincerely hoped he would find someone to make him happy someday.

Once Trevor was out of earshot, Lane quipped, "I guess no hellos for me."

Miranda chuckled. "Who could blame him when you have been nothing but cold to him in the past?

Lane shrugged nonchalantly. "He had what I wanted." She lifted their interwoven hands to her lips. "Who could blame me for not being friendly?"

Miranda laughed and started walking to her car. "Of course, you would see it that way."

Lane grinned, her eyes sparkling with satisfaction. "Yep, and I got the girl in the end."

Twenty minutes later, less than five minutes from Miranda's parents' house, Lane broke the comfortable silence they had existed in for the past ten minutes. "I really love this area. My lease is coming up for renewal and I've been thinking about buying a house around here. The commute to work might be longer, but the serene atmosphere is so much better compared to the hustle and bustle of downtown. Since I don't see myself leaving Seattle anytime soon, I guess I should invest in property here."

Before Miranda could overthink it, the words slipped out of her mouth, surprising even herself, "Or you could move in with me?" It was a spontaneous suggestion, unplanned and unspoken in their relationship thus far. Yet, as the words hung between them, she realized it was what she truly wanted. Irrespective of their relatively short time-span of six months together as an official couple, Miranda felt a deep certainty about wanting Lane to share her life more intimately.

Lane eased off the accelerator, glancing at Miranda with a mixture of surprise and hesitation. Miranda, sensing a shift in Lane's demeanor, hurried to clarify herself—not wanting Lane to feel pressured into a commitment she wasn't ready for. "I mean, that's if it's something you're ready for. You already spend almost every weekend at my house and at least two days during the week. You've mentioned on numerous occasions that you love spending time at my house and love the view from my backyard." She shrugged casually, masking her nervousness. "So, if you're open to it, I wouldn't mind living with you."

As Miranda spoke, she realized this was the first time she had ever suggested cohabiting with a partner. In her past relationships, it had always been the other way around—her partners pushing for her to move in with them before she wanted to. Now, being on the other side of it, she understood the uncertainty and hopefulness that came with waiting for a response. She also valued the importance of mutual readiness and respect for each other's space. Therefore, even though she deeply wanted them to move in together, she wouldn't be offended if Lane decided she wasn't quite ready. The car came to a stop, and Miranda realized with a jolt that they had arrived at her parents' house.

Lane turned to face Miranda, her expression contemplative as she searched Miranda's face. "Are you sure that is something you want us to do now? I'm not opposed to the idea because I do love being with you every second of every day, but I know how much you value your space. We don't have to move in together because it's expected of couples. I'm open to us having separate homes and still spending all the time together that we want."

Miranda reached for Lane's hand. "I'm absolutely sure, my love. I want to build a life with you. And except for those nights I have to be at the hospital, I hate not sleeping with you." She rubbed the back of Lane's hand with her thumb. "I want everything that comes with being in a relationship with you. Yes, I value my space, just as you do yours. However, we do have this uncanny ability to give each other space even when we're in the same house. You always sense when I need a moment alone and find something to occupy yourself with, and I do the same for you." Miranda gave her a soft smile that grew into a wide grin before she added, "Though, with you, I rarely feel the need to be alone. I always want to be with you."

Lane's lips curved into a wide smile, her eyes shimmering with happiness, and knowing she was the reason for that happiness made Miranda's heart go pitter-patter in her chest. "Okay, then yes, I'd love to move in with you, or find a place together. It doesn't matter as long as we're together." Closing the gap between them, Lane pressed her lips against Miranda's. Her tongue gently teased Miranda's lips apart, evoking a deep moan from her, instantly stirring a throbbing sensation at her core. Miranda knew they should probably stop kissing because, with the way Lane was kissing her, she feared they might end up having sex right there in her parents' driveway. However, instead of pulling away, Miranda drew Lane closer, deepening the kiss. The world faded around them, leaving Miranda captivated by Lane's demanding lips and the growing warmth between her thighs. God, she would never get tired of being kissed with such animalistic ferocity.

Miranda's heart leaped into her throat with fright when a knock sounded on the driver's side window. She hastily withdrew her lips from Lane's, glancing over Lane's shoulder to find Blake standing there with a wide grin on her face.

"Your friend has impeccable timing," Lane muttered wryly before she opened the door and stepped out. Miranda followed suit, joining them on the other side of the car.

Blake wagged a playful finger at them. "You know, Miranda, as open-minded as your parents are, I don't think they'd appreciate seeing their darling daughter getting hot and heavy in their driveway. It didn't seem like you two were going to stop if we hadn't arrived," she teased.

Miranda rolled her eyes dramatically. "Oh, be quiet. As if you're any better when it comes to keeping your hands off Alexandra," Miranda shot back, pulling Blake into a quick hug.

"She does have a strong point, sweetheart,' Alexandra chimed in, coming up beside them with Amara in her carrier. "Hi, Lane."

"Hi, Alexandra," Lane greeted Alexandra warmly, reciprocating with a quick hug. She then bent at the waist and greeted Amara, making cooing baby sounds. "She's so very beautiful and growing fast," she added.

Miranda always found herself fascinated whenever she watched Lane interact with Amara. Knowing Lane didn't desire children of her own made these moments particularly intriguing. In discussions about their future, Lane revealed that she had never envisioned herself in a family dynamic. However, now that they were in a committed relationship, she had expressed openness to the idea if it meant making Miranda happy. In other words, she was willing to adapt to whatever Miranda needed to find happiness together.

"We should probably head inside. We're on the verge of being late," Blake pointed out. "Though Alexandra and I have a valid excuse, you two were just making out in the driveway like teenagers."

"Sweetheart, your inability to keep your hands off me—which led to us having to feed Amara before coming here—might not be the strongest alibi," Alexandra joined in, kissing Blake on the cheek, her eyes twinkling with amusement.

"Hey now, you're supposed to be on my side," Blake protested.

"Facts are facts, darling." Alexandra looped her arm through Blake's, leading the way to the door.

Miranda glanced at Lane, who was watching the couple with a thoughtful expression. For the first time in her life, Miranda felt she had found the person with whom she could share the grand romance she had always dreamed of—have the same deep bond that Blake and Alexandra shared. Sometimes, the best things in life materialize from the most unexpected places. Falling in love with a woman was a surprise, but it was undoubtedly one of the best things that had ever happened to her.

Just as she was about to intertwine her fingers with Lane and guide them into the house, Lane turned to face Miranda, her eyes glistening with a mixture of love and vulnerability. "Now I understand how Alexandra could jump in front of a gun without a second thought for herself, taking a bullet meant for Blake. Why, even when everyone gave up on Blake in the operating room, she didn't. I think I'd do the same for you because of how deeply I love you." She reached up, cupping Miranda's cheek. "You make me want what they have, Miranda. You make me a dreamer of fairytale romances. I'm still learning how to love you the way you deserve, but I promise to continue trying—to give you every part of me, mind, body, and soul. You're everything to me and my life would become so desolate without you now that I've experienced what it's like to be loved the way you love me."

Miranda was caught off guard by Lane's impromptu heartfelt declaration, but she couldn't stop the tears from welling up in her eyes. Swallowing hard, she managed to rasp out, "You make it easy for me to love you. And you deserve all the love in the world. I'm so incredibly grateful that you chose me to be the one to love you. And I do love you so very much, my love. Just like you, I promise to continue trying my best to love you the way you deserve."

Lane's response was to close the distance between them, sealing their lips in another slow, passionate kiss. Miranda knew they needed to get inside but she just couldn't find the willpower to sever the kiss. Not when her need for Lane overpowered every rational thought, and all she wanted was to remain in Lane's arms, lost in this moment forever. Finally, she had found the love that her mother had encouraged her to wait for.

Chapter 29

.......one year later.......

"I can't believe you planned this entire trip without me catching on. It's breathtakingly beautiful here," Miranda commented, reaching across the table where they were dining on the terrace of their villa in Bali. She entwined her fingers with Lane's, her eyes shining with appreciation and love. "You really do give the best and most thoughtful gifts."

Lane's expression softened as she gently caressed Miranda's knuckles with her thumb. "You only turn forty once, and you deserve the best of everything life has to offer. Knowing how much you love gardening, it made perfect sense to bring you to one of the most beautiful garden resorts in the world."

Miranda's smile was radiant, her hazel eyes glowing with happiness. Knowing she was the reason for that joy made Lane the happiest person in the world. She had learned that Miranda loved celebrating her birthdays, a tradition her parents always honored with grand affairs, as evidenced by the extravagant party they had thrown for her fortieth. Lane had also wanted to do something extra special for her, despite Miranda's insistence that she didn't need to. But Lane was who she was and it was in her nature to give, especially to the woman she loved. She took immense pleasure in creating moments and memories that would make Miranda's heart soar.

But what do you give someone who has everything they need? In the end, Lane decided that the best gift she could offer Miranda was time together. She had secretly planned a two-week vacation in Asia, including stops in Malaysia, Singapore, and Indonesia. These locations were chosen specifically for their beautiful garden resorts, knowing Miranda's love for gardening. They were now on their final night in Bali, and Lane wished they didn't have to return so soon. She had cherished these moments of having Miranda all to herself, away from the demands of their lives in Seattle. Yes, they spend a lot of time together, however even after a year and a half, Lane still yearned to spend every second of every day with the woman who had become the best thing in her life. And this was why Lane's heart pounded with anticipation, hoping Miranda would say yes to the final gift she had saved for this special night.

"I have another gift for you. I saved the best for last, of course," Lane said teasingly, trying to quell the nervousness threatening to consume her.

Miranda shook her head in mock exasperation. "Sweetheart, you've already given me so much. But I know there's no point in arguing with you about it, so I won't even bother."

Lane stood from her chair, extending a hand to Miranda. "Let's go for a walk in the rose garden."

They strolled in comfortable silence, taking in the vibrant scenery. Moonlight filtered through the leaves, casting dappled shadows on the path, while the air was rich with the sweet scent of blooming flowers. The closer they drew to their destination, the more anxious

Lane became. She had spoken at multiple conferences throughout her career, debated with some of the most brilliant business minds in her field, and never once felt unsure of herself. Yet, for what could quite possibly be the most important speech of her life, no matter how hard she tried, she couldn't stop the nervous energy coursing through her body. Miranda's presence, the serene beauty of the garden, and the gravity of the moment all heightened Lane's emotions.

"I know gift-giving isn't a competition, but I'll really have to come up with something impressive for your birthday," Miranda stated halfway through the ten-minute stroll from their villa to the garden.

Lane brought their entwined hands to her lips, kissing the back of Miranda's hand. "I have full confidence in your capabilities, Dr. Hayes."

"I spoke to one of the horticulturists here, and she gave me a contact in Florida who can supply me with seeds for a variety of plants from this specific region," Miranda said as they arrived at the vibrant garden.

Lane nodded, her heart pounding—not from the walk but from the anticipation of what was to come. They paused at the entrance of the garden, surrounded by the fragrance of blooming roses and the gentle rustling of leaves. The tranquil beauty of the setting was the perfect backdrop for the moment Lane had been meticulously planning.

"This way," Lane directed, her throat suddenly tight as she steered Miranda along the trail she wanted them to take.

As they rounded a bend, they were greeted by a stunning rose garden, a riot of colors unfolding before them. Velvety red blooms stood tall beside soft pinks and sunny yellows, their petals glistening with evening dew. The delicate scent of jasmine intertwined with the heady aroma of roses, creating a sweet symphony that shrouded them.

Miranda gasped when they arrived at the center of the garden. Before them lay a heart-shaped floral arrangement, surrounded by small, flickering candles. Inside the heart were printed photos, each capturing intimate moments they had shared throughout their relationship. The photos were arranged chronologically, leading from the earliest days to their recent adventures on this trip. At the bottom, a message read: *"I want forever and a lifetime of memories with you."*

Miranda's eyes welled up with tears, her gaze moving from the photos to Lane. "It's so very beautiful. Thank you."

Lane enveloped Miranda's hands in hers, placing their joined hands over her rapidly beating heart. "That's just an accessory for the gift. I'm your gift, Miranda. Even though you're also mine." She squeezed Miranda's with tender affection. "Our paths crossed unexpectedly thirty years ago and again that night at Josephine's. Maybe it was fate—an unexpected fate. But whatever it was, I'm grateful that it gave me you. My love, you're such an unexpected gift that sometimes, I still can't believe that you're mine." Staring into Miranda's eyes, seeing all the love reflected in those beautiful hazel orbs, Lane felt some of her anxiety melt away. Miranda loved her, and that was why she was ready to enter into the riskiest contract of her life.

"I never dreamt of falling in love or having the type of relationship I have with you," Lane continued, her voice trembling slightly. "Before you, I was content with my life as it was, never feeling like anything was missing because I knew how to make myself happy. Now, I can't imagine happiness without you, and I hope I never have to."

Lane sucked in a shaky breath, trying to temper the overwhelming emotions. "I've never really believed in fairy tale romances or the idea of star-crossed lovers, but given our history, maybe we were always destined to end up here together." Lane began to lightly trace the length of Miranda's fourth finger. "You've always wanted a grand romance, and I want to be the one to give it to you." Lane took a full breath, mustering all her nerves and swallowing her doubt. "I want to give you everything you've ever dreamed of." Lane reached into her front pocket, pulling out a stunning 14-carat emerald-cut white gold engagement ring.

Miranda gasped, her eyes widening as they darted from Lane's face to the ring. "Is that what I think it is?" she asked tremulously as more tears welled up in her eyes.

Lane nodded, smiling nervously. "I'd go down on one knee, but that's too patriarchal for my taste."

Miranda chuckled, her tears now falling freely. Lane continued, "I saved the best gift for last... which is me. I'm giving myself to you in all the ways that matter because, while marriage is just a piece of paper, it's still one of the most powerful contracts in the world. It grants us certain privileges as each other's wives. I don't want—if anything should happen to me—for you not to have a say because we're not married. I don't want anyone to ever question your role in my life because we didn't have a piece of paper that signifies your importance to me."

She took a deep breath, hoping her eyes conveyed all the love burning in her heart for Miranda. "But that's not the main reason I want to marry you. I want to marry you because I'm so very much in love with you, and I want to spend the rest of my days living a grand romance with you. You've become so very vital to my existence, and my life would be unbearably empty without you."

Lane didn't realize her hand with the ring was trembling until she took a step back to place the ring on the tip of Miranda's ring finger. "Miranda Giselle Hayes, will you do me the honor of marrying me and making me even happier than you already have?"

Lane's heart thundered in her chest as she waited for Miranda's answer. While she didn't have to wait long, in those few seconds, she realized just how desperately she wanted Miranda to say yes. And when Miranda nodded and exclaimed, "Yes, yes, yes! I'll marry you, you wonderful, amazing woman." Lane released the breath she hadn't realized she was holding. Her heart felt like it might burst from the sheer love and joy overflowing within her. With shaking hands, she slipped the ring onto Miranda's finger, her soul alight with happiness.

Once the ring was on her finger, Miranda surged into Lane's arms, enveloping her in a tight embrace. She peppered Lane's face with kisses before their lips met in an all-consuming kiss. Each stroke of Miranda's tongue against hers, coupled with the overwhelming joy she felt, left Lane feeling like she was experiencing an out-of-body euphoria—intoxicated with love. At that moment, she felt completely whole, knowing that taking a chance on love with Miranda was the best decision she had ever made.

As the kiss slowed, Miranda eased back, holding Lane's gaze with tender intensity. "You're an unexpected dream that I never imagined could come true. But I'm grateful every day that you're the dream that became my reality. Thank you for making me the happiest woman alive. I love you so deeply, and I can't imagine spending forever with anyone else."

"I love you more. I intend to spend the rest of our lives showing you just how much."

Later that night, as they lay wrapped in each other's arms, basking in the afterglow of their lovemaking that had stretched into the early morning hours, Lane reflected on their journey together. How unexpected it was. She had always believed that life guided you down the path you are meant to travel—you just have to keep moving forward, even when everything feels like it's falling apart, embrace the risks along the way, and never stop believing in yourself.

She was happier than she had ever imagined possible, all because she had embraced the unexpected twists and turns that life had presented to her. As she lay beside Miranda, her heart full to bursting with love and contentment, Lane hoped that whatever other unexpected surprises life had in store for them, they would be met with peace, good health, and an abundance of happiness.

ACKNOWLEDGMENTS

To you, my readers, I want to express my heartfelt gratitude to all of you who have read or will read my books. Your continuous support means the world to me. It's still so very surreal to see my books being loved by so many of you. Knowing that through my art, I can be a source of comfort for many of you who, like myself, use books as an escape from this harsh world, is incredibly fulfilling. Words will never be enough to say thank you, but I hope to continue writing amazing stories for you.

Ah, Noella. Where do I even begin to express my gratitude for the care and attention to detail that you dedicate to my words. You make it hard for me to articulate what having you as an editor means to me. You're simply the best at what you do, and I hope I never have to publish a book without you being my editor. Just thinking about not having you to take care of my babies gives me anxiety. But whatever the future holds, just know that you have left an impact, and I'll forever be grateful for all that you have done for me. I appreciate you more than you know.

Clara and Erin, thank you for your steadfast support and friendship. Thank you for dedicating your time to being my beta readers. You know how much having your support means to me.

Casey, thanks for your constant encouragement and belief in my work. You're never afraid to express your faith in me and it means so very much. Thanks for sticking with me since the very first book.

A very special shout-out to my Dominican Republic gal, Coral. I'm laughing so hard writing this because that's the reaction you elicit! Thanks for always making me laugh. It's the small things in life that mean the most. So big up yourself, mami—my personal comedian.

To my family and friends whose names I cannot list here, you know who you are and how much you mean to me.

AFTERWORD

Thank you so much for reading my work! If you enjoyed this book, please leave a review on Amazon or Goodreads. Even just a rating makes a huge impact for authors and means so very much to us. I look forward to reading your wonderful reviews, many of which were the light at the end of the tunnel during some of my darkest moments. So, please believe that your kind words make a difference.

If you're interested, you can sign up for my newsletter for updates on upcoming projects, sneak peeks and giveaways, or follow me on Twitter or Instagram.

ABOUT THE AUTHOR

Skye Von Triessen

Skye lives in North York, where she is maybe one of the few who loves the long winter season. Despite being born on a beautiful island where it is warm all year round, she absolutely despises the summer months in her current home country. Skye spends her days as a corporate analyst and spends her nights dreaming up stories she desires to put on paper but oftentimes doesn't.

Her favorite thing to do is to lay in bed in the dark on Sundays, doing absolutely nothing but watching TV shows or reading a good book. She absolutely loves food, and despite her many attempts is unable to lower her monthly food bill to a reasonable amount, which is hard to do seeing that she believes in eating the best quality food, no matter the cost.

More than anything she believes that life is too short to be anything but happy.

Printed in Great Britain
by Amazon